ORIEL

for

Isaac, Leo & Jethro

ORIEL'S TRAVELS

An Archangel's Travels with St Paul

Robert Harrison

ORIEL'S TRAVELS

Published by Scripture Union, 207–209 Queensway, Bletchley, MK2 2EB, England.

Scripture Union: We are an international Christian charity working with churches in more than 130 countries providing resources to bring the good news about Jesus Christ to children, young people and families – and to encourage them to develop spiritually through the Bible and prayer. As well as our network of volunteers, staff and associates who run holidays, church-based events and school Christian groups, we produce a wide range of publications and support those who use our resources through training programmes.

Email: info@scriptureunion.org.uk
Internet: www.scriptureunion.org.uk

First published 2003, reprinted 2004
ISBN 1 85999 786 4

British Library Cataloguing-in-Publication Data: a catalogue record for this book is available from the British Library.

Cover design and photography by David Lund Design, Milton Keynes.

Maps by Sue Rann.

Internal design and typesetting by Servis Filmsetting Ltd of Manchester.

Printed and bound in Great Britain by Creative Print and Design (Wales) Ebbw Vale.

Foreword from the author

St Paul is not the best loved of the characters in the New Testament. People readily identify with the blundering yet well-intentioned Peter, but Paul is too sharp, too complex and too energetic for us to feel comfortable with him. Anyone who is familiar with the story of the New Testament will have a mental caricature of Paul, which they employ whenever his name is mentioned. What such caricatures easily overlook is the phenomenal length of his ministry.

Oriel's Travels retells the story of Paul's 30-year journey from being a militant young Jewish student in Jerusalem to arriving in Rome as a passionately Christian prisoner. It is not a history book, though I have tried to be historically accurate. It is not a biography; there are plenty of those available. *Oriel's Travels* is a very personal account of the life and work of this remarkable man.

The story is told from the perspective of Archangel Oriel, a fictional character built on an archangelic name from ancient Jewish tradition. I am not claiming that either Heaven, or the company of angels, are actually as they are presented here, although I am eager to present a robust and rounded view of spiritual realities.

Oriel's Travels is a work of imagination. I have taken the brief sketches of the New Testament account and coloured them in. I have given considered answers to some questions that have puzzled readers of the New Testament for many centuries: What was the personal problem mentioned by Paul in 2 Corinthians 12? Why did John Mark leave Paul and Barnabas in Perga, causing a rift between the two apostles that finally drove them apart? I am aware that many other answers have been given to these questions.

Some features of this story I must own as being the fruit of my own imaginings. It has always intrigued me that, according to Revelation 21, there is no sea in Heaven. This gave me the idea of angels having a pathological hatred of water. Also, in one account of Paul's dramatic conversion, the risen Jesus says to him, 'It is hard for you to kick against the goads.' This led me to the idea that the young Paul was scared of horses. Let me also acknowledge to readers with a keen knowledge of Biblical geography that

I have deliberately used the modern name, Turkey, rather than its potentially confusing ancient title, Asia Minor. Such things are part of the story teller's craft and I encourage you, after reading *Oriel's Travels*, to return to the official version, as written by St Luke, who was an eyewitness of much that he recorded in the Acts of the Apostles.

Finally, I would like to express my thanks to my daughters, Naomi and Grace; my editor, Lin Ball; and two theological advisers, Martin Davie and John Grayston for their help in trimming, shaping and polishing this story for publication. I would equally like to thank my wife, Katharine, for her patient love and support, and publicly apologise to her for all the Mondays that I have been late for supper because I was out travelling with Oriel and Paul.

Robert Harrison

Also by Robert Harrison:

ORIEL'S DIARY   (published October 2002)
ORIEL IN THE DESERT   (published October 2004)

In my office – free from the unrelenting pressure of time

'I have a challenge for you, Oriel,' my Boss said to me after a thought-filled silence. The word 'challenge' swept through my Angelic being like a great wave.

Serving the author of all creations is a challenge in itself. I shuddered to think what it might be that even he calls a 'challenge'.

'After your excellent work looking after my Son,' he began, glancing at the Heavenly man seated beside him, 'I would like you to look after another human for me.'

I have been responsible for Heaven's Angel guardian scheme since the very first humans stumbled across planet Earth. However, only once have I been a guardian myself and that was for Jesus, my Boss's Son, during his last months on Earth.

Father and Son looked intently at me while I digested their request.

'Who is it?' I asked, suppressing a rising tide of excitement.

'I have been looking for someone to travel to Rome,' my Boss explained, 'and tell its citizens about Jesus.'

I glanced at the Son, seated beside his eternal Father.

'What's so special about Rome?'

'It is the centre of the world's most powerful empire, at the particular moment in Earth's story that we are considering.'

I nodded thoughtfully. 'Who have you chosen?'

'A man called Saul, from Tarsus in Turkey.'

I was confused. 'You have picked a Turk to tell a Jewish story to the citizens of Rome?' I asked. I knew it was unwise to question his judgement but there was nothing to be gained from keeping my thoughts to myself; my Boss always knows them anyway.

'You know me, Oriel,' he replied with a disarming smile that invited me to ask further.

'What is it that makes Saul the right man for this job?'

'That is for you to discover,' my Creator replied, his eyes twinkling.

The Son joined the conversation. 'Saul is a Jew – he got *that* from his mother. And he's also a citizen of Rome – he inherited *that* from his father.'

This was an encouraging start. I waited for more.

'He has spent the last three years studying at the Rabbinical University at Jerusalem.'

'I like the man already,' I interrupted enthusiastically. 'I always said you should choose some followers from the university!'

'You did indeed,' the Son said. Now he was the one with a twinkle in his eyes. 'That's why you are clearly the Archangel for the job.'

'Where and when will I find the man?' I asked.

The communication that holds Eternal Father and Son in perfect unity is too deep for any Angel to fathom, but they allowed me to glimpse a ray of playful amusement that passed between them. I recognised it at once, and it set my spirit on alert. It warned me that there is something about this Saul that does not match the picture I was forming in my imagination. I shall just have to travel down to Jerusalem and meet the man to find out what.

Just outside Jerusalem – around 32 AD (I always struggle with human dates and calendars)

I arrived at a narrow, private gate in Jerusalem's wall which leads directly into the Temple complex. I spotted my man immediately. A small mob of angry priests were dragging a prisoner out into the sunlight from the labyrinth of passages behind the Temple. My Angelic eye was led directly to the shining spirit of their victim. He shone with the intense Heavenly brightness that illuminates all my Boss's human children. I quickly scanned the minds of the priests, to find out why they had turned against this wonderful man. The source of their anger was obvious: they were jealous of his faith. They were dragging him out of the city with one purpose – to dispose of this follower of Jesus just as they had wanted to get rid of Jesus himself. They were determined not to waste time pandering to the Roman Governor this time; they were going to do the job themselves – with stones.

The group was led by a thin, tight-spirited Pharisee whose mind was consumed by a determination to exterminate all memory of Jesus.

My first task was obvious: to rescue my man from his immediate fate and take him somewhere safe. The angry mob dragged their quarry down into the filthy valley where Jerusalem's rubbish is dumped. There they threw him to the ground and prepared to end his life by the crude method of throwing rocks at his head until his brain could take no more. Before this energetic execution began the priests removed their coats and handed them to their leader. I grabbed my moment.

I stood between hounds and prey, and called for the attention of all 23 Angel guardians present. 'Stop the hands of your charges and don't let them throw a single stone,' I ordered with the authority granted to all Archangels. 'Our Boss has chosen this Saul to tell the story of his Son right in the heart of the Roman Empire. He must not be killed.'

There was an awkward silence. Then a particularly depressed Angel spoke up. He was the guardian of the condemned man. 'This *isn't* Saul,' he said, nodding towards the prisoner.

'But he must be!' I replied.

'This is Stephen. He has just been condemned to death by the Jewish Council for asserting that our Boss's Son is indeed our Boss's Son.'

I was confused. I was sure that I had come to the right time and place to find the man my Boss had chosen.

'So which one *is* Saul of Tarsus?' I asked the assembled Angels, while the furious priests were gathering large stones to hurl at Stephen's head.

Twenty three Angelic faces looked in exactly the same direction. I turned round, following their gaze, and to my horror they were looking at the young Pharisee whose arms were laden with his companions' coats – the leader of the mob. As I watched, Saul gave a grim nod and the stones began to fly, crashing into Stephen's skull.

Jesus arrived.

'Ah, Oriel,' he said calmly. 'You've found your man, I see.'

I scowled back. 'We need to talk,' I said coldly.

'Drop into my office when you get back,' Jesus replied.

'They're killing one of your friends,' I pointed out. 'Don't you care?'

'That's why I'm here. I've come to take him home.'

We turned to look at Stephen. His human life was fading rapidly. 'Look!' he called faintly, 'I can see the Son of God.'

This prompted another volley of rocks, thrown with even more force and passion than before. They hit their target. Stephen's skull caved in and fragments of bone pierced his brain. The myriad of messages that had maintained his humanity throughout his life were silenced, his heart stopped pumping. As Stephen's spirit rose from its battered body I did not see the enslaved shadow that I have always seen before, tangled in the knots of its own selfishness. What emerged from Stephen's failing form was a vibrant spiritual body just like that of Jesus himself. With his last lungful of breath, Stephen said, 'Lord Jesus, receive my spirit.'

'I most certainly will,' the Son replied. He grasped Stephen's bright spirit by the hand and took him directly to Heaven.

Saul of Tarsus returned the coats to his fellow thugs and said, 'Good work! Now, come with me, we have much more still to do.'

They disappeared through the small gate in the city wall, leaving Stephen's shattered corpse where it was, on a heap of refuse. I remained there for some time until a group of frightened disciples arrived to remove the body for burial.

I must speak with my Boss.

In Heaven

I marched directly to my Boss's room. He instantly disarmed my fury with a forgiving smile. I knew there was no value in delivering the speech I had prepared during my lonely vigil beside Stephen's human remains, so I waited for him to speak first.

'Oriel,' he said, 'the potential for your mistake has been lurking in you since the day my Son chose a group of humble fishermen to be his first disciples.'

'I know,' I replied. 'I'm sorry.'

He smiled his full, radiant smile which reassured me that my mistake was completely forgiven.

I still needed to be sure that I had found the right man. 'But this man – is *this* the human you wish me to take to Rome,' I asked, 'to tell them about Jesus?'

'Yes,' was the united reply of Father and Son.

'But he hates you,' I said.

'He hates *me*,' the Son confirmed.

'He is utterly devoted to *me*,' the Father added.

I looked at the two expressions of Creative Love before me.

'That doesn't make sense.'

'That, Oriel, my dear friend,' the Son answered, 'is what you must help Saul understand.'

There was a knock at the door. In walked Stephen, liberated from the constraints and complications of time, and resplendent in his new, Heavenly body. On his face were carved the wounds of his bloody execution, but here in Heaven they were not the ugly scars that had disfigured Stephen's corpse. They were an elaborate adornment that proclaimed the beauty of their owner's love for my Boss.

Jesus stood up and hugged his friend. He introduced me. 'Stephen, this is Archangel Oriel, Heaven's chief administrator.'

Stephen embraced me. 'I saw you back there in Jerusalem,' he said, adding, 'I believe you mistook me for Saul.'

'Oriel is going to help Saul understand the truth,' Jesus explained. 'Then he will escort him to Rome so that he can tell my story there.'

'Quite a challenge,' Stephen observed with a wry smile.

'Do you have any hints?' I asked the man who had just experienced the full force of Saul's *devotion* to my Boss.

'Don't quote the scriptures at him,' Stephen replied. 'He is a bit sensitive in that department.'

I thanked him for his advice and left for my office. I have asked Archangels Michael, Gabriel and Raphael to join me.

Back in Jerusalem, at the place where Jesus died

My three Archangel colleagues responded to my call and we met in my office before I left for Earth. When I explained the situation to them, Michael was the first to comment. 'I don't think our army will be much use to you,' he said. 'Sorry, Oriel.'

We pondered the challenge in shared silence until Gabriel offered, 'I could go down and speak to him.'

'He deserves a fright,' I said to the great messenger, 'but, to be honest, I don't think he would notice you.'

We returned to our separate thoughts, brought back together again by Raphael. 'Before you can make any progress with this man, Oriel,' he said, 'you will have to learn to love him.'

The idea revolted me. I had viewed Saul with the same pure anger that I have for the Angels who have abandoned my Boss's service to join the Opposition.

'Impossible!' I replied.

'When you were looking after the Son during his human life,' Raphael said, 'didn't you listen to what he said?'

Raphael is the most thoughtful of my Archangel colleagues. I had no doubt that he was about to reveal a diamond of divine wisdom. I didn't answer his question but simply waited for him to continue.

'The Son said, *Love your enemies and pray for those who persecute you.* Does that sound familiar?'

Nothing else needed to be said. I thanked my friends for their support and came here, to the place where Jesus was executed. This is where my Boss showed the full extent of his love for his human enemies. Perhaps here I will find something to love in Saul of Tarsus.

I spent the Earth night alone on the barren hillock outside Jerusalem. At dawn, Raphael arrived.

'How are you getting on, my dear?' asked the conductor of Heaven's choir.

'Just thinking.'

'May I join you, Oriel?'

Jerusalem spun round into the yellow rays of Earth's Sun. Farmers and merchants leading donkeys laden with produce made their way up to the city's gates and waited for them to open. Nothing seemed to have changed since I was last working within the narrow stream of Earth's time. Two winters of rain had washed away the last traces of Jesus' human blood – they had been replaced with the stains of other men's deaths.

Raphael spoke. 'Cursed is the one who hangs on a tree.'

'What?' I asked, my mind emerging from dark memories.

'It is a line from the Jewish law,' my companion said. 'It may just be part of your Saul's problem.'

'How's that?'

'Jesus was hung on a wooden cross and so he became cursed under Jewish law,' Raphael explained. 'Saul is a Pharisee, so it is impossible – in his understanding – for Jesus to be anything other than an offence to all that is pure and holy.'

I considered Raphael's words. And the more I did so, the more hopeless my quest seemed.

'Is that supposed to help me?' I turned to ask my enigmatic friend. He had gone.

Saul's room – that evening

When the city gates opened, I made my way to the priests' offices behind the Temple and waited for Saul to arrive. Observing his thoughts yesterday, I saw that he's intent on eradicating all Jesus' followers as quickly as possible. So, assuming he would hatch his plans in the same ants' nest of dark corridors where Jesus' death was plotted, I settled into a vantage point that Raphael once used – a stone pillar – from which I could watch the comings and goings of the politician priests who rule the Jewish nation.

I was not disappointed. Saul of Tarsus strode arrogantly into the priestly headquarters as soon as morning prayers finished. He waited at the door to the high priest's office. The high priest, rounding the corner from another direction, was a different high priest to the one who engineered Jesus' crucifixion. He was an older man, Annas. I studied his mind and quickly learned that Annas is deeper and wiser than his predecessor.

Annas led Saul into his room and closed the door. I joined them. Before Annas had settled into his chair, Saul unleashed a tirade of anger against the followers of Jesus.

'These men and women are undermining the very structure of our nation,' he bellowed. 'They say it doesn't matter if you break the Law, because their Jesus will forgive you. The people, of course, lap it all up. They have water poured over their heads and say, *I'm living Jesus' way*. We have to stop them.'

'That's easier said than done,' observed the elderly priest. 'Caiaphas thought that killing Jesus would shut them up; it only made them more fanatical. Now they are claiming he is still alive.'

'We can't simply sit here and do nothing,' the young Pharisee asserted, his fists clenched in his lap.

'I'm inclined to agree with your old teacher.' Annas spoke slowly. 'Gamaliel said that if this Jesus movement is not from the Almighty, it will die out. But if, by some chance, it is blessed by the Almighty, then we will not stop it, whatever we do.'

'Jesus was not, nor ever could have been, the Messiah,' Saul thundered.

I was startled by the picture in Saul's mind. He saw Jesus nailed not to a cross but to a tree. Raphael had hit the mark with outstanding accuracy.

'Everyone who honours Jesus must be silenced.'

'What do you propose, Saul?'

'I propose we arrest everybody found proclaiming that this Jesus was . . .' He wouldn't allow himself to speak the words he was thinking. The very idea that Jesus is my Boss's Son is, to Saul, an unutterable heresy. He rephrased his reply. 'We must arrest anyone who claims that Jesus was more than a man, and charge them with blasphemy.'

'I don't want any more martyrs,' Annas said calmly. 'What happened yesterday, with Stephen, was unfortunate.'

Saul looked across the table at the old priest. He was irritated by the man's caution but knew he had to make concessions to get his own way.

'Have it your way,' he declared. 'No deaths. I'll leave them to rot in prison until they lose interest in their Messiah. You have my promise.'

Saul stood to leave. As he opened the door, the high priest said, 'Two more things, Saul.' The young man closed the door again.

'The first is that you and I never had this conversation. What you choose to do is entirely on your own initiative. Do you understand?'

'I do,' Saul said, nodding gravely.

'The second is that I don't want you to go anywhere near the fisherman, Peter.'

Saul scowled.

'I have already arrested him three times,' Annas continued. 'He is mine.'

Saul said nothing, but I saw his thoughts. 'Oh. no he isn't! That loudmouthed Galilean is at the top of my list.'

Saul made his way to the vast outer court of the Temple, to a shaded area called Solomon's Colonnade. A group of people were gathered there, most of whom shone with the spiritual light of my Boss's new-born children. Saul joined them, welcomed with warm smiles. None of those present seemed to know who he was. Matthew, the former tax collector arrived, his expensive Roman coat now worn and faded. A thrill of excitement spread through the small crowd; they were about to hear from one of Jesus' twelve chosen assistants. Saul listened for a while, shaking his head in disagreement at almost everything Matthew said. Then he slipped quietly away. I knew he would be back.

As Saul left I called to his Angel guardian, Harruel – a tortured-looking spirit – and informed him that I would be taking over the care of Saul with immediate effect.

'You're welcome,' he said, darkly. 'I'm off!'

Meanwhile, Matthew told of the day when Jesus walked into his tax office and invited him to join John and Peter as one of his followers. Matthew described his amazement, a year later, when he told a crippled child to stand up and she jumped into his arms and hugged him. He told the people that Jesus' friendship was the best investment they could ever make, that it would insure their lives against Death and judgement.

Saul returned. He sat at the back of Matthew's rapidly growing audience. At the same time, a group of Temple guards appeared at the end of the colonnade. Saul watched Matthew, and the guards watched Saul. He was waiting for an excuse to have the former tax collector arrested.

Eventually Matthew said, 'Brothers and sisters, whoever believes that Jesus is the Son of Almighty God will be forgiven, no matter how many of the laws they have broken.'

Saul looked to the guards and nodded. Two stepped forward and grabbed Matthew by the arms.

'You're under arrest for blasphemy,' one said, marching Matthew off to the Temple prison.

Undeterred, another of my Boss's shining children stood up in Matthew's place and began to talk of her meetings with Jesus. The moment she said something Saul considered to be blasphemous, he nodded at the guards, and she was escorted to the dungeons.

So the pattern continued throughout the day. Despite repeated arrests, the crowd grew, and every time a speaker was taken away someone else stood up and said what they knew about my Boss's Son. I studied the spirits and minds of these people. The news of Stephen's death had convinced them of the urgency of their cause. It didn't matter to them if they too were stoned to death; they believed they would see Jesus just as Stephen had done.

When the Temple horn was blown to announce the time for evening prayers, 17 of Jesus' followers were in prison. The remaining disciples assured their audience that they would return tomorrow. They then went further into the Temple to join the service of prayers and readings. Saul accompanied them.

The daily reading from the Book of their Law was an instruction given by my Boss through Moses when he was preparing the Jews to become an independent nation: *I will hand over to you the people who live in the land and you will drive them out. Do not make any deals with them or with their gods. Do not let them live in your land, or they will cause you to turn against me.*

The priest invited any of the men present to comment on the passage. Saul stood up awkwardly and walked to the front. There was about him none of the icy confidence he had shown in the high priest's office. He was intimidated by the size of the congregation and was desperately lacking in confidence in his ability to say what he wanted to say. I was surprised. 'I can't imagine this man speaking up for my Boss in the middle of Rome,' I thought.

Saul began to speak, or rather to mumble. Half of those present couldn't hear a word he was saying – but that was a blessing.

'Brothers and fathers,' Saul began hesitantly, 'our Law demands that we maintain the purity of our nation and of our faith. We have in our midst a greater and more deadly poison than the dumb idols of the Philistines but, like all false religion, we are commanded by our Lord to root it. . . '

I'd heard enough. My Boss has made me responsible for this angry young man; I didn't intend to do nothing while he spread his hatred of Jesus' new family. I grabbed hold of Saul's venomous tongue and wouldn't allow him to speak another word. The congregation waited for him to continue. Saul tried to force his tongue back into action. I held on tightly. The young Pharisee blushed, let out an incoherent gulping sound and fled. I did not relinquish my grip on his tongue until he was safely inside his own home. He collapsed onto his bed, furious, frustrated, desperate and defeated.

The following evening

Saul lives in the heart of the city, where he rents a spacious and richly furnished upstairs room overlooking a walled garden. This morning, after a breakfast of imported fruits, he returned to the Temple for morning prayers. He listened intently to the daily reading, investigating every phrase with the detailed attention of a hungry hawk, searching out anything that would further his understanding of the mind of God. He was like a man attempting to study the stars through a microscope. For all the industry of his research, there was no chance of him discovering anything whatsoever.

After prayers, Saul organised the despatch of a group of guards to Solomon's Colonnade.

'If you hear anyone claim that Jesus was anything other than the son of a human father,' he instructed, 'arrest them.' He followed the guards to their hunting ground to check that they were obeying his orders and then went down into the Temple basement to interrogate his catch from the previous day.

Saul recorded the names and addresses of all 17 prisoners and quizzed them for information about the movements of their leader, Peter. When he had spoken with each of them individually, he walked into the crowded cell where they were being held, intending to lecture them about the error of their beliefs. He surveyed his Creator's brightly shining children, but his eyes did not see what I could see; he saw only a jumbled assortment of rather vulgar, uneducated strangers. Saul held up his arm to attract the attention of his captives but suddenly became nervous and began to sweat. He remembered what had happened to him the day before and was afraid his tongue would seize up again. He changed his plan. He didn't even attempt to deliver the speech he had composed over breakfast. All he said was, 'You won't leave this prison unless you tell me that Jesus was a liar and a fraud.' He left – hot, anxious and agitated.

Armed with a list of addresses, Saul returned to the guardroom and selected a small arrest party, claiming he had permission from the 'highest authority' to arrest all blasphemers in the city. They set off at a swift march. At the first house, Saul ordered the guards to smash the door open and corner the inhabitants in one room. He had them brought out, one at a time, and asked each one the same question: 'Is Jesus the Son of the Almighty?' If they said 'Yes' they were arrested; if they said anything else, they were driven out into the street with the flat side of a sword.

He proceeded from house to house, terrorising my Boss's children. At each stop, I did my best to spoil Saul's work, advising the disciples that his question was a crude trap. As the day wore on, it was evident that the news had spread around the community of disciples. By the early afternoon, the guards were chasing people through the streets as they escaped from windows and back doors. By evening the houses were deserted; the residents had hastily packed some belongings and fled. When the horn was blown to announce evening prayers, Saul had taken nearly a hundred prisoners.

Early in the morning

During the night I stayed at Saul's side, watching the images that galloped across his mind in his restless sleep. Again and again the same dream returned. Saul dreamt that he was a horse, being ridden by a man he couldn't see. Saul was afraid of this rider, afraid where he might be taken. The rider was pulling on Saul's reins and spurring him with sharp spurs, trying to direct him down a particular road. But Saul – the horse – kept rearing up on his hind legs and turning away from that path. These images were as vivid as life in Saul's mind, but I couldn't make any sense of them.

I called on Jophael, a dream expert. Jophael patiently watched Saul's dream as it returned through the night, each time subtly different.

'He's afraid someone might take control of his life,' my specialist explained. 'The horse image comes from his childhood: he went riding with his father when he was seven and the horse was startled by a dog, turned from the track, and threw the boy into a thorn bush.'

'Why is he remembering a childhood accident?' I asked.

'He isn't,' Jophael replied. 'It's simply that since that accident Saul has been afraid of horses in rather the same way that you and I and other Angelic beings are afraid of water.'

'Why, then, would he dream that he is a horse?' I asked. 'I thought that humans dream about what they most want.'

'You thought incorrectly,' Jophael said carefully. 'Humans fantasise about what they most want, but often they *dream* about what they fear. Saul is afraid of becoming what he most fears.'

'You're not telling me that this highly intelligent man is afraid of turning into a horse!' I exclaimed.

'Of course not. This highly dedicated Jew is afraid of becoming a . . . a . . . a whatever they call someone who isn't a Jew.'

'A Gentile.'

'Thank you.' Jophael was still paying attention to Saul's ongoing dream. 'Your human is terrified of becoming a Gentile, of losing his Jewishness.'

We were interrupted by the arrival of another spirit. Lucifer, once an Archangel and now the leader of the Opposition, slunk into Saul's opulent room. Before the dramatic events of Jesus' execution and subsequent escape from Death, Lucifer had been a proud and powerful tiger among his Opposition forces. Now he's more like a bedraggled wildcat.

'What do you want?' I asked sharply.

'You are interested in this Saul,' my old enemy replied, 'and so, therefore, am I.'

'Get out,' I ordered.

'No.' He settled himself into a corner and watched Saul intently. After an awkward silence Lucifer said, 'I think you will find this man is one of mine.'

I said nothing. I nodded my thanks to Jophael and passed the rest of the night in stony silence in the company of the leader of the Opposition.

That afternoon

Today was a Sabbath, the Jewish day of rest and worship, but Saul has done neither. Unable to borrow any Temple guards because it's their day off, he determined to press the ordinary people of Jerusalem to join his campaign. As soon as it was light, Saul hurried round the city, finding out the times of synagogue services across the capital. Thus informed, he put together a schedule of visits that enabled him to cover as many synagogues as possible in one morning. (I must put on record that one thing I do admire about Saul is his attention to administrative detail.)

When he set out, he was followed by Lucifer as well as me. At the first synagogue, Saul informed the rabbi that he would like to address the congregation and was invited to speak. When he stood at the reading desk, he stretched out his right hand, as he had in the prison the previous morning. Once again he was overcome by fear of failure and the balanced rhetoric of his imagination gave way to short, disjointed sentences.

19

'Our religion is threatened. Our law is undermined.' These were sentiments guaranteed to open the ears of his Jewish audience, but Saul knew he was not managing to communicate well. He looked around the congregation who were waiting for him to identify the threat to their community. The more he looked at the faces in the packed synagogue the less he could remember of his prepared speech. Eventually he blurted out, 'The followers of Jesus must be stopped.'

At this, Lucifer leapt into action. He pounced from person to person, pricking their insecurities and anxieties. There were murmurs of agreement. Saul was encouraged.

'The followers of Jesus say it doesn't matter if you break God's law,' he continued, 'but I say it does.' He may have fired that observation into the dark, but he hit his target.

One man stood up and pointed across the room at a grey-haired Jew.

'He's involved with the Jesus thing,' he declared. I rushed to the side of the accused man, whose spirit was bright with the light of my Boss's love. 'Say nothing!' I whispered into the man's thoughts. 'It's a trap.'

I was overruled by a different voice: 'Just say what I put in your mind.' I was startled by this contradiction. The voice came out of the shining spirit of the same man; it was the unmistakable voice of my Boss. It wasn't either the Father or the Son; I would have noticed them the moment I entered the synagogue. It was the Director.

'Oh, I'm sorry, Sir,' I said. 'I didn't realise you were here. But, anyway, it *is* a trap. Saul is tricking people into supposed blasphemy and then arresting them. He isn't interested in truth.'

'I am,' declared the Director, 'and this child of mine is about to proclaim the Truth.'

The grey-haired man spoke up clearly and boldly. 'I am, most certainly, a follower of Jesus. And Jesus is, most certainly, the Son of God.'

There was uproar. Saul shouted, 'Arrest that man.' Prompted by the leader of the Opposition a number of men descended noisily on the ageing disciple. As they did, other men in the synagogue and women in the gallery, rose to their feet and started shouting that they too were followers of Jesus and that Jesus had fulfilled the Law, not undermined it. They, also, were mobbed. Within seconds, everyone in the place was involved. It might have been a terrible fight – apart from the fact that only one group was fighting. The Director was directing each of his children, telling them, 'Don't hit back. Let them hit you again. Just love them. Just pray for them.'

Saul shouted for order. He jumped up onto the reading desk, motioning with his hand to attract attention. 'Take the Jesus people to the Temple prison,' he instructed. 'I'm due at Mount Zion Synagogue in a few minutes. Who's coming with me?'

He strode into the street followed by an excited rabble and closely accompanied by Lucifer. Not wanting to lose sight of Saul, I went with the mob. As they charged through the city, I saw one of my Boss's new children, pushing his way to the front. I joined him. I needed to consult my Boss and I realised that where this disciple was, I would find the Director.

The man was a visitor from Antioch, called Nicolas. He had resolved to overtake Saul and warn his fellow disciples of their imminent danger. Over the top of Nicolas' urgent prayers I addressed the Director. Although I couldn't see him, I knew that he was somewhere in the heart of this shining man.

'Sir, Sir,' I called. 'It's Oriel here. What should I do?'

From the middle of this human chaos, my Master's voice wore its usual timeless calm. 'Do what I have asked you to do, Oriel.'

'Which is what?' I asked.

'Take Saul to Rome so that he can tell the people there about Jesus.'

'But he's trying to destroy Jesus' work,' I said, pointing out the obvious.

'He will not succeed,' the Director replied, pointing out the even more obvious. I did not know what to say, so I said nothing. The Director spoke again. 'Trust me, Oriel.'

I left Nicolas to run on ahead and went back to Saul, barging Lucifer out of the way as I did. Following the Director's example, I spoke calmly into the confusion of Saul's mind. 'Jesus is not destroying Jewishness,' I said. 'He is the fulfilment of Judaism.'

With these and similar words I addressed the deep-rooted fears from Saul's dreams. I repeatedly shoved Lucifer aside whenever he tried to get close. All to no avail. When we arrived at Mount Zion Synagogue, Nicolas was standing before the congregation, warning his fellow disciples of Saul's mission.

Saul shouted, 'Arrest all the Jesus people' and Nicolas was the first to be bundled to the ground.

While frightened Jews did Lucifer's work, the Director gathered his children into an orderly row in front of Saul. Each, in turn, declared that they were followers of Jesus and that Jesus was the Son of God. Saul had them all arrested. At the same time, other disciples were departing through back exits or windows and running to other synagogues in the city with a message of warning for their sisters and brothers.

By the end of the morning, the prison cells beneath the Temple were full. Such a large gathering of my Boss's children was too good an opportunity to waste. The Director prompted all those who had known Jesus during his earthly life to share their memories and experiences with the captive audience.

I stayed with Saul. He ran from synagogue to synagogue all day in search of the fisherman Peter, but without success. By evening a large number of my Boss's new human family had escaped from Jerusalem into the surrounding towns and villages, taking the story of Jesus with them. Saul returned to his lodgings, exhilarated yet frustrated, and most definitely exhausted.

Monday evening

Saul has spent the past two days interrogating his prisoners. He has not needed to force any of them into blasphemy because each, without exception, has opened their interrogation by stating, 'If I am on charge for my belief in Jesus from Nazareth, who was killed by your people, he is both God and Messiah.'

For myself, I quickly became irritated by this monotonous assertion. In Heaven we don't do or say the same thing twice; my Boss, though eternally the same, never repeats himself.

'This is ridiculous!' I snorted as the fifth disciple said exactly the same thing.

'What is ridiculous?' enquired the Director's voice from inside Saul's latest victim.

'They've already said that four times over.'

'Since when, Oriel,' the Director asked pointedly, 'has proclaiming the truth ever been a ridiculous thing to do?'

I did not attempt to answer the question. Saul took no notice of his prisoner's refrain but questioned him about the whereabouts of their leader, Peter. In time, an answer began to emerge.

Apparently Peter is in Samaria, the hated neighbour of Judea whose quasi-Jewish religion is more offensive to Jews than any of the petty gods of the Greeks and Romans. This news confirmed Saul's greatest fear: that the followers of Jesus are breaking down the very barriers that protect the purity of the Jewish nation.

After evening prayers today, Saul walked though Solomon's Colonnade, savouring its emptiness with satisfaction. The only followers of Jesus to be found in the Temple today are crowded into the dark cells below its ornate precincts.

Saul made his way to the office of Annas, the high priest, where he reported the success of his campaign. He also informed the high priest of Peter's movements. He knew that would increase the old man's concern.

'They have scattered,' Saul explained, 'and that introduces a new problem. This Jesus disease will quickly infect the Jewish communities in big cities like Antioch and Damascus. When the Jesus crowd set up a rival power-base in, say, Alexandria, your leadership of all Judaism will be seriously threatened. If you don't move quickly it may be too late. We must weed them out before they put down roots.'

The old priest was thoughtful. He is a man of books, not a natural politician, but the news that the Jesus movement is becoming established in Samaria frightened him. He was well aware of the threat to his own power.

'Give me until tomorrow, Saul.'

'We don't have until tomorrow,' the young man pressed. 'There are only four days to the next Sabbath. You can be sure that these Jesus people will take their heresy straight to the synagogues when they reach those cities.'

'Where will they go first?' asked Annas.

'Damascus,' replied Saul.

'By this Sabbath?'

'Yes.'

'And you?'

'I don't understand,' Saul replied.

Annas was anxious and irritated. 'Can you reach Damascus before the Sabbath?'

Saul calculated the journey in his mind. 'It would only be possible with . . . horses.'

'Leave at first light,' the high priest ordered. 'Take horses and men from the Temple Guard. I'll prepare papers introducing you

23

to the Jewish leaders in Damascus which you can collect from me at the stables tomorrow morning.'

The focus of Saul's mind blurred slightly at the prospect of four days on a horse but his attention was held in place by a much greater fear.

Very early the next morning – Tuesday

Saul did not get to bed until late after packing for his misguided mission. I tried repeatedly to attract his attention but to no avail. I even employed the risky strategy of making things go wrong for him as he prepared his supper, in the hope it might awaken a negative superstition to alert him of the stupidity of his plan. However, spilt wine, a broken plate, rancid cheese and rotten fruit did absolutely nothing to dissuade him. Saul is not a superstitious man. Which is, of course, a good thing – but it didn't help me very much. Far from becoming uneasy about his latest project, Saul was so excited that his various *misfortunes* failed to bother him at all.

However, when he finally drifted into sleep, he was repeatedly disturbed by the violence of his dreams. The horse that has become a regular feature in his sleep was wild with terror and uncontrollable. Again and again Saul dreamed that he was resisting his rider's spurs and rearing up away from the road. As he rebelled against his nightmare rider, he fell against walls and into ditches, he sank into deep mud or became lost in featureless deserts. Every time, at the point when his dream self was lost and alone, Saul woke up.

I left him to this torture and returned to Heaven, afraid that my mission was on the brink of failure. I needed to consult my Boss.

'I thought you might pay me a visit, Oriel,' he said in greeting. 'And, yes, I do know what Saul is intending to do.'

As he had anticipated my opening question, I paused to consider what to say next.

'Your instructions remain exactly the same, Oriel,' my Boss asserted, before my thoughts had fully taken shape.

'But. . .'

'I do not want Saul taking captives in Damascus,' my Boss informed me. 'I want him captivating hearts and minds in Rome.'

I pondered the full meaning of these words. 'Are you saying that you want me to turn Saul around before he reaches Damascus?'

'It is not Saul's horse that must be turned around, Oriel.' There was an intensity in my Boss's voice. 'But his life.'

I slipped into my office to contemplate my Master's instructions. As I turned the words round and round in my mind, I became aware of being watched. Raphael was standing in the doorway.

'You have to love him, my dear friend,' he said. 'You will get nowhere until you do.'

'He is not a loveable man,' I snapped.

Raphael looked straight at me. 'Do something to help him – something that will not advance your own cause in any way, something that is utterly for him.'

I returned to Saul's lavish home, wondering what this man might need that I could provide.

Midmorning Tuesday

As soon as the sun's light was seeping over the horizon, Saul left his house and jogged through the deserted streets to the stable-yard at the back of the Temple, and I followed. By arrangement, Hagogue was waiting for me – the Angel who helped my Boss with the design and development of horses, donkeys and zebras.

Saul was greeted by the high priest and introduced to the five Temple guards who were to accompany him to Damascus. The group made their way into the stables to select horses for the trip.

'I have allocated twelve horses,' Annas explained. 'With a spare mount each, you can travel faster.'

Saul's nerves quivered at the sight and size of the horses. 'You pick two for me,' he instructed the officer of the guard brusquely, heading for the door and the pale morning light. 'You know more about them than I do.'

'Yes, sir,' the man replied in an unquestioning military style.

'Come on, Hagogue,' I called to my fellow Angel. 'Do your stuff.'

'I'm no good with people,' the rather wild-looking Angel replied. 'You'll have to deal with the man yourself, I'll take care of the horses.'

25

I began to talk into Saul's mind. 'No one here knows you're afraid of horses, and the horse certainly won't know.'

'Hmm. That's not actually true,' Hagogue interrupted. 'The horse will notice almost immediately.'

'Well, what should I tell Saul?' I asked crossly.

'Tell him to relax and control the horse with a firm hand.'

This was not going well. I worked on Saul's agitated nervous system, easing the tension in his mind and muscles. When the horses clattered out into the cobbled yard I spoke to him again. 'Now go up to that horse, give it a firm pat on the side and stroke its neck.'

'The *it* is a *he*,' Hagogue informed me.

As Saul stretched out his right hand towards his first horse, I held it tightly to keep it from shaking.

'Saddle it up, officer.' Saul kept his order short and sharp so as not to betray the panic steadily growing in his mind.

'Now that's the kind of treatment this horse needs,' Hagogue observed. 'Tell Saul to take control of his mount in much the same way that he does the humans.'

While the guards prepared the horses, Annas spoke quietly to Saul. 'Remember,' he said, 'I don't want any more deaths. Arrest the leaders and bring them back here for trial, but please don't bring me every man, woman and child; the prison's not big enough.'

The five guards were already mounted and waiting for Saul. As soon as the young man turned to face the magnificent black beast awaiting him, Hagogue started issuing instructions.

'Get him to hold firmly onto the horse's neck,' he instructed.

'Hold firmly onto the horse's neck,' I repeated.

'Push up with the left leg, pull with the arms and swing the right leg over the back of the horse.'

'Push up with the left leg, pull with the arms and swing the right leg over the . . . Oh!'

Saul was beached like a whale across the saddle cloth, his head and arms on one side and his legs dangling down on the other. I sensed the amusement of the guards as they looked down on the young intellectual who was supposed to be their leader. The horse shifted restlessly.

'Get him on, quick!' Hagogue implored.

I thinned my Angelic substance sufficiently to get a firm hold of Saul's backside and shoved him firmly into position. No sooner was he in the saddle than the horse began to skip around the yard bouncing Saul up and down like puppet with a broken string.

'Tell him to squeeze firmly with his knees,' Hagogue instructed urgently, 'and pull down hard on the reins.'

I passed on Hagogue's message, while forcibly manipulating Saul's limbs in the required fashion. 'You can do it, you can do it,' I repeated into his mind, while Hagogue whispered calmingly to the horse. The creature settled down and eventually stood still. I quickly glanced around the minds of the guards searching for a little sympathy towards Saul. I found some in the officer and pointed it out to the man's Angel guardian. 'Can you see that sympathy?' I asked. 'Work on it. This poor soul of mine needs a friend.'

The Angel responded immediately and the officer drew his horse to Saul's side. 'You'll be fine, son,' he said quietly, so that his men couldn't hear. 'I'll ride with you 'til you get the hang of it.'

Saul smiled breathlessly at the older man. 'Thank you.'

The six humans and twelve horses set off towards the eastern gate of Jerusalem. Hagogue kept up a constant conversation with Saul's horse, updating me with instructions concerning the rider's posture and horsemanship. When the group reached the open road and were trotting towards the rising sun, I gradually loosened my grip on Saul's arms and legs, allowing him to ride on his own.

The group are now resting and changing horses. Saul is taking a lesson from Nathan, the officer, in how to fit a saddle cloth. Hagogue is studying the spare horses to decide which is best suited to a novice rider.

Pella – late evening

The group rode, rested and rode on again throughout the daylight hours and stopped for the night at an inn on the edge of Pella. Nathan and Saul ate their supper together while Saul explained the purpose of their mission in greater detail.

'Actually, my wife was a bit of a fan of that Jesus,' Nathan informed his companion. 'He told cracking stories, I gather.'

'Did you ever hear him yourself?' Saul asked.

'A couple of times. But I haven't got time for getting religious, if you'll pardon me for saying.'

'And what did you think of Jesus?' Saul pressed.

'I thought he was a good man.'

Saul was surprised by Nathan's reply. 'Why?' he asked.

'Don't know. It's just the impression I got, that's all. And now, if you'll excuse me, I need to check the horses.'

Saul was alone. For the first time since I met him, there is in his mind the possibility of a positive image of Jesus. I need to work on that.

Next day – Wednesday

Saul slept more easily last night. In part, I don't doubt, he was exhausted from his ride. But there was a significant difference in his dreams. Though he was still dreaming of himself as a horse, the horse was less frightened. As on previous nights, the same dream was recycled in Saul's sleeping mind but now I could perceive the slightest hint that the rider could be right, that his chosen path might just be passable.

Saul woke with a fresher mind. The state of his body, however, was not so encouraging. Almost every muscle was stiff from yesterday's exertions. After various attempts at hauling his body out of bed, he eventually had to roll onto the floor and crawl across to a chair before painfully pulling himself into an upright position. When the Temple guards saw the agony he suffered in the simple act of sitting at the breakfast table, they failed to conceal their laughter.

'You'll feel fine by this time next week,' Nathan assured him with a smile. Saul grunted through a mouthful of bread. 'I'll get your horse ready.'

When Saul stood beside his horse, the prospect of mounting it seemed akin to vaulting an elephant. 'I'm sure it's grown overnight,' he thought to himself.

'Come on, Saul,' I urged him, 'we can do this.' I gave him a great shove and launched the man onto his mount. That achieved, I settled myself behind him and spent the day whispering into his thoughts. 'Remember what Nathan said. Why should you be afraid of Jesus?'

With these and similar ideas I attempted to re-draw the negative image of Jesus which dominates Saul's mind. For some reason, perched precariously on top of his horse, Saul was less deaf to my encouragement.

At the second rest stop, I was further encouraged by a conversation between Saul and Nathan.

'Tell me more about Jesus,' Saul said. 'Tell me one of his stories.'

Nathan became embarrassed and tried to turn the conversation to practical details about their journey – but Saul was not going to be distracted.

'Nathan, you said yesterday that Jesus told cracking stories – so tell me one.'

'I'm not sure I can remember any of them now,' he said.

Saul persisted.

'Well,' the officer started hesitantly, 'he was a carpenter before he was a story teller and he told us about this man who had a speck of sawdust in his eye. And there was this other man who was trying to take the dust out of the first man's eye, but the second man . . .' Nathan started laughing.

'Go on,' Saul urged, irritated.

'Well, the second man, who was trying to get the speck out of his friend's eye, he had a ruddy great plank in his own eye!'

Nathan, chuckling, had clearly finished.

'Is that it?' Saul asked, grim-faced.

'You had to be there, really. It was the way he told it,' said Nathan, awkwardly.

Back on the road, Saul had closed his mind to any positive thoughts about Jesus. 'A teller of silly stories' were the words running through his mind.

Gamala – Thursday morning

I saw evidence during the night that the horse rider in Saul's dream is undoubtedly Jesus. Saul dreamt that every time the rider prodded his bronze spurs into the horse's flanks he also told an inane story, giggling like a child as he did so. Unsurprisingly, it was in a dark mood that the intense young Jew hobbled his way down to breakfast this morning. He was consciously ignoring the pain in his back and legs, because his mission is far more important to him than the discomforts of horse riding; he is more determined than ever to silence the stories of Jesus.

When they set off, I let Saul clamber up onto his horse on his own. I was angry with him and did not want to contribute in any way to his quest to wipe away all memory of my Master's life.

Raphael arrived. He took one look at Saul and exclaimed, 'Oriel, dear old thing, you have done it. Well done!'

'Done what?' I asked curtly, not in the mood for Raphael's obscure humour.

'You have been *loving* him, my dear,' he replied enthusiastically. 'Look at him. If I'm not mistaken, you helped him overcome his fear of horses.'

'Well, I had to. . .' I began.

'No you did not *have* to,' Raphael interrupted. 'You *chose* to. And that, my dear friend, is love.'

I watched as Saul guided his horse onto the road. All I could see was his arrogant determination to complete his mission.

'That's all very well,' I said glumly, 'but I haven't made any impression on his hatred for the Son.'

'That's our next task,' Raphael said breezily.

'*Our* task?'

'I've come to help you, Oriel. Our Boss suggested you might need a little . . . assistance.'

I was tempted to insist I was getting on fine, but that wasn't true. 'He's quite right,' I conceded.

The men and horses were setting off on the next leg of their journey.

'What did you have in mind, Raphael?' I asked.

'I thought I would give him a scripture lesson.'

'Stephen advised me not to quote scripture at him.'

'I know,' Raphael said. 'What I had in mind was more a guided tour than a bombardment with biblical missiles. Would you like to come along?'

I'm all too familiar with the painful detail of Raphael's discourses. 'Thanks,' I replied politely, 'but I will take the opportunity to catch up with some other business.'

I left Saul in Raphael's dependable, if long-winded, care.

Ituraea – Thursday night

When I rejoined Raphael at Saul's third and final stop before Damascus, he was dull with disappointment.

'He agreed with me on most points,' Raphael reported. 'But whenever I brought him close to a new understanding of our Boss's plan, he would simply come up with, *I must arrest them all, every single one*, or something indecipherable about specks of sawdust.'

'I'm going to call Michael and Gabriel,' I told Raphael. 'Tomorrow's our last chance. He'll be in Damascus by nightfall.'

Shortly after Saul was asleep, the two other Archangels arrived. We left the confines of time and place in order to forge our plans without Earthly rush; we certainly needed that freedom.

'The question is,' Gabriel began, 'how do we move a human mind forward from acknowledging facts to embracing truth?'

When we had carefully considered all the possibilities, all the dangers and all the limitations of our task, we agreed on a specific plan and divided its numerous details between us. After what would have been many human hours of intense discussion, I returned to Saul's side, only to find the leader of the Opposition feeding his mind with guilt and fear.

'Get away from him,' I yelled, angry with myself for leaving Saul unprotected at such a crucial moment.

'I want this one,' Lucifer whined.

Midday Friday

Before Saul woke, Michael arrived in full battle gear and wrestled Lucifer away. I escorted my human charge to the breakfast table, where he sat with considerably more ease than on previous mornings. When the meal was over, Saul and Nathan rode ahead of the other guards, surrounded by a squadron of Michael's most experienced Angelic soldiers. Lucifer was nowhere to be seen.

Once everyone had settled into the rhythm of the ride, Raphael set about his allotted task. He scanned through every sentence of Jewish scripture stored in Saul's brain, searching for something important to him, which contradicts the uncompromising edifice of his pharisaical beliefs. My task was to repair the damage done in Saul's mind by Lucifer's meddling during the night, and to reassure him that there's no need to be suspicious of Jesus. Gabriel should be in position somewhere near the end of the day's journey, preparing for his part in the operation.

As the morning drifted on, we were joined by an increasing number of Opposition spirits; first four, then another three, and so on until there were nearly a hundred enemy spirits around us. Michael expanded his militia to twice that number. The horses seemed to travel faster for their spiritual company. We are now in the hills that look down on Damascus sprawled across the plain below and the humans have stopped for lunch.

A short while ago, something significant happened. An Arab herdsman came up the road from the Damascus, leading a large flock of sheep and goats.

Nathan, with a mouthful of cheese, pointed to the man and said to Saul, 'That reminds me of one of the stories Jesus told us.'

Saul responded impatiently. 'What?'

'It was about a shepherd,' Nathan continued, undeterred, 'who was taking a hundred sheep to market. He stopped at a well for a drink and noticed that one of his ewes had wandered off.' The officer paused for a mouthful of wine and then continued, 'I bet you'll never guess what the idiot did.'

Saul had no intention of guessing.

Nathan let out a small snigger. 'He left the 99 perfectly good sheep right there on the road and ran back to find the stupid bleater that had got itself lost. And then . . .' He paused for effect – Saul waited impatiently – 'then, when he found the ridiculous creature, he picked it up, put it over his shoulder, carried it straight back to his home and held a massive party in its honour!'

'And what, in Heaven's name,' Saul asked angrily, 'does that have to do with the kingdom of God?'

'Someone asked Jesus that,' Nathan went on, buoyed up by several more mouthfuls of wine. 'All he said was, *God's like that.*'

'May Angels defend us!' Saul exclaimed, to which there was a great cheer – one he couldn't hear – from the large gathering of Angels who were doing just that!

Outside Damascus – Friday afternoon

The afternoon began much as the morning had ended. Our Angelic escort grew in step with the increasing Opposition force. Raphael returned to his methodical search of Saul's memory and I worked on his feelings about God. Sadly, he imagines my Boss as a kind of humourless, nit-picking accountant.

As we drew, step by equine step, closer to Damascus, and therefore to Gabriel, I began to feel uneasy about our plan. We had based it on a method we have used before to good effect, but things have changed since the days of Balaam.

When we descended onto the flat plain that surrounds the city, my reservations grew. A short distance in front of the gates of Damascus, Gabriel was waiting in the middle of the road. Between him and us there were two long lines of Angels, forming a funnel to channel Saul towards the Archangel.

Raphael, who had been utterly focussed on the intricate networks of Saul's brain, suddenly exclaimed, 'I've got it!'

'Got what?' I asked, but he had already set off to tell Gabriel. 'Raphael!' I shouted after him, 'I need to know. What is it?' If he heard me above his excitement, he did not respond.

I looked at Michael. 'There's something not quite right about all this,' I said.

'We agreed on the plan,' he reminded me. 'To change anything now would be reckless.'

I knew he was right, but my unease was rising. Saul had entered the Angelic funnel and it was closing behind him; he was surrounded. Opposition spirits began to attack Gabriel's ring of Angels from the outside and Michael's troops counter-attacked.

I was still unhappy. My doubt centred on Raphael's advice about love. Our plan was an act of coercion. Saul was no more than a hundred paces from Gabriel. I had to make a decision: to continue with the plan or follow my own intuition?

As Saul approached, Gabriel began to slow his Angelic form down to the spectrum of energy visible to the human eye. But he was not slowing to the human-like form he uses to deliver messages – we couldn't take the risk of Saul missing him altogether. On this occasion Gabriel intended to terrify Saul by deliberately appearing as a vast shining figure, towering above his skinny body.

Saul could not fail to see the bright light above him. Gabriel began to boom down at Saul the words delivered to him by

Raphael, 'Abraham believed God, and it was credited to him as righteousness.'

I decided to abandon our plan. 'It's all right,' I shouted into Saul's mind over the top of Gabriel's message. 'God loves you, just as you are. He loves you, Saul. Do you hear that? He simply loves you.'

Chaos! All around there was a full-scale spiritual battle between Angels and Opposition spirits. With all the spiritual fervour of that conflict, it took me a while to focus on the human drama in front of me. Gabriel had overdone it. The horses bolted in terror, hurling their riders to the ground. Saul himself had been physically blinded by the brightness of Gabriel's Heavenly appearance and further injured by his fall. There was shouting and screaming, much of it aimed at me. Then the Son arrived.

Angels and Opposition spirits halted mid-fight and watched as the Heavenly man Jesus crouched down next to the frightened Jew, Saul. Jesus held Saul's trembling hand and spoke to him in his own native language.

'Saul?' he asked gently, 'why are you persecuting me?'

Saul could hear the voice, he could feel the presence beside him, but could not see a thing; his eyes were completely burnt out. Jesus continued to talk soothingly to the terrified young man. 'Saul,' he said, 'it's hard when you are fighting against the spurs.'

Saul, oblivious to the hordes of loyal and rebellious spirits which surrounded him, was aware of the firm touch and reassuring voice of someone he had never met before.

'Who are you?' he asked.

The Son raised Saul up until he was sitting on the road and said simply, 'I am Jesus. The one you are persecuting.'

Saul grasped those hands which were the only fixed points in his dark world, and Jesus pulled him carefully to his feet, brushing the dust and dirt from his clothes.

I watched in awe as Saul's mind and spirit responded to the Son's love.

'What do you want me to do, Lord?' he asked.

At the word *Lord* all my stress and anxiety evaporated. The Son had achieved in a few moments what I had completely failed to do over days.

'Go into the city,' Jesus instructed Saul. 'You will be told why I have chosen you.'

The Son turned round and called forward one of the Angels who were gawping at the scene.

'Haziel, go with Saul and find him suitable lodgings in a quiet part of the city. Stay with him until Oriel returns.'

Then he turned to me. 'Oriel! Find Raphael, Gabriel and Michael, then come and see me.'

In my office

The Son told the four of us to wait in my office until we were called. Not one of us spoke. There was nothing to say. In our meeting last night, we had considered all the options we were aware of, and around those considerations we had constructed our plan. I was angry with Gabriel for blinding Saul. I expected that the others were even angrier with me for abandoning my part in the plan at the last moment, and yet I still felt in the depths of my spirit that I had made the right decision.

When our Boss's voice eventually called us into his office, the area outside his room was deserted and eerily silent. I pushed the door open. My Boss's room was filled with serious faces: Angels, Cherubs, Humans, and numerous other creatures for which there are no human words. In the middle of them all was our Creator: Father, Son and Director. Everyone was looking at us. We made our way into the centre of the room and stopped. There wasn't a sound or movement in the entire assembly.

I looked into my Boss's eyes and saw there a sparkle of brightness that reassured me that he still loved me. At that same moment the room exploded with a great cheer. Music started and there was dancing and jumping and waving and singing and clapping all around us. Our Boss, in the middle of this, seemed to be doing all of these at once.

'Oriel, Raphael, Gabriel, Michael,' he sang over the top of – yet still in harmony with – all the sounds that filled the room. 'Well done!' There was another great cheer. 'Well done and well done indeed.'

Then my Boss called my name, and the room seemed to become quiet, although I do not think it really did.

'Oriel, especially well done. You loved Saul and you risked your own reputation for that love. Thank you.'

I was amazed.

Stephen and Moses both stepped forward and gave me tight

embraces. I turned around to see Raphael dancing with Abraham, and Michael shaking hands with King David. We celebrated until every nuance of Heavenly delight had been expressed. Saul had accepted his adoption as a child in my Boss's family – what a party!

Judas' house, Straight Street, Damascus

When the celebration was over and everyone returned to their different activities, the Son approached me with Gabriel at his side and said, 'Come on, Oriel, we have work to do.'

'Yes,' I replied, gathering my thoughts after the excitement of the party. 'We have to deliver young Saul to Rome.'

'One thing at a time,' the Son said, carefully pruning my expectations. 'Gabriel and I are off to visit a brother of mine called Ananias, who lives in Damascus. Tell Saul to expect a visit from him.'

We returned to Damascus and went our separate ways. Saul was easy enough to find; his spirit was shining brightly with its new-found faith in my Boss. His body, however, was in a bad state. His skin was scratched and bruised after falling from his horse, his muscles were stiff from sudden inactivity after four days' riding, his eyes were still not working at all and in addition to all that he hadn't eaten or drunk anything for three days.

I looked accusingly at his temporary guardian, Haziel. 'What have you done to him?'

'He won't eat,' the inexperienced Angel replied. 'He has resolved to starve himself for a week as a penance for all he's done against our Boss.'

'Didn't you tell him he's already forgiven?'

'Is he?'

'Weren't you there when the Son died?'

'Yes,' the Angel said, 'but . . .'

'What's your usual job?'

'I work as an archivist in Gabriel's department,' he replied.

I took a fresh look at this Angel and his temporary charge. Perhaps he hadn't done such a bad job, for someone who's had no training in guardianship. Saul was in excellent health spiritually, even if his body required some attention.

'Would you be interested in a transfer into the Human Guardian Scheme?' I asked.

He looked at me with an expression of mild shock. 'No thank you,' he said politely.

When Haziel had gone, I turned my attention to Saul. He was lying on his bed, deep in prayer. When I pushed at the door of his mind, which had been firmly locked against me three Earth days ago, it swung open. I introduced into Saul's thoughts the image of a man called Ananias, coming to visit him, sent by Jesus.

Almost immediately there was a timid knock on the door to Saul's room. 'Yes?' Saul called out, his voice as sharp as ever.

The door opened slowly and in came a bright but anxious-looking man who had a startled look in his eyes – which I must say is common to almost everyone who has just been visited by Gabriel.

'Excuse me, I'm sorry to bother you.'

'What is it?' The acidity of Saul's reply dispelled the remaining euphoria from the party. Although Saul has changed sides, he hasn't changed.

'Are you, by any chance, Saul from Tarsus?' Ananias asked hesitantly.

Saul did not sit up to greet his visitor. His unseeing eyes stared emptily at the ceiling. 'You must be Ananias.'

The timid disciple affirmed his identity. He closed the door and stood up a little straighter, then began the message he had obviously prepared as he walked across the city.

'My brother Jesus, who you met on the road, asked me to come.'

'I was expecting you,' Saul stated. 'You've come to put your hands on my eyes and restore my sight.'

He had picked up my input to the last detail – I was greatly encouraged!

'Yes, that's right,' Ananias replied in his hesitant way, 'and also so that you will be filled with God's Spirit.'

'Well, you'd better get on with it, man.'

'Yes, you're quite right,' Ananias agreed. He stepped carefully across the room to Saul and gently laid a hand over each of Saul's eyes. 'Brother Saul,' he said, 'receive your sight.'

When Ananias removed his hands it was as if dark scales were falling, one at a time, from Saul's eyes. Piece by piece, his eyesight returned. Saul was overcome by the experience and the two men looked at each other in awe-struck silence. When Saul's vision was completely restored, Ananias stepped back with the relief of a man who had just disarmed a large bomb.

'If I am to be a disciple of Jesus,' Paul announced, 'I must be dipped in water like all his other followers.'

A broad smile crept over Ananias' face. 'There's a water trough in the yard,' he suggested.

'Let's do it,' Saul urged.

The two men walked out into the bright sunlight, down the steps at the side of the house and across to the stone trough used for watering horses and camels. Saul stood at one end of the trough and asked, 'How do we do this?'

'Just bend over a bit,' Ananias suggested, taking a confident lead for the first time since meeting his former persecutor. He stood beside Saul and grabbed the hair at the back of his head. Then, without warning, he plunged Saul's head and shoulders down into the cold water. What I saw next sent a shudder throughout my being. As Saul was forced into that suffocating liquid, his human spirit began to fade dramatically. The water was killing him.

'Saul,' Ananias said excitedly, 'I dip you in the name of the Father . . .' He pulled Saul's head, dripping, out of the water and as soon as the young man had taken a gasp, he pushed it back down with a splash and the words, 'and of the Son . . .'

I was unsure what to do. I desperately wanted to intervene, to stop Ananias from destroying the life I had worked so hard to rescue, but I knew that this dipping was one of the instructions left by the Son for his followers. I watched closely. Although water can easily destroy a man's physical life, it was only Saul's spirit that was being affected.

Again Ananias pulled him up for a quick breath, then down into the trough for a third time, to the words, 'and of the Holy Spirit'. Ananias pulled the soaking torso out into the life-sustaining air and let go of him. Saul's spirit was completely dead. Ananias then raised his hands and placed them on Saul's forehead.

'Brother Saul,' he said, 'receive the Holy Spirit.' This phrase was new to me and I was not sure what to expect. I watched carefully as the Director stepped from the depths of Ananias' spirit and settled equally securely in the body of the young Jew. Immediately, Saul's spirit came alive again, shining with a renewed, Heavenly light. Saul had become one of my Boss's sons.

The effect of the Director's arrival was remarkable to watch. Not only was Saul's spirit completely reborn, but his body responded too: tight limbs were loosened, his exhausted mind was refreshed. He smiled at Ananias and said, 'Gracious, I'm hungry.'

A great cheer of Heavenly delight erupted from behind me. I turned to see my Boss in the middle of the yard, both Father and Son, accompanied by Gabriel and Haziel. They were clearly enjoying the spectacle; I had found it quite terrifying.

Saul arranged for bread, meat and wine to be brought and the two humans sat in the sunshine while Saul told Ananias the story of his mission to Damascus and his unexpected encounter with Jesus. Ananias listened, carefully studying the slight man whose reputation is so monstrous. The Son himself, unseen by the two men, sat with them at the table, joining the modest party.

Ananias' house – five days later

The evening of his dipping, Saul left the house of Judas, accepting an invitation to stay with Ananias and his wife Joanna. Since then, he has enjoyed the homely charm of the couple's simple life and has met many of the followers of Jesus who had escaped his clutches only two weeks earlier in Jerusalem. Like Ananias before them, these faithful people approached Saul with considerable caution, anxious that his apparent conversion might be a trap, but without exception they have returned to their own lodgings reassured and glowing with joy.

Saul has been eager to learn about Jesus from his former victims; he has been especially interested to hear, again and again, their accounts of Jesus' cruel execution and subsequent return from death. This one story fascinates him more than all the homely parables of Jesus' teaching. In fact, I perceive that Saul is still struggling to understand how the powerful acts of God can be appropriately contained in such worldly tales.

Yesterday evening, at the Sabbath meal, Ananias was once again timid and faltering in Saul's company. All week the older man has been conscious that he still had one more message to deliver to Saul from Jesus. In the excitement and busyness of so many visitors, he had failed to find an appropriate moment to complete his mission, but yesterday, at a quiet meal with just Saul and Joanna, he knew it had to be said. Nonetheless, Ananias was unsure how Saul would respond to the instructions he had to pass on.

'Saul,' he said in a deliberately serious way to mark a significant turn in their conversation. There was silent anticipation round the table. Ananias had not even shared these thoughts with his wife.

'When our Lord, Jesus, sent me to you to heal you and dip you,' he continued cautiously, 'there was one more thing he asked me to tell you.' Ananias waited while Saul finished a mouthful of boiled chicken and could pay full attention to his host. 'Jesus told me he had chosen you and called you for a specific reason.' Again Ananias waited. This time he was waiting for the courage to continue.

'Come on man, spit it out,' Saul urged.

'Jesus said . . .'

'Yes, I've got that bit.'

'He said, *I have chosen his man to tell my story to the Gentiles and to their kings.*'

Saul's blood pressure fell dramatically and he struggled to keep his body upright in his seat. Among his fellow Jews Saul is brash and bursting with confidence, but the prospect of meeting with non-Jews, or Gentiles as the Jews call them, was more intimidating for him than his fears of riding any horse. He was afraid, very afraid, and fought hard to master the horror that rose, like backed up sewage, through his being.

'Did Jesus say anything else?' Saul enquired weakly.

'That was all.'

'Thank you for the meal, Joanna.' Saul pushed his half-empty plate away and said, 'I think I shall go to bed.'

He did not sleep. He lay on his bed and again and again he called out to Jesus who had spoken with him outside the gates of Damascus. 'Is it true Lord?' he asked. Above the jangling noise of his own ingrained prejudice and fear, he repeated the question. 'To the Gentiles, Lord? The Gentiles?'

When I first met Saul, the delicate balance of his mind was held together by his energetic hatred of all things related to Jesus. Since he met Jesus, human to human, that hatred has been replaced by an equally energetic excitement. At supper this evening, his energy crashed. I am concerned for the balance of Saul's mind. I sent for Raphael, asking him to join me immediately. Raphael quickly understood the problem and engaged Saul in conversation in his prayers.

'Remember, my dear Saul,' he said, 'how the prophets said that the kings of the nations would bring their offerings to God in Jerusalem.'

'I remember,' Saul replied, 'but they expected the Gentiles to come to Jerusalem. Ananias said that I must go to them, right into their sinful, lawless cities.'

'How will they come to Jerusalem, friend Saul, if they have not been invited?' Raphael explained. 'And how will they be invited, unless someone goes to them? And who will go to them unless they are sent?'

That is how Raphael began. He went on all night and Saul got very little, if any, sleep until the sun was once again spreading its thin light over the city of Damascus and Raphael returned to his Heavenly duties. Joanna had to shake Saul awake so that he could have breakfast before the short walk to the synagogue.

By the time Saul and Ananias arrived, the synagogue was already pulsing with excitement. Nathan and his Temple guards had spent the week with the chief rabbi, as planned, and they still expected Saul to turn up with the high priest's papers and arrest the leaders of Jesus' disciples. The leaders of Jesus' disciples, on the other hand, had turned up early in order to pass on the news of Saul's dramatic conversion. Where these two rumours met, confusion reigned. No sooner had Saul stepped through the doorway than he was invited to address the whole synagogue. Everyone was eager to hear what he had to say. As he made his way to the reading platform, Nathan grabbed his arm.

'What do you want me to do?' he asked.

In all the excitement of the week, Saul had largely forgotten that Nathan would be awaiting his orders and he was not sure what to say to the loyal soldier.

'Do whatever you believe is right,' Saul informed him.

Saul reached the platform, climbed it and swept an out-stretched arm slowly in front him to call for attention. Then, as has happened before, his mind froze at the sight of so many people waiting to hear him speak. There was a long silence. Every person in the room was eager to hear Saul speak and the wait did not dampen their expectations. Indeed, their excitement merely grew.

I was about to take control of the situation when the Director served a single sentence into Saul's mind. Saul spoke it.

'My fellow Israelites, I am here today concerning Jesus from Nazareth who was crucified and who, it was reported, rose from death.' Every single person in the room listened eagerly. Whatever their position on the Jesus issue, they anticipated that Saul was on their side.

'This Jesus,' Saul continued, repeating the words placed in his mind, 'has been called the Son of Almighty God – a claim that is held by many to be blasphemous.' A variety of murmurs rippled along the benches of the synagogue. 'I have met this Jesus,' he said clearly. The murmurs evaporated. Every mind focused again on Saul. 'I have spoken with him, and I am here to tell you the truth about the storytelling carpenter.'

Those who opposed the Jesus movement sensed victory. Nathan nodded to his men, checking that they were ready for action.

'I have met with this Jesus,' Saul repeated, his voice gaining strength. 'I met him last week.' There was a gasp of shock from the anti-Jesus lobby. Saul continued. 'I can tell you that Jesus is very much alive and that he is, without doubt, the Son of Almighty God.'

Saul has a knack for reducing synagogues to chaos and today was no exception. The Jesus followers stood and cheered, their Angels with them. The chief rabbi slumped back in his chair. Those who resisted the influence of Jesus started shouting and pointing accusing fingers. Those who were undecided chatted excitedly among themselves. As far as I could see, there was only one calm person in the entire gathering, and that was Nathan. He sat with his hands on his knees, an amused but satisfied smile on his face.

That night

Saul returned to Ananias and Joanna's home in a thoughtful mood. He ran through the events at the synagogue in his mind, trying to determine whether his appearance there had been a success or a failure. He did not know about the numerous con-versations struck up between Jesus' disciples and those who were fascinated to hear more about the death-defying rabbi. All that Saul had seen was the chaos; all he had heard were the partisan cheers of one group and the accusing shouts of the other. These memories did not encourage him.

At first I considered broadening his understanding so he could see how my Boss's new family had grown through his outspoken courage. But I decided against it. My task is to prepare Saul to tell Jesus' story in the streets of Rome, not in the synagogues of Damascus. 'Don't worry about the synagogue,' I told him as he sat in his room with his head hidden in his hands. 'Your calling is not to the Jews – but to the Gentiles and their rulers.'

He stood up and began to pack his bags. Once again he had heard my words, echoing round his mind.

Next morning

At breakfast, Saul told Ananias and Joanna that he was going away for a few days to visit the Arab villages around Damascus, just as Jesus had toured the towns and villages of Galilee. I could see in Ananias' mind a longing to go with Saul, but he knew that he needed to stay in the city and work to support his family. He suppressed his desire to join Saul, convincing himself that Joanna would not be happy to let him go.

Before they had finished eating there was a knock at the door. It was Nathan.

'We're going home. Our work here's finished,' the soldier announced with a warm smile.

'Thank you for all your help,' Saul said. Then, after a pause, he added, 'What will you tell the high priest?'

'I'm not sure,' Nathan replied. His smile broadened. 'Maybe I'll tell him you've changed tactics and are trying to convince the Damascus Jews of the truth about Jesus.'

'I'm sure he'll misunderstand you,' Saul said, seriously.

Nathan chuckled. 'I hope so.'

The two men embraced, said their farewells and Nathan left. At the door he stopped. 'I'm leaving you the two horses. You need a bit more practice!'

As soon as the door closed behind him, Joanna said excitedly, 'Two horses! Ananias, my love, why don't you go with Saul? It's not good for a man to be alone.'

There followed a delicate conversation about who needed who most and who would provide for who how. Saul left them to it and attended to the horses. When he returned, husband and wife were still tiptoeing around one another's sensitivities regarding money.

'I'm a fully qualified tentmaker,' Saul announced. 'There will be plenty of work for me among the Arabs. We'll come back here at regular intervals to share our earnings. Come on, Ananias – if you're coming there's nothing to be gained from waiting around!'

My thoughts exactly.

Kanata – that evening

As the two men rode side by side out of the city, I spoke to the Director, residing deep in the spirits of both disciples.

'Where are we going?'

'Forwards,' he replied.

'What do you want me to do?' I enquired.

'Go ahead of us and find an Arab with a broken tent?' he suggested.

Searching for a broken tent – for an Angel – is a far from simple task. It was easier to search for a Angel guardian with a human who had a broken tent. At each Arab encampment en route I stopped and called for the attention of all the Angels and asked if any of them had a human in need of an expert tentmaker. This is not the kind of activity I anticipated when I took on Saul of Tarsus.

Eventually I came across a group of Angels whose family were distraught at the state of their old and much-patched tent. They could not afford a new one but no longer fitted their growing children into their present dwelling. I explained that help was at hand and raced back to find Saul.

Saul and Ananias reached the family at midday. They were greeted with customary Arab hospitality and invited into the shabby tent for refreshment. During a lull in the conversation, Saul looked around him and commented, 'It looks like you could do with an extension.'

'We could,' the woman replied anxiously, 'but the local tent man said ours was too old to extend.'

Her husband added, 'He said we need a completely new one.'

'Nonsense!' Saul exclaimed, and began to explain in bewildering detail how he could cut, sew and re-appoint the present tent.

I admit I quickly lost track of the conversation. So, while Saul was talking tents, I had my own conversation with the Director.

'Where did he get all this tent know-how from?'

'His family have been in the tent business for generations,' he replied. 'His father won a contract to supply the Roman army and they were so impressed with his work – and his price – they rewarded the whole family with Roman citizenship.'

Saul's discussions with the Arab family had moved on to the tricky subject of payment. 'All I ask,' Saul insisted, 'is food and accommodation for my colleague and me while we do the work and some supplies to take with us when we finish.'

The couple nodded in overwhelmed gratitude.

'Plus,' Saul added, emphasising that this was the important part of the deal, 'I ask that you allow us to tell you all about a friend of ours called Jesus.'

They readily accepted Saul's terms, handing him a sandal as confirmation of the deal. Saul detailed a long list of things he would need and work began immediately.

During the afternoon, the man tried to extract some information from Saul about 'this Jesus' who he was insisting on telling them about. He is suspicious that Saul might be from some oppressive religious cult and is uneasy about letting his children be exposed to such matters.

I asked the Director about it. 'Could the wonderful growth of your new human family be understood as being an oppressive *religious cult?*'

In reply, the Director showed me how he had been guiding the Arab man's thoughts and feelings about religious matters, preparing him for the occasion when he would hear the story of the Son's human life.

This evening, when the sun's light had faded, the man gathered his whole family around a fire and invited Saul to tell his story.

Three days later

The tent extension is finished. Saul employed the entire family in the work and the newly enlarged tent looks stronger than it has for years (according to the opinion of the family's Angel guardians). Far more important than the growth of the tent, has been the growth of the nightly gatherings around the fire. Relatives and friends have been invited to hear the tentmaker's stories of a carpenter who defeated death.

This morning, after Saul and Ananias had packed their few possessions on the horses and were taking their leave of the family, the father said, 'My good friend Saul, we wish to become disciples of this Jesus. Will you help us mark our decision by dipping us in the same way that Ananias dipped you?'

Saul was startled. The strength of his Jewish prejudices about Arabs had kept him from believing that his nightly audience would ever fully embrace his very Jewish message about a very Jewish Messiah. I was not surprised. I have watched the spirit of both the man and his wife grow in brightness until they far outshone the fire around which they sat. Last night, as they lay in their bed, they prayed together, 'God of the Jews, if you will hear our prayer, don't let Saul leave us until we can share the new life that he speaks of.'

Saul's immediate thought was to offer to circumcise his Arab friend instead of dipping him. It was clear to me that such a suggestion would not be well received. The man wanted to be a friend of Jesus, not a servant of Moses.

Ananias intervened. He doesn't suffer from the complex quandaries induced by his partner's highbrow education. He said, 'Take us down to the stream where you water your flocks and I will dip you there, just like Saul and I were dipped.'

The whole family set off immediately, followed a short distance behind by an indecisive Saul. The stream was narrow and cut deep into a rocky gully. This presented a logistical problem.

'The only way you could dip them here,' Saul observed, 'would be to hold them by their ankles and lower them, head first, into the water. Maybe we should come back another time.'

This was obviously an attempt to escape the situation.

'No problem!' Ananias asserted. 'If we can't get them to the water we will just have to bring the water to them.'

He asked the oldest child to fill one of their water jars. While she did, the Son arrived accompanied by a number of senior Angels who were only vaguely familiar to me. They were the Angelic representatives of the Arab race and, in particular, of the Nabataean kingdom. When, Ananias had been handed the jar, he asked the father, 'Do you believe in God, our Father, in Jesus his Son, and in his Spirit who gives us life?'

'Yes, I do,' the man said solemnly. The resulting Angelic cheer was far from solemn!

Ananias lifted the jar above the Arab's head and drenched him with three generous pourings of water. This time I knew what to expect. The water swept the man's doomed spirit away as easily as the desert wind disperses dried leaves. Jesus stepped forward and embraced the dripping man, causing his spirit to spring to new life with incandescent Heavenly brightness.

Ananias proceeded to ask the same question to each member of the family in turn, down to the youngest, and soaked them all. Saul watched thoughtfully, blind to the spiritual transformations before him, struggling to broaden his mind to accommodate my Boss's love. The Son enthusiastically embraced every member of the family and left each one glowing with the familiar light of his new brothers and sisters.

As we made our way back to the tent, the Son said to me, 'Well done, Oriel!'

'What should I do with Saul?' I asked. He was still profoundly unhappy about what Ananias had done. As Saul understood it, the Son had not simply become a human, he had become a Jewish human. He could not imagine it possible to follow Jesus without becoming a Jew.

'He'll learn,' the Son reassured me. 'Are you staying for the party?'

'I'd love to but I can't,' I explained. 'We have another tent to repair for your new friend's second cousin's husband's brother.'

Saul was anxious to set off as soon as possible. He doesn't want to be late for a customer who is offering generous payment. But he also needs to do some serious thinking. I may ask Raphael to come down and help him.

Back in Damascus – three days later

Saul finished his second job in time to return to Damascus with Ananias for the Sabbath. They shared out their earnings between Joanna and the synagogue fund, and shared their news with all the disciples they met. This morning Saul visited a different synagogue. Ananias is highly respected in the local Jewish community and the rabbi was happy, when asked, for Saul to speak. Saul managed to speak with more composure than last week. Nonetheless, he is much more comfortable speaking with a small group of people than he is addressing a large formal gathering. At my suggestion, he did not mention the growing interest about Jesus amongst the Nabataean Arabs. I could see in the minds of the congregation that such information would have caused another riot.

Tonight Saul is staying at Ananias' home. Tomorrow he intends to purchase some new tools, then return to the Arab camps.

Meanwhile, Raphael has spent many hours helping Saul wrestle with his conscience regarding non-Jewish Arab disciples.

'How's it going?' I asked casually.

'It will take much more than a few brief chats, Oriel, to prise open this mind.'

Many months later

I have not written for some time because nothing much new has happened. Saul and Ananias have travelled widely in the Arab territories, repairing tents in return for attentive ears. The response has been polite.

As they have travelled further afield, their returns to Damascus have become less frequent and this is possibly a good thing because the anti-Jesus Jews are becoming suspicious of Saul's activities. They are trying to get him banned from the synagogues.

Tomorrow is a very important day for Saul's Arabian mission. The King of the Nabataean Arabs, Aretas, has commissioned a new tent for his latest wife. Saul insisted on the usual condition of an open ear to his stories about Jesus. King Aretas accepted the deal.

The Nabataean Royal Encampment – the next evening

Saul is angry. He arrived this morning as early as he could, had a site meeting with the king and his new bride, surveyed the imported Roman cloth he'll be using for the tent and set to work immediately. Come the evening, Saul expected to be allowed to join Aretas and his entourage for dinner and be invited to speak about Jesus. It didn't happen. He and Ananias were brought their supper in their own small travelling tent. Saul sent a message to the king reminding him of the terms of their deal. Aretas replied that he never pays for work until it is completed.

While I was trying to encourage Saul's disheartened spirit, none other than Lucifer, leader of the Angelic Opposition, arrived in the tent.

'Get out of here!' I scolded him. 'I have enough problems without you turning up.'

'Get out yourself, Oriel! I'm going nowhere,' Lucifer replied coldly. 'I have more than enough troubles without you and this Saul interfering.'

'Get out of here, Satan!'

This second command came, not from me, but from Saul. Lucifer stared at him in sudden horror. Saul's voice was not the only one he had heard; joined with the thin human sound, in subtle duet, was woven the unmistakable command of the Director. Lucifer had no choice. He left.

Some weeks later – back in Damascus

Saul finally got his audience with King Aretas one evening about a month later when the work was complete. I stayed outside the royal tent to keep an eye on Lucifer. Since being evicted from Saul's tent, he's been working hard on the king, hardening his thoughts against Saul. Some of that work, however, was undone when Aretas saw the quality of Saul's workmanship.

'You are truly a master tentmaker, Saul,' the king declared as he inspected the fine workmanship. 'Come to my tent this evening and we will find out if you are also a master storyteller.'

Sadly, Saul is not.

The king's tent was full of loud and drunken courtiers and the Director had his work cut out preventing Saul from seizing up altogether.

King Aretas quickly became bored with Saul's intellectual explanations of the Son's life and death. He was hoping to be entertained and had no desire to be educated. But Saul, as I have discovered, does not give up easily. He ploughed on with his message while the king's disappointment changed to irritation, then to frustration and finally to outright anger. When Saul informed the king that he was an incurable sinner and liable to unending Death, the first minister stood up to defend his king.

'How dare you say such things of our king,' the man thundered. He proceeded to banish Saul from the entire Nabataean kingdom, concluding with, 'If you are still in the royal camp by sunrise, I will have your tongue sliced out immediately.'

It was not an idle threat. The king concurred, adding, 'I will gladly perform the operation myself. It would do the world a favour.' These were Lucifer's sentiments more than the king's. Saul stared at Aretas with dark eyes, searching for a reply.

'Just leave, for Heaven's sake!' I bellowed into his brain. Saul was waiting for the Director to give him something suitable to say to the king. Nothing was given. In the end, he pursed his lips tightly together, turned and strode out of the tent.

'Run, you fool,' I urged, but Saul was too proud to respond. He maintained a steady stride until he reached his small tent and gloomily informed Ananias, 'We have to leave.'

Not wanting to put Saul's tongue at any further risk – he'll need it when he gets to Rome – I impressed on Ananias the urgency of the situation and he was sensible enough not to ask for explanations. He persuaded Saul to get on his horse at once and abandon both tools and tent.

Free from the weight of their luggage, the two missionaries travelled fast, outpacing the news of Saul's banishment. They did not relax until they were safely within the walls of Damascus, which is not governed by King Aretas. The disciples of Jesus welcomed them warmly and were excited and impressed to learn that Saul had even proclaimed his message to the King of the Nabataeans.

Two days later

News spreads quickly, especially – it seems – bad news. Today, the spice market in Damascus was humming with the rumour that a crazy young Jew from Damascus tried to convert King Aretas to Judaism and only narrowly escaped death for his efforts. Angels working among the market traders sent word to me and by the time I arrived two different chains of events had begun.

One chain followed a packet of saffron destined for the Governor of Damascus' dinner. I pursued the trail and soon discovered that the Governor is not as politically independent as he is supposed to be. When he heard that his city was harbouring a fugitive from the king, he ordered that every exit from Damascus be watched by armed guards, and that Saul be arrested if he attempts to leave. The governor is keen to earn King Aretas' favour.

I returned to the market to investigate the second chain of events. An Angel informed me that information about Saul's activities had accompanied a few grams of cumin that were now in the house of the leader of the city's largest synagogue. I quickly checked that Saul was safely asleep and visited the synagogue leader.

The news that a self-appointed Jewish preacher had been mixing with Arabs, and had even tried to ingratiate himself with an Arab king, sparked fury among the Jews. As the fire of that fury spread from Jewish household to Jewish household, I watched and waited patiently for it to reach the home of one of Jesus' followers so that I could divert the information towards Saul and advise him to leave Damascus as soon as possible.

My job was still only half done. I returned to the Governor's villa in search of someone who could deliver a second warning for me. No joy. I left the villa and made my way round the city wall. I was not surprised to discover that the Governor's guards had already been posted. At the third gate on my tour, I found what I was looking for. The gatekeeper's wife was bright with the spiritual life that is characteristic of all the Son's disciples. I reminded her that Saul needed to be told what was happening and she left her work immediately.

Saul is now safely – I hope – hidden in the home of a Greek historian whose house Joanna has been cleaning to supplement her income. The man is neither Damascan nor Jewish nor Arab nor a follower of Jesus – perfectly qualified for the task! Meanwhile, Hannah, the gatekeeper's wife, is working on a plan to smuggle Saul out of the city tonight.

A mile outside the city – the same night

During the afternoon, Saul's horses were led out of Damascus by the historian's manservant. Then, well into the night, when the city streets were largely deserted, Saul was escorted to the western gatehouse, dressed in Greek clothes. At Hannah's house, built into the wall above the western gate, they watched the guards and made further plans for Saul's departure. That done, everyone waited for the guards to be distracted from their duties.

It was a long wait. Saul was anxious to get on his way and willing to gamble on his ability to outrun the guards. Hannah, thankfully, was more level-headed – after all, her husband's job was at stake as well as Saul's life.

Eventually I opted for a little Angelic intervention. My initial idea was to put the men to sleep but their Angel guardians wouldn't let me, saying that their charges would be severely punished for such neglect of duty. Hannah's guardian suggested that we provoke the guards into an argument, but again their Angels were unhappy. In the end, one of the guards' guardians spoke up.

'I have an idea. Archangel Oriel, get your man ready and wait.'

Before I could ask him to explain his plan he had gone, but something in his manner reassured me that he knew what he was doing. I returned to Hannah's house with her guardian, who informed Hannah that it was time to install Saul in the laundry basket she had borrowed. Saul fitted in easily. Hannah tied a rope around the basket and Ananias lifted it onto the ledge of a window that looked outwards from the city wall.

We waited.

Suddenly there was a great crash from further along the wall. The guards immediately ran to find out what had happened. At that moment Ananias, with the help of Hannah's husband, quickly lowered Saul to the ground in the basket. After a relatively gentle landing, Saul climbed out of the basket and sprinted down the western road, dissolving quickly into the darkness. He reached the horses as planned and began the lonely ride back to Jerusalem. It's strange to remember that when he last rode along this route, three years ago, he was in full swing of persecuting my Boss's children. The hunter is now the prey, fleeing from a persecution that he himself began.

Gadara by Lake Galilee – a week later

Saul has not hurried on his return trip to Jerusalem. He has much to think about and important decisions to make about his future. My first priority is for Saul to meet with Peter and the other leaders of Jesus' earthly family so that he can learn more about Jesus' life from them before he sets off for Rome. For the moment, though, he needs rest. I fixed him up with lodgings at the home of a local man dramatically cured by Jesus some years ago. This man, a pig farmer turned goatherd, has had some casual contact with Peter and the other disciples in Jerusalem and has told Saul how to find them when he gets there.

Jerusalem – two days on

Saul's arrival in Jerusalem caused considerable commotion among the disciples. As advised by his Galilean host, he went straight to the *Lost Sheep Inn* and ordered a meal. As he ate his mutton in red wine sauce, both he and I were aware of the staff staring uneasily at their customer. They knew who he was; they remembered him as the man who had imprisoned dozens of their fellow disciples last time he was in Jerusalem. Saul continued to eat and, following the instructions of Simeon the Gadarene goatherd, he was careful to leave a substantial pool of sauce on his plate. As Saul finished his mutton and vegetables, he picked up his one remaining piece of bread and drew a simple fish shape in the sauce on his plate. Simeon had made him practise this manoeuvre several times over as it is a secret symbol used by the family of believers to identify themselves to one another.

When the waiter looked down at the message Saul had carefully drawn on his plate, he was momentarily paralysed by fear. I tried to sow some reassurance in his mind, but failed. Saul, now well used to the company of other disciples, smiled warmly, but the waiter abandoned Saul's plate and fled to a back room. I followed.

'He has infiltrated us,' the waiter informed the other staff. 'He knows about the fish.'

'He's one of you, you silly sheep,' I shouted, but they were too frightened to hear me.

'I'll run and tell James and Peter,' a young woman said, referring to Jesus' younger brother and fisherman friend. She shot out the door and pounded down the street like a startled badger, looking for the fisherman and Jesus' younger brother.

'For Heaven's sake,' I yelled, this time addressing myself to the Angel guardians in the room, 'tell them that Saul is on their side now.'

'We'll have to think up a new symbol,' the owner of the inn continued. 'And somehow, we'll have to get the news around very quickly.'

'How about a cross?' one suggested. The others stared in disbelief. The speaker continued less confidently, 'Well, it's easy to draw.'

'That's grotesque!' was the disgusted response.

I returned to Saul, who is quietly pondering the effect he has had on his fellow disciples.

At the same table – two hours later

'Just wait here, sir,' were the only words the inn staff dared to say to Saul, when three of them arrived together to snatch away the offending plate.

While I wrote my diary, Saul penned a letter to the high priest, thanking him for the loan of the horses and, more importantly, outlining in considerable detail his discovery that Jesus is indeed the Son of Almighty God. I was interested to note how much more freely Saul manages to express his thoughts when he is writing. His speech, especially in public, tends to be cumbersome.

Our wait finally ended when a tall, broad, brightly shining son of my Boss walked into the *Lost Sheep Inn* and strode boldly up to Saul.

'I'm Barnabas.'

Saul stood to receive the greeting, looking like a meerkat meeting a lion. 'I am Saul.'

'I know,' Barnabas replied with a disarming smile. 'Your message caused something of a stir among my friends.'

Barnabas, I quickly noted, has an honesty rare among humans. And he got straight to the point.

'Perhaps you could tell me how you heard about this inn and discovered our fish message.'

Barnabas was no less afraid of Saul than the inn staff, but his fear was outweighed by his love for my Boss. Saul proceeded to tell Barnabas his story and, as he did, the staff slowly emerged like nervous rabbits from the security of the kitchen.

When Saul had finished, Barnabas announced, 'I must take you to Peter.' The staff scurried back into their burrow.

'I need to deliver these horses and this letter to the Temple,' Saul replied. 'Would it be possible to do that on the way?'

A secret location in Jerusalem – later that night

Saul's meeting with Peter did not go as smoothly as his conversation with Barnabas. It seemed to me that Saul looks on the Galilean fisherman as though he were from some lesser subspecies. And Peter, for his part, nurtures a deeply conditioned distrust of Pharisees from Jerusalem. Both men were polite and each had a list of issues that they wanted to discuss with the other.

Despite the noticeable chill in the air, Peter invited Saul to stay with him. I encouraged Saul to accept. I am keen that Saul should learn more about the life and teaching of Jesus. Peter is the ideal tutor, whatever Saul may think about being taught faith by a fisherman.

Fifteen days later

Saul's presence in Jerusalem has significantly unsettled the community of disciples. He has been with Peter for two weeks now and their discussions have been long and intense. On most days, James the brother of Jesus has joined them. Much time has been devoted to the issue of Saul's work among the Gentile Arabs. Both Peter and James have been profoundly challenged by Saul's news. Over his three years in Arabia, Saul became familiar with the idea of Jesus having non-Jewish disciples and began to understand that my Boss's love is not exclusive to the Jewish race. Peter, however – as Saul did at first – finds the idea of mixing with Gentiles most unsettling. He is a solidly traditional Jew in both lifestyle and principle.

Yesterday being the Sabbath, I encouraged Saul to visit to the Grecian synagogue. His mission to Gentiles may still be 'under consideration', but I thought it would be useful for him to meet some Jews who are visiting from Rome and other great cities of the empire.

I am sorry to have to report, however, that once again Saul and synagogue proved to be an explosive combination! What was intended as a sermon rapidly deteriorated into a verbal brawl. I had not anticipated that expat Jews would be so stringent in their Jewishness. The Greek-speaking congregation instantly took exception to Saul's assumption that they would be familiar with the ways and attitudes of their pagan neighbours and, in the end, Saul was asked to leave the building before people started throwing punches as well as insults.

This morning, Barnabas arrived with grim news. An ultra-pharisaical group from the Grecian synagogue have made a suicide pact to kill Saul and stamp out his anti-Jewish behaviour. Hurried plans were laid to escort Saul away from Jerusalem as soon as is humanly possible. Barnabas has run home to pack a travel bag and will accompany Saul.

This is Saul's third forced flight in little more than a month.

Caesarea, on the Mediterranean coast

Saul, royally paid for his last tent shortly before upsetting King Aretas, purchased two horses from the Arab market outside Jerusalem. He and Barnabas made swift progress on the coastward road; it has been interesting to watch Saul trying to improve his new partner's riding technique.

They arrived in this very Roman city today and their minds immediately turned to the question of where Saul should go next. Urged on by me, Saul suggested going straight to Rome but Barnabas advised against this. He insisted that any mission to Rome would need the blessing of Peter and James in Jerusalem, and advised Saul to wait for them to catch him up on the issue of Gentile disciples. Sensing an argument looming between the two men, I recommended to Saul that they both sleep on it and consider the matter in the morning.

In the meantime, I have asked Barnabas' guardian, Asphiel, to watch over both men while I consult our Boss in Heaven.

Back in Heaven

I explained the situation to my Boss as I understood it.

'How can it be right,' I concluded, 'for Saul's mission to Rome to be delayed by Peter's opinion, when Peter is so clearly in the wrong?'

'Peter is the leader of my earthly family,' he replied.

'Yet he's holding the whole thing up,' I stated, with more than a hint of exasperation.

'I know.'

My Boss knows everything.

'Well, if – as you've told me – you are working on Peter and James' opinions, and if – as is the case – it will take Saul a long time to actually get to Rome, then can't Saul and I set off now, on the understanding that Peter will be willing to approve Saul's Roman mission by the time it actually begins?' I ran through the question in my mind twice, just to check that I had said what I intended to say. Only then did I look up to my Boss for a reply.

He had been waiting for me and said, calmly, 'No.'

'Why not?'

'Because I have put Peter in charge of my family down on planet Earth and I cannot let you go about undermining his leadership.'

'Even if he's wrong?'

'Even if he is wrong.'

I was more than a little perplexed by his answer.

'It is simply a matter of time, Oriel, and, as you are working within Earth's time, you will simply have to wait.'

'For how long?'

'For as long as it takes.'

'And what should I do with Saul in the meantime?'

My Boss smiled. 'As I have put you in charge of Saul's mission to Rome, I am happy for you to make that decision.'

'What if I get it wrong?'

The patient smile widened on my Boss's face but, before he

could reply – if indeed he intended to – the door flew open and in came the Son, leading his mother Mary, and followed by her Angel guardian, Maphrael. Maphrael, who insists on being called Maff, is the leader of my special operations team. My Boss greeted Mary.

'My child, welcome home.'

Mary was taken up in an embrace of pure and unending love. She looked wonderful, freed from the deterioration of time and clothed in her new, Heavenly body. The beauty that had been hinted at in the human flesh of her youth was now in full bloom. Yet even more beautiful than her Heavenly body was her outstanding faith in my Boss and the unparalleled love that she has for the Son.

The Son stepped forward to greet the one who had wiped his nose and bottom in babyhood with such devoted care. 'Mother!' he exclaimed, and then introduced me. 'This is Oriel, who looked after me through my last two years on Earth.'

'It's lovely to meet you, Oriel.' She threw her arms around me – a startling experience. I have never before been on the receiving end of such human affection.

'Jesus has told me so much about you.' Mary pulled back from me and studied my face intently. 'I have never seen you before,' she said, 'but there is something very familiar about you.'

'Mary, my dearest daughter,' my Boss said, 'let me show you the rooms I have been preparing for you.'

'Hang on a moment!' interrupted Maff, turning to our Boss. 'If Mary is your daughter and Jesus is her son, then . . .' He paused long enough for me to brace myself for whatever outrageous suggestion this brilliant but tactless Angel was about to make. 'Then you must be his . . .'

'Maff!' I burst out. 'I need to see you in my office. Right away.'

I ushered him out of the room and down the corridor, not daring to even look at the others. Though my Boss's sense of fun is undoubted, it is not the role of Angels to make fun of him.

Maff thought I had over-reacted. 'He's all right,' he said to me when I had safely closed my office door. I decided to change the subject.

'Maff,' I said, 'I want you to look after another human for me. But this time, only temporarily.'

'You're landing me with Saul of Tarsus, aren't you?'

'You know about him?'

'Everyone in Jerusalem knows about Saul,' Maff replied, 'and, from what I've heard, he's rather short of friends there.'

I had not expected Maff to be quite so well informed.

'I want you to take him home to Tarsus,' I said, 'and look after him until certain other matters have been resolved.'

'Where's he now?' Maff asked.

'At Caeserea with a man called Barnabas.'

'The big fellow?'

'Yes. They are currently working out what Saul should do next. I want you to take him home and reacquaint him with the ways of the Roman Empire.'

'Sounds simple enough.' He was silent for moment while he thought through his commission. 'Only one question, Oriel: how will Saul be travelling to Tarsus?'

There was something in the tone of Maff's question which indicated it was not quite an innocent enquiry.

'By sea,' I replied, well aware that my junior colleague had anticipated this.

'Oriel,' he asked pointedly, 'is it just possible that you are handing Saul over to me simply to avoid a boat trip?'

'Certainly not,' I was indignant, although I was also relieved to realise that I would be spared several days on the loathsome brine. I explained the situation regarding Peter and James and their fear of non-Jewish people and said, utterly truthfully, that if Maff could look after Saul, I would be able to get on with other matters. He was not interested in my explanation.

'And I have to go – by sea – with a man who is banished by the Arabs, hated by the Jews and not even trusted by his brothers and sisters in our Boss's new family?'

I did not reply. Maff did not expect me to. I simply looked directly at him and waited for him to accept the task. Instead, he said, 'What if I say *No*?'

Our Boss walked into the room. 'Maff,' he said, 'please remember that I made the sea, and I am of the opinion that it is very good.'

'If seas are so wonderful,' replied the impertinent Angel, 'why don't we have one here in Heaven?'

'We do not need one,' our Boss replied, 'and neither do you need to travel across it. You can meet up with Saul in Tarsus.'

Maff smiled a greatly relieved smile, but when he turned it towards me I thought it contained an element of smugness.

'Who will look after Saul on his journey?' I asked.

'Oriel,' my Boss replied, 'it occurs to me that Saul is very unlikely to *walk* all the way to Rome.' My spirit slumped in anticipation of what was coming next. 'I think you could do with some practice.'

Tarsus Quay

The entire journey was horrible. Barnabas wanted to visit his home, on the island of Cyprus, so we had to cross over the open sea. The two disciples found a boat that was taking the quick route to Tarsus, via Salamis on Cyprus. We didn't stop at the Cypriot port for more than an hour and were off again on the restless waves. During my brief respite on Cyprus, the land appeared to be as agitated as the sea was. I cannot imagine travelling all the way to Rome in such an unsettled environment. I shall have to look into land-based alternatives.

When we finally reached the river port of Tarsus, I collapsed on the quayside like a beached jellyfish and left Saul to find his own way home. I need a break – I'm off to my own home. It's Maff's turn.

In sealess, timeless Heaven

My recuperation was disturbed by the unexpected and, I have to confess, unwelcome return of Maff.

'I can't find him,' the finest of my specialist Angels informed me. 'I can't locate him in Tarsus.'

I found it hard to believe, but Maff's harassed look informed me this wasn't a joke.

'How many new-born children of our Boss are there in Tarsus?' I asked. 'There can't be many.'

'A fair few,' Maff replied, 'but not one of them is called Saul.'

'Come with me,' I ordered impatiently, heading straight to eastern Turkey.

As we arrived over the city, I spotted Saul immediately. He was stooped over a broad workbench sewing some tent cloth.

'There's your man.'

'I've visited *him*,' Maff told me. 'He's not called Saul.'

'I tell you, he is.'

'Well I tell *you*,' Maff replied, his frustrations getting the better of him, 'that human is called *Paul*. I'll show you.'

Maff took me around to the front entrance of Saul's workshop. There, over the door, was a freshly painted sign which read *Paul's Tents*.

I was astounded. We went into the workshop, where I spoke to the Director, deep in the man's spirit.

'What is all this Saul / Paul business about, Sir?' I asked.

'Saul is his Hebrew name,' the Director explained, 'but in the language of the Romans, the name is Paul.'

Maff and I looked at one another with parallel exasperation.

'These humans and their names!' I exclaimed. 'First we are obliged to cope with three different Marys, two Jameses and two Judases. Now it's spun round the other way and we have one man with two different names.'

'It is quite common,' the Director informed me. 'Barnabas, who you dropped off at Cyprus, is known to his family as Joseph.'

'We've had a couple of Josephs already,' Maff added. Then, 'So in Jerusalem and among the Hebrew Jews this man is known as Saul – but here in Greco-Roman Tarsus everyone calls him Paul?'

'That's right,' the Director affirmed.

I returned to Heaven.

Next entry

Several years have passed on Earth – and still Paul, as I suppose I should now call him, is nowhere near Rome.

I have kept an occasional eye on him. He has busied himself with three activities: making tents for the Roman Army; studying Greek and Roman philosophy at the local university (I especially praised Maff for achieving this); and being a leading member of the small but growing family of disciples in Tarsus.

A short while ago I was visited by Gabriel.

'We are making our move on Peter and his dislike of non-Jews,' he informed me.

'At last!' I exclaimed.

'I've got to visit a man called . . .' Gabriel studied his instructions. 'Cornelius – a Roman centurion based in Caesarea.'

'Sounds hopeful!' I said.

'After that,' the great messenger Archangel continued, 'I will be speaking to Peter, who is in nearby Joppa. That bit is all rather complicated but the Boss has given me precise instructions, so it should go smoothly. If it all works, you could be back in business with your old friend . . . what's his name?'

'Paul.'

'I'll be off then.'

'Gabriel!' I postponed his departure a moment. 'Don't frighten them.'

'I'll try.' He smiled and was gone.

Next – in Antioch

Since Gabriel's mission, as well as keeping an eye on Paul's progress, I've been keeping a careful watch on developments in Jerusalem.

Peter got into serious trouble with his colleagues for formally dipping Cornelius' houseful of Romans. Peter explained to James and the others that the Director had undoubtedly embraced these Romans as his own children and that there was nothing for him to do but allow them the outward sign of what had already taken place. After a lengthy exchange of questions and answers, the leading disciples were uncomfortably delighted. I believe it will be some time before their emotions catch up with their thoughts, but they have cautiously admitted that they had been wrong, and reluctantly welcomed the Romans into their spiritual family.

Not long after that, news arrived in Jerusalem from Antioch that numerous Greeks have become disciples there. Our old friend Barnabas (known also, apparently, as Joseph, but don't let that confuse you) has been sent on the long journey north to investigate.

I sensed that this was the opportunity I had been waiting for and spoke with my Boss about it. I explained Barnabas' mission as I understood it and said, 'I plan to get Barnabas and Paul together in Antioch and, once Paul is up to speed on things, I'll take him to Rome for you.'

As I left his office, I noticed a knowing smile on my Boss's face. 'What?' I asked.

'You'll find out,' he replied.

I joined Barnabas in Antioch. This wonderful, encouraging man was delighted to see the dramatic growth in my Boss's family here and decided to stay so he can help the leaders with the challenge of integrating Jewish and Gentile disciples. As he visited the numerous different groups of my Boss's sons and daughters, I placed in his mind the suggestion that what he really needs is a partner, someone with a formal training in Greco-Roman philosophy, who can help these Greek disciples to understand the Jewish Messiah they have chosen to follow. Barnabas accepted the idea immediately and as soon as he began wondering where he might find such a person, I jogged his memory about the unscheduled voyage to Cyprus that he took ten Earth years ago.

Tomorrow, Barnabas is departing for Tarsus.

In Tarsus – a Sunday evening

I went ahead of Barnabas' sloth-like progress and met up with Maff at *Paul's Tents*. Maff has given me a thorough debriefing about the last ten years of Paul's life. The impetuous young man has evidently grown into a wiser and more thoughtful impetuous older man. Recently, Paul has been growing impatient with life in his home town and – I was delighted to hear – his thoughts have turned towards Rome and his calling to announce the message of my Boss's love there.

Yesterday was the Jewish Sabbath but Paul did not go to the synagogue. He has been banned. Today, however, Maff and I accompanied him to a meeting at the home of Demetrius, a Greek disciple who learned about the Son from Paul. All Jesus' disciples in Tarsus – Jews and Gentiles alike – meet together at Demetrius' home every Sunday to celebrate the day when the Son led Death's captives to his home in Heaven.

The meeting was very similar in structure to the services in the synagogue, except that their worship was addressed directly to my Boss's Son. Much to my surprise, just as proceedings were about to begin, Archangel Raphael arrived.

'What, on Earth, are you doing?' I asked.

'I could ask you the same question,' the leader of Heaven's choirs replied.

'I have come to prepare Paul for his mission to Rome.'

He floated away from me and whispered into Paul's thoughts. I tried to follow what was being said, but it did not make a great deal of sense.

'What was all that about?' I asked my colleague when he returned.

'Paul and I are working on some hymns to celebrate the Son's life, death and . . . what do they call it?

'Resurrection?'

'That's the word.'

I was intrigued. 'I didn't know he was a musician.'

'He isn't. He sings enthusiastically but tends to go flat on the high notes. However,' my friend continued, 'he *is* something of a poet, when in the mood. Paul has been writing new words to some traditional Jewish hymn tunes. You will hear one shortly. It's a new one. I've just given it a little polish.' Raphael had a slightly pained look on his face as he looked towards the modest band of human instrumentalists in the home meeting.

'The music will be lamentably poor,' he continued, 'but their intentions are honourable.'

I didn't have to wait long. As soon as Demetrius had welcomed his fellow disciples he announced that they would begin with Paul's new hymn. It went something like this:

> *He didn't hold being like God*
> *as all that he wanted to be*
> *but he made himself almost as naught*
> *the humblest of servants like me*
> *yet when he had come as a human*
> *he humbled himself even more*
> *and consented his life to be nailed on a cross*
> *and to die with the violent and poor.*
>
> *But God didn't let it all end there*
> *and exalted him up to the heights*
> *and gave him the name which exceeds every name*
> *and devotion in all hearts ignites.*
> *In heaven and on earth they adore him;*
> *when the hour of our worship is done*
> *the Angels of Heaven will sing 'Jesus is Lord'*
> *to the glory of God and his Son.*

Raphael winced all through Paul's energetic rendition and said quietly to me, 'It still needs rather a lot of work on it, I feel.' Nonetheless, when the song was sung he led the gathered Angels in a raucous round of applause.

Paul was evidently one of the leaders of this gathering. After reading from the book of the prophet Joel, he embarked on a long, faltering and tedious analysis of all the different types of locust mentioned. During this sermon a good deal of work was done by the assembled humans: shopping lists were drawn up; plans for the week were forged; the complete redecoration of Demetrius' house was severally considered; and a good deal of lost sleep was regained. I suspected that the complexity of Paul's argument showed signs of Raphael's influence but my colleague assured me that it was all Paul's own work.

When Paul had dissected his last locust, they sang again and turned their minds to prayer. At this point the gathering was transformed into one of the most remarkable events I have ever witnessed on Earth. I am tempted to describe it in minute detail but, unlike Paul, I will be brief. Demetrius invited his guests to join him in inviting the Director to speak to them. The Director was quick to accept the invitation. Rather than saying numerous things to everyone, as Paul had done, the Director spoke different messages into the thoughts of each and every disciple, all at the same time. He put words in one person's mind which, when spoken out, were great encouragement to another person. He spoke to, and through, one of them in a language that none of rest understood and then inspired someone else to translate the message for the benefit of everyone present. Through all of this I recognised an old and familiar characteristic of my Boss's work with humans: never do something on your own if you can find someone to help you. (On reflection, I suppose, the same is true of his work with Angels.)

It was a wonderful experience and everyone returned to their homes refreshed, reassured and inspired.

I followed Paul back to his shop and put a question to the Director as we went. 'Why do they bother with Paul's rambling sermons when they can learn so much directly from you?'

'There are times,' he replied, 'when they become almost completely deaf to my voice. When that happens, they need their preachers.'

65

Later that week

Paul's spirit is restless. He feels constrained and limited, sometimes even bored by life in his home town. He is looking for a new challenge, a new beginning. He is tired of hearing his parents' friends asking him, 'What are you getting up to now, young man?'

I am expecting Barnabas to arrive soon and I hope Paul will then find the open door he has been searching for.

Several days later

Asphiel, Barnabas' Angel guardian, arrived today. Maff and I were discussing the problem of Paul's soporific preaching when Asphiel all but crashed into the house. He seemed greatly relieved to find us.

'I was expecting you last week,' I said.

'Barnabas can't find Saul,' he announced. 'He's been searching the city for days.'

Maff laughed and announced unhelpfully, 'He isn't here.'

I rescued the dismayed Angel. 'He's there.' I pointed to Paul's workshop. 'Making the Governor of Tarsus a marquee for his daughter's wedding.'

Asphiel took one look, recognised Paul immediately and let out a bewildered 'Oh!'

'Here in the Roman world he's always known as Paul,' I explained. Then I added, with a sideways glance at Maff, 'You're not the first Angel to be caught out by that.'

The Director's voice emerged from Paul's workshop. 'If you Angels were not so obsessed with names, you would look into the spirits of the people themselves.'

'Tell Barnabas to ask for *Paul's Tents,*' I told Asphiel.

Two days later

Yesterday, while Paul finished off the governor's tent, he and Barnabas had a long discussion about managing a mixed community of Greek and Jewish disciples. Barnabas was very excited to hear about the Sunday services at Demetrius' house and Paul accepted Barnabas' invitation to travel to Antioch without hesitation.

Paul has packed up his tools, taken down the shop sign and purchased a donkey to carry his possessions.

'So you're off?' Maff said, as Paul and Barnabas loaded up the young donkey.

'Yes,' I replied.

Maff continued, 'Is Paul responding to the Boss's call to tell the people of Rome about the Son?'

'Yes.' Maff does not usually ask such basic questions. I wondered what was coming.

'And are you heading for Antioch?'

This time I replied more cautiously, 'Yes.'

'Which is in exactly the opposite direction from Rome?'

His trap closed around me. Not wanting to give Maff an easy victory, I quickly asked myself what my Boss would say if I put such questions to him. I looked at my assistant and said, 'Do you trust me, Maphrael?'

The momentum of his Angelic play was halted and he simply replied, 'Yes.'

Antioch – again – a month later

Antioch is a vast city sprawling across the broad fertile valley of the River Orontes. Second only to Rome among the cities round the north of the Mediterranean Sea, I was sure that this was a good place for Paul to begin the work to which he had been called. He was astounded at what he found. In Tarsus there is one small gathering of disciples. Here in Antioch there are hundreds of people who have decided to live by the teaching of Jesus.

After speaking to numerous Angels, I learned that Antioch has been in spiritual confusion for many years. Under successive empires, Syrian deities were re-defined as Greco-Roman gods and people became disinterested in the whole charade. Before news of Jesus reached the city, a considerable number of local people went through the long – and for men painful – process of becoming Jews. The Son's story has fallen on this parched ground like long-missed rain.

The task before Paul and Barnabas is to bring order and organisation to the muddled groups of disciples that meet in scattered communities across this huge city.

I have learned one other interesting thing in the past weeks. Local people have devised a name for all these energetic young children of my Boss. They call them *Christians*. This had to be explained to me several times. The people of Antioch have noticed that once a man or woman embraces the Son, as their Messiah, they never stop talking about it. So they started calling them the *Messiah People*. The Greek word for Messiah is *Christ*, hence the name *Christians*.

Months later

Paul has been very busy – far too busy to make tents. He and Barnabas have been employed by the Christians as their teachers and leaders. They travel around the four wards of the city, addressing large gatherings made up of numerous separate groups of disciples. Paul leads the people in worship, based on the model he developed in Tarsus, then Barnabas inspires and encourages them with stories about Jesus, many of which come from his own experience. Finally, Paul, in his hesitating, faltering way, tries to educate the assembled Christians, teaching them about their new-found faith.

Today was the first of a special tour of these assemblies. This tour includes a particular excitement for the already excitable people of Antioch: a group of disciples are visiting from Jerusalem. Brothers and sisters from Jerusalem are always especially honoured guests among the Antioch faithful, because many of them bring firsthand stories about Jesus. However, at this afternoon's gathering, the disciples were most struck by the words of a man called Agabus. Agabus has a mind finely tuned to the Director's voice and, helped by the Director, he has come to understand that the shortage of food being caused by a drought across the Roman world will be particularly severe in and around Jerusalem.

The Antiochenes were characteristically energetic in their response. They immediately organised a collection of money from among every group of Christians in the city. They requested that Paul and Barnabas should represent them in taking their gift to Jerusalem.

A week later

Paul is on the road again. Laden with gold and silver coins, he, Barnabas and one of the Greek-born Christians called Titus, are travelling to Jerusalem. I have to concede that this journey takes Paul even further from Rome, but I am hoping that he might be able to meet up with Peter in Jerusalem and get an official blessing for his mission to Rome.

Jerusalem – Passover time

Rather than the joyful Passover parties I was expecting, we found the Jerusalem disciples in shock. Peter is in prison. King Herod – the same man who dressed Jesus in a purple cloak on the morning of his death – arrested the other James, John's brother, a week ago and had him killed. When Herod realised how popular the execution was among the Jews, he had Peter arrested as well. Peter is due to be tried and executed as soon as Passover is over.

Paul and Barnabas have joined the local disciples, or Christians, in their prayers for Peter. The trial is tomorrow. I'm off to speak with my Boss.

In Heaven

'I'm glad you came so promptly. I would like you to rescue Peter for me.'

I was somewhat taken aback. I had knocked on my Boss's door armed with the question, *What are you planning to do about Peter?* I wasn't expecting to be part of the plan.

'How?' I asked.

'I'm sure you can work something out,' he replied. 'If you can release all the resurrected captives of Death from a small tomb, you should be able to rescue one man from a Jewish prison.'

I went straight to my office and called Maff.

John Mark's house, Jerusalem – that night

Maff and I checked out the prison where Peter was being held and worked out the simplest route from Peter's cell to freedom. We then worked our way back though the labyrinth of steps, tunnels and dark cells, putting everyone into a deep sleep. Peter was already deeply asleep. I tried to rouse him several times without success.

When I had used the whole spectrum of Angelic speech, from gentle whisper to anxious yell, Maff said, 'You'll have to get physical with him.' He was right.

I thinned my Angelic being to something near the shadowy existence of humans and called out to Peter's ears rather than his mind. I had a small measure of success; he gave a loud snort and started snoring loudly. Unexpectedly, another Angelic light appeared in the cell. I turned round to see Gabriel watching me, an amused grin on his face.

'Do you want any help?' he asked.

'No thank you.'

I returned my attention to the sleeping form of Peter and gave him a firm shove in the side. It worked. He opened his eyes and looked straight at me with dumbstruck horror.

Gabriel cheered.

'Quick, get up!' I told Peter, concerned that the guards might be woken by Gabriel's racket. Then, to Maff I said, 'Take those chains off his arms.'

That done, I handed Peter the clothes and sandals that were in a heap on the damp floor. 'Put these on,' I said.

He was still staring at me with his mouth hanging open.

Maff handed me a cloak that one of the guards had been using as a blanket. 'This is Peter's, too,' he said.

I had to physically haul the burly fisherman to his feet. 'Put this round you and follow me.' I turned around to discover that Michael had joined Gabriel.

'Well done, Oriel,' Gabriel called with amused delight.

Michael added, 'The way you barked out those orders, we'll make a soldier of you yet.'

Maff swung open the heavy wooden door and I led Peter out of his cell. Peter seemed dazed. I don't think he had much clue about what was actually happening. Past two sets of sleeping guards we eventually came to a heavy metal gate, again opened by Maff. It led directly into a deserted street.

I walked with Peter, still in something of a dream, to the end of the road. Maff called to me from above the houses, 'Come on Oriel, hurry up. He's out of the prison now and he's lived here ten years. He doesn't need a tour guide.'

I looked at the man, a string of dribble now swinging from his lower lip. He needed something. I resorted to a method I've seen humans using on one another and gave Peter a firm slap on the cheek. Then I resumed my usual form, joined Maff, and we returned to Paul's lodgings at John Mark's house where a large crowd of disciples were hard at prayer. They were imploring my Boss for Peter's freedom. I told Paul that their prayers had already been answered but he was too distracted to hear.

I spoke to the Director, 'Can't you tell him that his request is received, understood and granted?'

'He's not listening.'

Maff and I waited as the roomful of Heaven's children pleaded desperately to their divine Father with such energy that not one of them could hear his reply. After a while there was a knock at the door. It was Peter. Nobody responded. Some decided that their prayers were more important than any visitor who might be knocking in the middle of the night, others were afraid that the knocking might be Herod's soldiers, come to arrest them too. Peter knocked again, harder. Those who feared arrest redoubled their prayers. Eventually one of the household's servants, a girl called Rhoda, took it upon herself to find out who was at the door.

'It's me. Peter!'

Rhoda ran back into the main room and declared, 'Peter's outside the door!'

'Don't be stupid,' came the reply. 'Peter's in prison. That's why we're all praying for him.'

'But I recognised his voice. It's him,' the poor girl insisted.

'It must be his Angel guardian,' someone suggested.

Rhoda stared around the crowded room, now quiet, searching

for someone who might believe her. Then a voice boomed from behind her, 'For goodness sake, will somebody let me in.'

Stunned silence. No one moved. Finally, Paul spoke up.

'Well, let him in then.'

When Peter was finally admitted he told the astounded gathering, 'It's easier to get out of Herod's prison than it is to get in here.'

Some days later – on the road to Caesarea

More delay! Paul never did get to speak to Peter. The former fisherman went into hiding that night. Paul and Barnabas did have a meeting with James, who gave his full support to the work they are doing among the non-Jews in Antioch, but he agreed with Barnabas that Paul would have to speak with Peter about Rome.

Today the pair began their journey back north. They are taking with them an even more valuable cargo than the money that they brought to Jerusalem; they have been joined by John Mark. John Mark has been compiling a collection of stories about Jesus and offered to share it with the Christians of Antioch. Barnabas, in return, has agreed to sponsor the expensive process of making copies of John Mark's book when it is completed.

Antioch – a year later

Returning to Antioch, Paul and Barnabas resumed their work here. In their absence the numbers of Christians had continued to grow, but, without clear leadership, numerous petty quarrels and squabbles sprang up between different groups and certain individuals. It was not long before there was more to be done than the two men could manage and three more were released from their occupations to become full-time ministers. Of these, two were Africans and one, Manaen, was a Jew – a reflection not only of the diversity of this great city but also of the universal appeal of the Son's story.

Today, at the initiative of the Director, these five men have called a special meeting of the leaders of the many groups of disciples across the city. They all know they need to discuss future plans but the Director has something more radical up his proverbial sleeve – not that he actually wears clothes as humans would understand them. He sent a separate message to me, telling me to be sure to attend.

Sounds exciting.

Later

The assembly began with some singing, Raphael having continued to pay occasional visits to Paul. This was followed by John Mark reading an extract from his book about Jesus. After that came an airing of the assorted whinges, whines, mutterings and murmurings without which no human gathering is complete. It was late in the evening when Simeon, one of the two African leaders, called all present to stop listening to their own frustrations and start listening to the Director. There was silence as over a hundred men and women tried to focus their attention away from themselves and onto their Creator. The room grew brighter and brighter to my eyes during this time, until the dazzling moment when every one of these Heavenly children was looking to their Father.

Then, in one glorious instant, the Director said the same thing to every one of them. Usually he sends different messages *to* different people *through* different people, but this time they all found the same thought emerging in their minds: 'Let Paul and Barnabas get on with the work I called them to do.'

I leapt into the air and gave out a great yelp of delight, much to the astonishment of the 127 other Angels present. The Director explained my action. 'As you can see,' he informed the Angels, 'our friend, Oriel, has been waiting for this moment for many Earth years.'

While my field staff congratulated me and wished me well in the next phase of my mission, the humans were excitedly sharing what they sensed their God telling them. Despite the petty rancour of the first part of the evening, the generous-hearted Antiochenes were quick to release their two leaders. It was rapidly agreed that all the groups of Christians should devote a month's prayers to Paul and Barnabas' expedition while the two of them make plans and prepare for the journey. A departure date was set.

I have been waiting for this day through 14 orbits of the watery planet round its pale sun. Rome, here we come!

The next day

If I was rather euphoric yesterday, the feeling hasn't lasted. This morning Paul and Barnabas began to consider what route to take and which cities they might visit on their way. Barnabas said he has a deep longing to tell the stories of Jesus in his home town. Barnabas' home town is Salamis. Salamis is in Cyprus. Cyprus is an island. There is only one way for humans to get to an island in this particular stretch of their history and that is by boat. I hate the sea. I hate boats. I especially hate sailing boats. Why didn't my Boss send his Son to Earth in the age of aeroplanes?

They then decided they would sail from Cyprus to mainland Turkey. I did my best to point out that Cyprus was no more than an unnecessary detour and that Turkey could be more easily reached by road. I was outmanoeuvred at every turn. Barnabas is a man whose enthusiasm is infectious and irresistible. Paul was quickly won over and he is as stubborn as a wine stain.

I appealed to the Director.

'Oriel,' he said, 'there are thousands of your Angels on the Island of Cyprus whose only prayer is that their humans have a chance to hear the story of Jesus. Would you deny them that for the sake of a boat trip?'

Salamis on Cyprus – five weeks later

The sea was polite and well behaved for our crossing from Seleucia but, nonetheless, I hated every moment of it. Throughout the voyage I had a sensation – familiar to humans – that time had slowed to an imperceptible crawl. I even wondered if it had started flowing backwards. I asked Asphiel, as he stared down into the hungry depths of the sea, how he coped with these things, being the guardian of an islander.

'When I first left the island with Barnabas,' he told me, 'I spoke to the Angel responsible for the captain of the ship. He advised me to look carefully into the water and showed me that it is filled with billions of tiny animals and plants, each of which is made by and loved by our Boss. He told me that humans can only see a tiny fraction of them.'

He was quite right, but it brought me no comfort whatsoever. I closed my mind to planet Earth and thought instead of the graceful rotation of distant galaxies spinning away from the moment of their creation.

When we finally drew into the port of Salamis, Raphael was waiting for me at the quayside.

'Well done, my dear old friend,' he said warmly. 'Let me look after your Paul for a short while. You go and have a rest.'

Normally I would have declined his offer. Raphael is to guardianship what a frightened rhinoceros is to diplomacy. But his face was beaming with such generous love that the prospect of a few days off was too good to reject. I have just had a quiet word with Asphiel and John Mark's guardian Paruel, asking them to call me if there is any trouble. Now to escape from the Universe altogether.

Next – a Friday

I've not had a chance to calculate how many Earth days have passed since Raphael relieved me of my duties, but Asphiel sent out a distress call, pleading with me to return.

'Paul and Barnabas are having a raging argument,' he informed me and then added cautiously, 'Archangel Raphael is not exactly helping the situation.'

I only knew it was Friday because the disagreement is over which of the two disciples should preach at the synagogue tomorrow. Paul is insistent that what is required is a thorough analytical presentation of the divine purpose behind Jewish law. Barnabas is in favour of interspersing a few sections from John Mark's book with some stories about how his own life has changed since meeting Jesus. Raphael was throwing all his Archangelic muscle behind Paul's case and Asphiel asked me to act as counsel for John Mark and Barnabas.

'Paul puts his fellow humans to sleep,' I told Raphael.

'They simply need to learn to concentrate and take their eternal destiny more seriously,' was his uncompromising reply.

I switched tactics. 'Raphael, which is better: to give a discourse on the complex interplay between harmonies, melodies and counter-melodies, or simply to listen to the music itself?'

'My dear Archangel,' he said, slightly irritated that I had apparently changed the subject. 'Music is to be listened to as love is to be shared.'

'And as stories are to be told,' I added firmly.

He looked at me with a slightly dazed look and I could sense Asphiel and Paruel trying to restrain triumphant giggles behind me.

'Barnabas is offering to play the music of the Son's human life,' I explained. 'Paul is threatening to dissect it and display it in minute parts. Have you ever seen the effect that Paul can have on a synagogue?'

'No.'

'You might like to call into Jerusalem or Damascus or Tarsus on your way home,' I suggested. 'They're probably still clearing up the mess.'

Raphael was not yet ready to rest his case. 'But Paul does have important things to say and teach, my dear Oriel.'

'I know. And he will. But for now, let's allow Barnabas to do the talking.'

'I'd better leave,' Raphael said, deflated. He turned to go.

'Raphael,' I called after him. 'Thank you for my rest and thank you for looking after Paul. It means a lot to me.'

Next day

Barnabas did an excellent job. The people were enthralled by his stories and a good number of them stayed on after the service to hear more about the Son from Paul. A special meeting has been arranged at the other synagogue in the town this evening.

Tomorrow the three disciples plan to tour the island.

Paphos – the other end of Cyprus

Paul, Barnabas and John Mark have now travelled the length of Cyprus and spoken at most of the synagogues along the way. The Jewish faith seems to be well respected here and both Jews and Gentiles have been keen to hear Barnabas' story. The missionaries have left behind a considerable interest in Jesus.

The tension between Paul and Barnabas, however, has not been left behind. Paul has been eager to press home the advantage, to capitalise on the interest they've stirred up, and to stay longer at each town, holding open meetings at which he could explain in more depth how the life of Jesus is the fulfilment of all Jewish – indeed all human – hope. But their itinerary has been determined by the complex network of Barnabas' many friends and relations.

By the time they reached Paphos, news of their tour had preceded them. Tomorrow morning they have an appointment with Sergius Paulus, the proconsul of the island. Saul has claimed the primary speaking role for himself, stressing that 'Sergius is an intelligent and educated man, well capable of managing a *decent* discussion.'

Next morning

I discovered how significant this morning's meeting was in the middle of the night. Archangel Michael sent a messenger to tell me that Lucifer has been seen entering the proconsul's villa. I left Paul with Asphiel and Paruel and made an exploratory visit. I discovered that the leader of the Opposition gained his entrance with the unwitting help of a Jewish mystic who is favoured by the proconsul. This man is far more interested in his own career, wealth and popularity than he is in the mystery of my Boss's love, and his self-interest provided Lucifer with the opportunity he sought. Would you believe it, this pathetic so-called mystic goes under the name *Bar-Jesus*? What more evidence could one require to prove that the human system of names is woefully inadequate! I shall call the man by his alternative name – Elymas.

When Lucifer noticed that I was watching him, he came close and said, 'I am going to stop this Saul, Oriel.'

'Paul,' I corrected him.

'Stop means stop,' Lucifer continued. 'You and I both know what that means.'

I returned immediately to Paul's side. If Lucifer is intent on destroying him, I need to stay with him all the time. When I arrived at the home of Barnabas' sister (where they are currently staying) I found two Opposition spirits lurking in the shadows, keeping a careful watch on Paul.

Later

Sergius Paulus welcomed Paul, Barnabas and John Mark warmly. He had heard news of their progress and was very interested to learn more about the Jewish teaching they represent. Lucifer had taken a firm grip on Elymas' mind and was using it to distract Sergius' interest. Whatever Paul said, Elymas undermined. He would say, 'That's only an opinion, sir,' or exclaim, 'The most outrageous interpretation I've ever had the misfortune to hear!' Most of the time he simply tutted or whistled or took audible lungfuls of air. The effect of all this was to confuse and befuddle the proconsul.

I countered Lucifer's assault by speaking into Paul's mind. 'Shut him up, Paul,' I urged. 'As one of the Boss's children you have authority to deal with things like this. Jesus did. Don't you ever listen to John Mark's stories?'

At that point the Director backed me up. 'Oriel is quite right,' he informed Paul. 'Whatever condemnation you declare against this man, I will honour.'

Paul got the message. Looking straight at Elymas, he said, 'You are a child of the devil, full of tricks and lies. Will you ever stop twisting God's truth?' Elymas, Lucifer and Sergius Paulus all looked at Paul with startled faces: Sergius in wonder, the other two in dread. Paul continued, 'You will be blind. Unless you return to the truth you will never even see the light of the sun.'

The effect was instant. At Paul's word, the Director acted. Elymas groped around the room asking for someone to lead him home, and Lucifer slunk out, muttering, 'I'm going to stop this Paul. And stop means stop.'

In Sergius the result was quite different. The enlightenment in his mind was as dramatic as the darkness in Elymas' eyes. While

Elymas begged for a guiding hand, Sergius grasped the truth. Lucifer's departure was followed by the arrival of the Son, come to witness the birth of a new disciple, a new brother. There will be another party in Heaven tonight. There might even be one here in Paphos.

Pamphylia – on the Turkish coast

Paul, Barnabas and John Mark stayed another week in Paphos, during which Paul paid daily visits to the proconsul's villa. They had booked a berth on a boat to the mainland and were waiting for their ship to be ready.

The voyage was bad enough in itself but it was made far worse by a great storm of an argument between Paul and John Mark. Paul – never one to be timid in his opinions – had just finished reading the latest draft of John Mark's book and took the opportunity of the journey to say exactly what he thought of it.

'You waste far too much space on simplistic little stories and barely begin to explain the real significance of our Master's life.'

This was not an encouraging start. He then proceeded to comb his way through the entire work, detailing everything he considered inadequate.

'Let's begin with your opening sentence,' he said. '*The beginning of the good news about Jesus Christ, the Son of God.* Firstly, if you really want the beginning you will have to go all the way back to creation. Secondly, the book itself doesn't come across as good news because you have ended with everyone being terrified and confused. Thirdly, you can't assert that Jesus is the Christ, the Messiah, without comprehensive reference to all the prophecies of the Jewish scriptures. In fact, such a claim, and the one that he is God's Son, each deserve an entire book in themselves.'

I won't torture you with any more of Paul's criticisms, but in a similar way he worked his way, sentence by sentence, right through to the last word. Barnabas tried to defend John Mark at first but soon gave up and retreated to the far end of the ship. It seemed that John Mark's only defence was to say, 'But that is how Peter told it to me.' This did not do great service to Paul's opinion of Peter.

The critique, and the voyage, took a full three days. At supper tonight, in a harbourside inn, the three disciples ate in preoccupied silence. Barnabas is cross with Paul, Paul is disappointed with John Mark, and John Mark is deeply hurt. In the gloomy quiet the Director said to me, 'Not one of them can hear me over the din and clatter of their own opinions.'

Next day

When Paul and Barnabas woke up this morning they discovered that John Mark had gone, taking both book and baggage with him. The two men ran out onto the quayside and asked everyone they met if they had seen a heavily laden young Jew. Their enquiries all pointed in the same direction, to a ship bound for Caesarea which – to their weak eyes – was already just a dot on the horizon.

Paul and Barnabas quickly packed up and left the coast. They are walking inland to the Roman city of Perga, where Paul hopes to find some opportunity to proclaim his message. I think they will need to offer a little forgiveness to one another before their message will have much effect.

Perga – ten days later

Wherever he has travelled, Paul has always visited the synagogue first, and usually managed to cause enough of a commotion there for his name to spread rapidly. Perga does not have a synagogue and both Paul and Barnabas have been searching for a suitable opening. They visited the amphitheatre and the Roman sports stadium but no one showed much interest in two talkative tourists. In order to build up money as well as contacts, Paul sought out the local tentmakers and offered his services. This work has provided him with a number of challenging conversations but the local people are too interested in earnings and entertainment to have much time for eternity.

In the midst of this disappointment and frustration, Paul has become ill. Human diseases are not my speciality, but his body is dangerously hot, to such an extent that his thoughts occasionally go hopping and skipping down the uncharted pathways of his brain. The Director – and he should know – assures me that Paul will not be dying in the near future. A local doctor advised Barnabas to take Paul up into the mountains where the clean air will, apparently, aid recovery. Barnabas is presently searching for suitable cart or carriage for Paul to travel in.

I am quite sure that the continuing tension between Paul and Barnabas concerning John Mark's departure contributed to the collapse in Paul's health. It's also true, however, that this illness has prompted them to put aside their differences and work together again.

Pisidian Antioch

My frustration concerning human misuse of human names has doubled. After the confusion caused by individuals with multiple names and multiple individuals with the same name, we are now staying in a town called Antioch which is hundreds of miles from Antioch and nothing like it. It's all the fault of some vain and arrogant king, I'm told. What is more, Pisidian Antioch is not even in Pisidia! For all that, up on its high grassy plateau, this smaller Antioch has fresh air and clean water and is a very suitable place for Paul to recover. There is a substantial Jewish population here, which has responded energetically to Paul's need. Paul was so impressed by their support that he declared, 'You have welcomed me as if I were an Angel,' which only shows how little he knows about Angels. Humans habitually ignore us completely, and Paul is one of the worst offenders!

A few weeks later

I have used Paul's convalescence as an opportunity to work on the 'who should do the preaching?' question. The Director is firmly in favour of Paul being the primary spokesman and won over my unswerving support for the Paul camp by saying, 'If Paul is going to announce the message of the Son's achievements to the people of Rome, he'll need to practise.' He went on to acknowledge that

Paul's preaching style is currently tedious and complicated (my words, not his) and encouraged me to ask Archangel Gabriel to help.

Gabriel arrived while Asphiel and I were locking antlers over the story-versus-analytical-truth debate. He listened intently while we pushed our argument backwards and forwards over the sleeping forms of Paul and Barnabas. Eventually, capitalising on a brief pause in the duel, Gabriel said, 'The truth *is* the story.'

He got our silence if not our understanding.

'The truth *is* the story,' he repeated. We still stared at him with blank faces.

'Our Boss teaches humans through their stories. You cannot explain the truth without telling the story and there is no point in telling the story without expressing the truth.'

Asphiel and I were quiet while we digested Gabriel's words. At last Asphiel asked, 'Does that mean that we are both right.'

'Certainly not,' my colleague replied bluntly. 'You are both wrong.'

Asphiel and I looked at one another apologetically.

Gabriel said brightly, 'In my experience, humans are particularly open to the business of Heaven when they are ill. I suggest that you start working on Paul before he gets any better. I'll be off now.'

During the days that followed, while Paul looked out of his window at the stony hillsides of nearby Pisidia, I took him through the stories of the Jewish people and of the Son's human life. I showed him how the truths he values so highly are all part of the story, just as flowers are part of the plant on which they grow.

Tomorrow, now he's through the worst of his illness, Paul will be speaking at the synagogue. They have already heard Barnabas' anecdotes and are keen to hear Paul.

The following day – a Sabbath

Triumph! Paul has managed to deliver an entire synagogue sermon without causing a riot or being thrown out. He started with a story – actually, the entire story of the Jews from Abraham all the way through to Jesus. After that he was able to restrain his analysis to just one subject, showing how the plan for Jesus' resurrection can be found in earlier parts of the whole saga.

It seemed a bit ambitious but they loved it. At the end of the service, Paul was immediately booked for next Sabbath and a considerable number of Jews and converts to Judaism followed him and Barnabas to their lodging to discuss the whole thing further. They would have stayed all day but Paul's hostess threw them all out in the afternoon, saying that her guest was still unwell and needed rest.

A week later

Since last Saturday, word has spread from neighbour to neighbour, from customer to trader to customer, from child to adult and from sister to brother, all saying there is a man visiting the Jewish synagogue who can relieve people of their guilt and offer them a new start in life. Excitement is not a frequent visitor to isolated provincial towns and well over half the population turned out to hear Paul. There was simply no way that they were all going to fit into the synagogue.

Barnabas suggested that they follow Jesus' example and preach in the open air. The vast congregation decamped to the Square of Tiberius in the town centre. Among them I spotted a significant number of Opposition spirits, eagerly looking for some way to disrupt the assembly. They found the opening they needed in the minds of the most dedicated synagogue worshippers. The more the non-Jews expressed their excitement about Paul, the more jealous the Jews became. These jealous Jews gathered in a grumpy group at the back of the square and fell into a quiet discussion about all the things that irritate them concerning Paul.

Barnabas, with a little help from Asphiel, noticed what was happening and slipped up the ornamental staircase from which Paul was preaching to let him know what was happening. Paul was characteristically direct. He attracted the attention of the disgruntled Jews and said to them, 'We came to you first with our message, but if you reject it and can't be bothered with eternal life, we will concentrate on the Gentiles because they *can* be bothered.'

The assorted Romans, Greeks and Celts, who make up the population of Pisidian Antioch, were delighted by this and readily took Paul and Barnabas to their hearts. The Jews marched back to their synagogue – to have their own service in their own building in their own way.

Paul's synagogue record is back on track.

On the shore of Lake Beysehir – three weeks later

The leader of the Jewish community made use of influential contacts among the wives of prominent city councillors. These women drew up a petition and, within days, had Paul and Barnabas banned from every shop, inn and market in Antioch. A few days later the council passed a second motion – expelling them altogether.

However, as they left Pisidian Antioch they could take consolation in leaving behind a large and energetic family of new-born brothers and sisters.

At present, needing to consider Paul's health, they have stopped in a lakeside village overshadowed by tall, snow covered mountains on the main east-west road.

Iconium – two weeks on

To my utter dismay, when Paul and Barnabas set off again on their mission, they headed east – away from Rome. Inexplicable! I appealed instantly to the Director, asking him to make them change their minds. He refused, adding, 'Oriel, I am trusting Paul. Aren't you?'

Our route brought us to Iconium, a modest town at an important junction on the east-west road. Paul and Barnabas timed their arrival for the main Sabbath service at the synagogue. After lengthy discussion, they agreed to take turns at addressing the congregation, and to great effect. There was considerable excitement among the attendant Angels and they stirred up strong interest in the thoughts and emotions of their charges. The lives of both Jews and non-Jews were illuminated by a renewed love for my Boss.

The air of celebration was shattered when the same Opposition

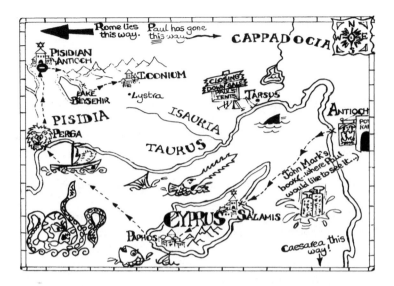

spirits who caused trouble in Pisidian Antioch entered the synagogue. The spiritual atmosphere cooled rapidly as these agents of Lucifer sought out people whose minds were darkened by prejudice or selfish interest. These men and women began to answer Paul, raising objections, questioning assumptions. The clear, refreshing good news of forgiveness and Heavenly life became muddied by partisanship and controversy. The Angels, especially those nurturing newly-given spiritual life in their humans, became restless.

While the Angels grew quieter, debate between the humans grew stronger and sharper. Paul, prompted by the Director, had an answer to each objection raised by the Opposition spirits. He regained the initiative and before long my Angels had something to cheer about. The brightness of Heavenly hope returned to the room and Angels responsible for doubters fought hard against the Opposition spirits to gain the attention of their humans.

There was another significant turn in the proceedings when one doubter, a wealthy Roman official called Lucius, a worshipper in the synagogue for many years, spoke up. 'Paul,' he said, 'I would love to stay and follow this argument through, but my wife is ill and I must make sure the children are being cared for. Why don't you and your friend come to my house on Wednesday to continue the discussion.' He then addressed the whole congregation, saying, 'You are all invited. We need to get to the bottom of this Jesus business and see what's what. Any time after sunset is fine.'

Wednesday night

Lucius' grand home was already packed when Paul and Barnabas arrived. Paul asked after the man's wife and, hearing she was still gravely ill, offered to pray with her before addressing the guests. That done, he entered the crowded main room and Saturday's debate was resumed.

The meeting might have lasted well into the night had it not been interrupted by Lucius' wife opening an internal window and shouting, 'It's time you lot went home to your families.'

This was greeted with a stunned silence. Eventually Lucius stammered, 'Chloe, you're up!'

Chloe had been on the last orbit of her earthly life when Paul arrived. No one knew how long that orbit would last, but they had accepted she would not get better. Next to her, as she leaned into the room full of health and life, was an even livelier face, unseen by the humans but unmistakable to the Angels present. It was the face of Jesus.

Chloe explained her recovery. 'Paul came into my room and prayed in the name of his Jesus – and I've been feeling better and better ever since.'

One of those who had just responded to the story of Jesus with simple but wholehearted faith, spoke up. 'Paul and Barnabas,' she said, 'come to my home tomorrow evening; I would like to be dipped. Everyone is welcome. Now, let's leave Chloe and Lucius in peace.'

A month later

Day after day, Paul and Barnabas have been invited from house to house. Gradually the meetings developed into two distinct kinds: those where newly committed disciples encouraged each other and hungrily dined on the stories of Barnabas and insights of Paul; and other meetings which always included at least one

Opposition spirit, meetings which often degenerated from debates into confrontations.

This morning, the two missionaries were discussing the rising tide of opposition when an Angel arrived from the home of one of Paul's most outspoken critics, the synagogue secretary Ben-Judah. 'They've been turned,' the flustered Angel announced. 'Take Paul with you and go.'

'Hold on, hold on,' I said, trying to calm the distracted spirit. 'Start from the beginning. Who has been turned? From what to what?'

'First thing this morning my human, Ben-Judah, met with various other anti-Pauls and they resolved to drag Paul out and stone him next time he says anything they say is blasphemous.'

'Wait there,' I instructed the Angel. I butted into the conversation between the two humans in the room.

'Time to move on,' I instructed Paul. Asphiel said the same to Barnabas.

Our contributions certainly had an effect on their discussion, but not the one we hoped for.

'I am not going to let Ben-Judah frighten me out of this city,' Paul asserted.

'Quite right,' Barnabas replied. 'We need to stay to encourage the new Christians. They're not yet strong enough to stand on their own.'

I turned to Ben-Judah's Angel. 'Were there any humans at this meeting still open to persuasion about our Boss's Son?'

He thought for a while. 'I think Gershal's human was rather shocked at their decision,' he said. 'Yes, I think her mind is still open.'

'Go and speak to Gershal,' I instructed hurriedly. 'Between the two of you, get the human to come and warn Paul and Barnabas about the plot.' As the Angel was leaving I said, 'Ask the Director to help you, he's bound to be around somewhere. Look in this human's spirit, you may find him there.'

While Asphiel and I waited, Paul and Barnabas continued to discuss how they might strengthen the faith of their Iconian brothers and sisters.

At last, Gershal arrived. 'She's coming,' he announced.

A few minutes later there was a knock on the door. I was shocked to see that the undecided opponent was Chloe, the wife of Lucius, so recently rescued from an early descent into Death. How dull humans can be to spiritual realities – especially rich humans!

As Chloe waited for Paul to open his door, I noted it was her gratitude to Paul that kept a hopeful doubt in her mind.

'Chloe,' Barnabas said, 'it's lovely to see you. You're looking well.'

'They're planning to kill you!' she said, looking from Barnabas to Paul. 'They want to do it the Jewish way, to stone you to death for blasphemy. Please leave. Go now! The plan is to stop you in the street near the Jewish shops, to confront you with a loaded question and then drag you off as soon as you answer it.'

There was silence. Barnabas looked at Chloe, trying to understand the dramatic news. Paul was deep in thought and I did not like the thoughts I was seeing. 'If I live, I will carry on the work of my Messiah,' he reasoned to himself. 'But if I die, I shall go to live with him. Which is best?'

While Paul considered his options, I rained into his thoughts just one idea: 'Rome, Paul. We've got to go to Rome. It can't end here in an obscure Turkish trading post.'

He wasn't listening. I appealed to the Director. 'Go on, Sir, you tell him. He won't take it from me.'

This time my desire matched the Director's. He lit up the numerous mental pictures of Rome stored in Paul's mind. There were a considerable variety, from the romantic images of his childhood to the violent prejudices of his youth. To accompany these, the Director caused the voice of Ananias to echo around Paul's thoughts: *Jesus said, This man is my chosen instrument to carry my name before the Gentiles and their kings.*

Paul grasped the vision of Rome. Asphiel and I embraced in relief.

'We must leave,' Paul announced gravely. Barnabas accepted the decision without question. Paul turned to Chloe. 'Chloe, our Lord did not heal you for nothing. Will you please guide us safely out of the city?'

The state of Chloe's mind concerned me. She was teetering on a tightrope of indecision between her husband's admiration for Ben-Judah and her own gratitude to Paul. I was about to shout out, 'Paul, how do you know you can trust her?' when the Director stopped me.

'Trust her, Oriel.' he said.

Lystra – two days after

Chloe smuggled the two disciples out of Iconium, setting them on the southbound road which would take them across the border into the region of Lycaonia. 'There,' she told them, 'you should be safe.'

How wrong she was!

Urged to leave as quickly as they could, it wasn't possible for Paul and Barnabas to gather all their belongings or buy horses. They left on foot, taking only what they could carry, and they walked all day. It was already dark when they reached the Roman colony of Lystra and the city gate was closed and bolted for the night. The two men retraced their steps a short way and slept under the archway of an imposing pagan temple beside the road.

At first light, they joined the queue of assorted travellers and traders waiting for the city gates to open. Never one to miss an opportunity, Paul began to address the people around him, telling them of a God who is greater than Zeus – in whose temple he had slept – and inviting Barnabas to share his stories of meeting Jesus. By the time the gatekeeper performed the first duty of his working day, Paul had already stimulated considerable interest in the Son. He and Barnabas were invited to continue their tale at an inn situated at the edge of the Square of Augustus, just inside the northern gate.

Lystrans who regularly take their breakfast at the inn joined a growing audience. The human simplicity of Jesus, as described by Barnabas, contrasted sharply with the expensive pomp of the cult of Zeus, the official religion of the city. One man who responded readily to this more accessible faith was a lame beggar, seated in his customary post at the city gate. The man's dull life brightened dramatically when he opened his mind to the news of a God who heals sick people and cares for the poor.

I drew Paul's attention to this crumpled man. Paul was telling his audience that Jesus is not a religious cult exploiting vague myths from the forgotten past, but is alive, touching and changing the lives of those who follow him. Without acknowledging my help, Paul strode over to the beggar, who had never walked a step in all his sad life, and said to him, 'Stand up!'

The man, overflowing with newly-discovered faith, literally jumped to his feet and began to walk. The crowd erupted with amazement, in their excitement abandoning the Greek language, which they only use for business and conversation with outsiders. Reverting to the local dialect they shouted to one another, 'The gods have come down in human form.' Pointing to Paul, who had done most of the talking, they announced, 'This must be Hermes, the messenger of the gods.' Then, with great awe, they looked at Barnabas, whose body is considerably bigger than Paul's in every dimension. 'This,' they said in quieter voices, 'must be Zeus himself.'

Paul and Barnabas, of course, were completely ignorant of all this. They could see that they were being considered with great honour, but neither of them understood a word of the Lycaonian language. They were led by reverential hands to two large chairs placed in the very centre of the square, and their guides retreated to a discreet distance.

The Square of Augustus filled up as word spread round the city that Zeus had appeared in human form and had healed a beggar. It was clear to the two disciples that everyone was waiting for something to happen. They waited too.

The square became packed with excited people – the excitement focused on the two men in the centre. Eventually a way was cleared through the crowd at the North Gate. In through the gate came a procession of priests, with acolytes carrying bundles of wood and lighted torches. Behind them were servants dragging sacrificial white bulls. The priest at the front of the procession was carrying two wreaths of flowers, and when he made to place these over Paul and Barnabas' necks, the disciples suddenly understood what was happening.

Paul jumped up from his seat and ran into the startled crowd, shouting in both Greek and Latin to avoid any further confusion, 'What are you doing? We are ordinary men, just like you. We came here to tell you to give up your worthless gods and worship the true and living God.'

It was a difficult task. The priests of Zeus proceeded to build a sacrificial pyre and Barnabas had to physically restrain them from slaughtering a bull in his honour. The people couldn't understand it. A man, crippled since birth, had been miraculously cured – there was no doubt about that. These visitors must therefore be gods, but they insisted they were nothing of the sort.

I assembled all the Angels present and instructed them to

do their best to explain the situation to their charges. Years of ignorance and spiritual abuse, however, cannot be quickly overcome.

Late into the morning confusion still reigned. Many people returned to their homes and jobs but the Square of Augustus remained busy and the priests were still trying to perform their now-ragged ritual. Into this mayhem rode a small group of Iconian Jews, led by Chloe's husband, Lucius, and the secretary of the synagogue Ben-Judah. They were accompanied by a familiar group of Opposition spirits.

Lucius had forced Chloe to tell him where Paul and Barnabas had gone and furnished Ben-Judah's assassination squad with fast horses. When they galloped into the square and saw their intended victims being worshipped as pagan gods, they needed no further evidence of blasphemy.

'These men are not gods,' Ben-Judah informed the crowd from his horse. 'They are liars and cheats. They have perverted the minds of the people of Iconium and, after escaping from our city yesterday, they came to peddle the same poison to you.'

The people listened. Ben-Judah was making sense. Paul's claim that he was just an ordinary human made no sense because he had undoubtedly cured a crippled man. It seemed much more likely that he was a cheat and a liar.

'We have come here as fast as we could,' Ben-Judah continued, 'to save you from these evil men.'

No one objected. The Iconian hit squad dismounted, grabbed the two disciples and dragged them out of the city. Through the gate they turned right along the foot of the wall. Asphiel and I followed, shadowed by six Opposition spirits. Around a corner and out of sight from the road, Lucifer was waiting. He had chosen his spot carefully, beside a pile of abandoned builder's rubble.

I had, of course, seen a human stoned to death before. There were no formalities, just hatred and brutality. Barnabas was restrained. Paul was thrown against the city wall and without a moment's pause rocks were thrown at him. The leader of the Opposition said nothing; he did not need to.

I leapt into the middle of the rock shower and tried to divert the missiles from Paul's head. It was difficult to have much influence on something as faint and vacuous as rock but I did my best.

Asphiel shouted to me, 'There's no point doing that. They'll just carry on until he's dead. All you'll achieve is postponing his end. You won't stop it.'

Still shielding Paul from the bombardment, I struggled to think. Being stuck in time, there was no opportunity for careful consideration. Before long, Paul's brain would be reduced to mush.

Lucifer jeered, 'I win, Oriel!'

That spurred me into action. I grabbed Paul firmly. 'I'm sorry about this,' I said. 'It's the only way.' With that I gave Paul a sharp blow on the back of the head and he slumped to the ground, unconscious.

The stoning stopped. Ben-Judah and his mob looked at the motionless figure. Barnabas cowered on the ground nearby, expecting he would be next. I stood beside my man, numbed by what I had witnessed and shocked by what I had just done, but triumphant none the less.

Lucifer cut my victory short. He whispered into Lucius' mind. Lucius turned to Ben-Judah. 'We'd better check that he is really dead. Listen for his heartbeat.'

They were only a few paces from Paul's bruised and unconscious form. I had to do something even more drastic. I had no choice.

As Ben-Judah stooped down over Paul's prostrate body, I too leaned down. I reached inside the disciple's chest and took hold of his flabby heart. As Ben-Judah pressed an ear to Paul's ribs, I squeezed the heart into submission. Ben-Judah was conscientious in his work. He called for silence, listening carefully, first with one ear, then with the other. All the while, I held the heart from beating.

I know enough about human bodies to understand the terrible risk I was taking. I didn't need Asphiel to ask, 'Will you be able to start it again?'

Ben-Judah shook his head. My wait was nearly over, but Lucifer knew exactly what I was doing. He prompted Lucius again. 'Let *me* listen,' the man said.

Lucius bent down and pressed his ear to Paul's chest. I poured out my panic to the Director who was still there in Paul's fading body. 'There was nothing else I could do,' I whimpered. 'Have I done something awful? Have I ruined your plan?'

As Lucius turned his other ear to Paul's silent torso, I watched the light of my human's life growing dimmer and dimmer. It would not be long before I extinguished that light altogether. Yet I knew that if I released Paul's heart, Ben-Judah would simply release a second bombardment of stones.

My Boss's gentle, powerful voice came up from the dying man. 'I have this situation under control, Oriel.'

I wanted to reply, 'You don't seem to be doing much to help!' but said nothing.

Eventually, Lucius stood up and pronounced Paul dead.

Lucifer shouted desperately, 'He isn't, he isn't. You've been tricked.'

But there are few humans who will trust their spiritual senses above their physical ones and the voice in Lucius' dark soul could not overcome the conviction of his well-trained brain. The mob drifted away. Not triumphant. They knew they'd done a terrible thing. They only excused the terror by telling themselves that it was necessary.

The men mounted their tired horses and as they rode away, I gave Paul's heart a series of precisely measured slaps. To my great relief, it began to beat again.

Lucifer looked at me, his face dull and expressionless. 'You know me, Oriel,' he said. 'I don't give up.'

Though alive, Paul's body was seriously damaged and his brain was concussed by my blow to his head. He had two broken ribs which were also my handiwork. Barnabas, who had no reason to doubt Lucius' pronouncement of Paul's death, remained curled into a rather large ball by the wall. I sent Asphiel for help, not daring to leave Paul's side.

For a time, neither man moved. Eventually, a groan from Paul roused Barnabas from his grief and terror. The big man crawled on hands and knees over to his companion and gently coaxed him into consciousness, then after that, into conversation. When Barnabas had determined the extent of Paul's injuries, he set about the serious matter of praying for him.

'Dear Jesus,' he prayed, placing a large hand on the back of Paul's head where a rising mound marked the site of my life-saving assault, 'heal the bruising to his head.' Then, moving his hand and attention to the sharp pain in his friend's chest, he prayed, 'And mend these broken ribs.'

As soon as Barnabas' prayers were out, the Director was at work, restoring soft flesh, re-assembling bones. I was enormously relieved to see the ill effects of my blundering rescue reversed. The Son arrived.

'Nice work, Oriel,' he said breezily. Then, with a reassuring smile, he added, 'You were nearly the first Angel, in all Heaven, to purposefully destroy the human in his care.'

'I had no choice.'

'There is always choice,' he replied.

'How would you have handled it?' I asked, still pricked by feelings of guilt at the damage I had caused.

He did not answer my question. 'You will have to excuse me,' he said. 'Asphiel needs my help.' He left.

'So, what *could* I have done differently?' I said, continuing the conversation with the Director.

He was still working on Paul's injuries as Barnabas' prayer continued. 'You acted in love, Oriel, and that – as I said – was *nice work*.'

When Paul's most serious injuries were tidied up, leaving only cuts and bruises, the Director brought an end to Barnabas' prayer, saying, 'Alexander can deal with those.'

I had no idea who Alexander was, but as Paul and Barnabas started to consider their own *coulds* and *shoulds*, I repeatedly suggested to them that they should wait for Alexander.

And Alexander duly came. Arriving with Asphiel, he was, I discovered, the formerly disabled man whose healing had set off the whole disastrous chain of events. Alexander was accompanied by a group of other Lystrans, all former colleagues in begging at the North Gate.

Asphiel reached me ahead of them. 'He healed every one of them, with the Son's help,' he informed me, excitedly. 'When I arrived, he was busy telling his fellow beggars what had happened and they asked him if this Jesus could cure them too. At that moment, the Son turned up, said *Of course I can* and spurred Alexander into action. He worked his way along the line saying, *In the name of this Jesus character, walk*, and, *In the name of this Jesus character, see,* and *In the name of this Jesus character, stretch out your arm.* Here they all are.'

Alexander walked straight up to Paul, his new-found confidence showing itself in his new-found gait. 'You all right, mate?' he enquired.

'I am now, thank you very much,' Paul replied. He tried to sit up but his bruised muscles were in no hurry to respond. He winced at the mass of minor aches across his body.

Alexander was quick to respond. 'In the name of Jesus, get up,' he said.

'That's what I'm trying to do,' Paul assured him.

'Come on,' Alexander urged. 'Your Jesus chap sorted me out, and all this lot.' He indicated his friends, who all smiled enthusiastically at Paul.

'Lovely to meet you,' Paul said, trying to struggle to his feet.

Alexander hadn't finished, 'So he's not going to miss you out now, is he?'

'He hasn't,' Barnabas intervened helpfully. 'You should have seen him a few minutes ago. He was dead.'

Alexander looked at Barnabas as the leader of a pack of hyenas might look finding itself face to face with a lion. There was a respectful silence during which Paul finally hauled his bloodspattered body upright. No one quite knew what to say.

A young man spoke up. 'We need to get you somewhere safe,' he said, 'and wash all those wounds.'

Everyone turned to look at him. Without exception, every mind asked the same question, 'And who might you be?' though none actually said it.

I looked at the glowing Angel accompanying the young man and posed the same enquiry. 'Who is he?'

The Angel beamed at me with proud delight in his newly enlightened human. 'Timothy.'

The next day

Timothy led the ragged and battered procession around the perimeter of Lystra, through the East Gate and down the neat streets of a fairly wealthy quarter that led to his parents' home. His mother – a Jew – was pleased to welcome Paul and Barnabas into her home and immediately set to cleaning Paul's wounds. She was less certain, though, about her son's collection of ex-beggars. But Timothy was so excited about everything he had witnessed that morning that it was infectious. His mother just looked on as he raided the family's wardrobes in order to supply Alexander and his friends with fresh clothes.

Paul, Barnabas and Alexander stayed the night. I learned that Ben-Judah and his henchmen were also staying in Lystra.

With the help of at least four Angel guardians and three humans, I arranged for this information to be passed to Paul. (It would be so much easier if he would simply listen to me.) Over breakfast, the two disciples thanked Timothy and his family for their hospitality and explained that they needed to be on their way. Alexander, having slept in a real bed for the first time since he was a child, volunteered to take to the road with them.

'Having never walked in over thirty years, until yesterday,' he explained,' I could use the practice.'

He will get it. It is sixty miles to the next significant settlement, the town of Derbe.

In Derbe – some months later

The three travellers did not hurry. They went at Alexander's slow pace. Never having travelled outside his home town before, he was distracted by every new sight along the way. He was equally excited by all Barnabas' many stories about the Son (though less so by Paul's impatient attempts to explain the truths behind them).

When they finally reached Derbe, just on the Galatian side of the border with a neighbouring kingdom, they learned that there's no Jewish community here and therefore no synagogue to preach in. Alexander was quick with an alternative.

'Let's go back to the city gate and start with the beggars – like you did at Lystra.'

It worked! There were no wealthy Jews to supply the three missionaries with accommodation, so Paul returned to his old trade, training Alexander and the now healthy beggars of Derbe in the craft of tentmaking. While Paul and his novice workforce built tents, Barnabas concentrated on building the growing community of Christian disciples. The testimony of restored bodies and changed lives spoke for itself.

Today, Paul and Barnabas have announced their departure. They have learned the value of an ordered community of disciples and are keen to retrace their steps so they can bring some order to the chaos left behind them. They informed their dumbfounded brothers and sisters that Alexander will take over as the head of the Christian family. No one disagreed. This man, whose only responsibility in life had been the needs of his own belly, has emerged as a shrewd businessman and, more importantly, a disciple with a keen ear to the Director.

Lystra

The return journey to Lystra took just two days. Eager to avoid the catastrophe of their last visit to the city, Paul and Barnabas timed their arrival for the half-light of evening, just before the gates were closed. They rode swiftly to Timothy's home, where they were enthusiastically welcomed.

The Christian family in Lystra has grown significantly since their hurried departure. The growth has been along two very different branches. One branch has grown out of the thriving community of Jewish merchants and wealthy citizens who worship at the synagogue but have not fully converted to Judaism. The second branch is formed from the shady underclass of city life to which Alexander's former beggar friends belonged. What a combination!

Much as Paul wanted to stay and sort out this fragmented community, he knew that his visit had to be brief and quiet.

Yesterday, at Paul's suggestion, and after considerable diplomatic effort from Barnabas, all the Christians gathered together in Timothy's parents' garden – the house not being big enough. Paul and Barnabas addressed the uncomfortable gathering in their different styles, all the while looking for some guidance as to who they might appoint as a leader for this deeply divided community.

This morning the two men discussed their thoughts and feelings.

'What about Archippus?' Paul asked, unenthusiastically.

Archippus is the leader of a network of underground businesses that used to redistribute stolen goods around the region. To his credit, Archippus has tried very hard to transfer his efforts to legitimate enterprise – not altogether successfully.

'No,' said Barnabas with confidence.

'He's well respected,' Paul observed. 'The Lystrans admire him for his former life, and the Jews for his new one.'

'Only because he has opened up new trading contacts for the Jewish businessmen,' Barnabas explained.

'Exactly,' replied Paul, beginning to get excited about his suggestion. 'He's a survivor and a natural leader.'

I joined the conversation. 'It is not a *natural* leader that you are looking for,' I interjected. 'You need a *spiritual* leader.' My contribution went unheeded.

'Archippus has a wife and five children at his father's farm in the country,' Barnabas continued. 'He also has a girlfriend with two other children in the city. I think he has quite enough family commitments already.'

More thinking.

'The person who would do the job best,' Barnabas began, 'is the person who's doing it already. Eunice – Timothy's mother.'

'No,' Paul replied.

'Why not?' asked Barnabas.

'Yes, why not?' I echoed.

'Because she's a woman'.

'She *can* do the job,' Barnabas returned, teasing out the issue.

Barnabas was quite right. I looked to the Director, to see what light he could cast on the problem. He was waiting for Paul's reply.

'The Jews would never accept it,' Paul declared. 'Leadership is, and always has been, the responsibility of men. If a woman cannot lead the Jewish community, she cannot lead the Christian community.'

I looked deep into Paul's mind and noticed a certain unease regarding women. It rose, like his earlier fear of horses, out of a sticky web of childhood experiences tangled with ancient traditions of Jewish faith. I didn't want to see as good a woman as Timothy's mother set aside for such an untidy pile of reasons, and so appealed to the Director, asking him to overrule Paul's reservations.

'The leadership of this part of my human family is Paul's responsibility, Oriel,' he reprimanded me, 'not yours.'

'But Eunice would be excellent,' I protested. 'She understands the Jewish faith; she cares for the Lystrans; she's respected by both groups.'

I would have continued, but the Director stopped me. 'Oriel. We have had this conversation already. When I give my children authority, I trust them.'

I was just sliding into a sulk when he added, 'I do not treat you any differently, my friend.'

I spoke to the Director again. 'Who's your tip for the task, then?'

'They haven't asked me yet,' he replied.

I pointed this out to Paul and somehow, for once, he must have picked up the message because when Timothy's mother popped her head round the door to invite them to lunch, he said, 'Thank you, Eunice, but we have some urgent praying to do instead.'

'Can I join you,' she asked, 'when I've sorted the family out?'

Later

Throughout the afternoon the three of them struggled to listen to the Director over the din of their own prejudices and fears. Their spiritual hearing was not helped by an irritated rumble of annoyance in both men that the other had rejected their best suggestions.

I spoke to the Director. 'Why have you not said anything?'

'They would not be able to hear me,' he replied.

Eunice excused herself to prepare supper for the family and then returned to join the prayers. Neither Paul nor Barnabas had eaten since breakfast and hunger was beginning to focus their minds. I watched and waited. Without warning, the silence was pierced by the sound of Eunice's younger children squabbling over their dessert. The Director said to me, 'Oriel, could you go and fetch Terathiel.'

Terathiel, Timothy's Angel guardian, was in the family dining room where Timothy was trying to settle his siblings' dispute. When we returned, the Director asked, 'Terathiel, how are you getting on with Timothy? Do you think he's ready?'

The Angel was thoughtful. 'He could be. He would need a lot of help.'

'Of course he would,' the Director replied.

The door opened. It was Timothy. 'I've sent them both to their rooms,' he reported to his mother.

All the knotted hairs of Paul, Barnabas and Eunice's anxieties were straightened out by a single stroke of the Director's comb.

Every strand of tangled prayer suddenly pointed in the same direction.

'But he's only a kid!' I exclaimed.

'Timothy,' Paul said calmly, 'could you gather all the Christians together again this evening? I have to leave tomorrow and need to appoint their new leader before I go.'

'I should think I could,' the boy replied.

'But he's only a cub.' I repeated my reservation, this time specifically to the Director.

His response was brief. 'So was King David.'

Perga

Paul and Barnabas learned as they went. In Iconium they made a point of praying and fasting *before* they started any discussion about who might be the budding leaders in the Christian community. The Iconian Christians were divided by religious tradition rather than social class; Jew against Gentile. The Gentiles were further divided into pro-Jewish and anti-Jewish lobbies. The Director inspired Paul to appoint a group of leaders to represent these divergent backgrounds.

They moved on. In Pisidian Antioch, Barnabas perceived that whoever was appointed as leader would need some kind of formal inauguration to highlight the fact that their leadership carried my Boss's authority. Paul was not quickly convinced, but he revived the early practice of Peter in Jerusalem, of laying hands on people to mark the Director's work in their lives.

There can be no doubt that the Director has been working among these novice disciples but I have to admit that I would never entrust so much to Angels who were so inexperienced. My Boss does not share my sense of caution.

After leaving Pisidian Antioch, Paul and Barnabas retraced their steps southward towards the coast, keen to have another crack at the synagogue-less city of Perga. Resolved to repeat what they had done in Derbe, they headed for the beggars. They found an interested audience, but their message of Heavenly glory did not arouse as much interest as its gladiatorial equivalent. In Perga even beggars dream of becoming champion charioteers.

Admitting defeat does not feature in Paul's repertoire and

Barnabas is a virtuoso optimist. The Director reminded me of Jesus' instructions to his disciples, 'If the inhabitants of a village are not interested in your message, move on.'

Paul and Barnabas debated their next destination. Paul's vote was for travelling west, into Greece. Barnabas was for returning to Antioch to encourage the Christians there with news of their mission in Galatia. I, quite understandably, was about to throw my weight behind the Romeward option, when the Director said, 'Before you say anything, Oriel, take a close look at their motives.'

I looked. Paul is fuelled by a fear of failing; he has no wish to be like Jonah who fled by boat in the opposite direction to God's call. (What a dangerous place to put yourself when doing such a stupid thing!) Barnabas, however, is drawn by love: love for the Christians of Antioch who released him for the journey; love for the churches he and Paul have founded, and a longing to gather them into the Son's family. Thus confronted by fear and love, I knew which road we had to take – or rather, which boat we had to catch.

'Anyway,' Barnabas said to Paul as they boarded a ship bound for Antioch, 'your mission to Rome has *still* not been approved by Peter.'

Antioch

The voyage from the little fishing harbour of Attalia was as uneventful as it was unpleasant. As soon as the coastal trading ship splashed its way out of the relative safety of the harbour into the unpredictable restlessness of the open sea, both Paul and Barnabas relaxed. The disciples were free from the demands and dangers of their missionary work. There were no Opposition spirits around, no Jews to plot against them, no speeches to be prepared, no debates to engage in, no hungry crowds to feed with the story of the Son's ugly death and triumphant resurrection. They seemed blissfully ignorant of the terrible dangers presented by the vast expanse of poisonous liquid that surrounded them.

Each time the boat moored, Asphiel and I jumped quickly onto solid ground but Paul and Barnabas tended to stay on board, content to gaze across the empty flatness of the sea, and rest. I have never known Paul so placid. Could sea travel have a redeeming feature?

The travellers' fellow leaders in Antioch were as relieved to see them as I was to arrive in the safety of that violent city. In over two years of travelling, no news of Paul and Barnabas had returned to the Christian community who had so generously sent them on their way. After the initial joy that they were alive came an even greater delight at the news that so many and such variety of people had joined the ever-growing family of Jesus. For the past weeks, the two travellers have visited group after group around Antioch, telling their story.

For Paul, this process has involved more than simply polishing his narrative. As he's retold his story, his understanding of it has grown. What excites him above everything else is the coming together, in faith, of both Jews and Gentiles – just as Jewish prophets had foreseen centuries before.

This afternoon Barnabas ran breathlessly to Paul's lodgings and announced, 'We have some visitors from Jerusalem!'

Paul had been straining his eyes to read a scroll of ancient Jewish prophecies and was not enormously excited by the news.

'They want to meet you,' Barnabas continued. 'They're eager to develop ties with the churches here and in Galatia.'

Something in the word 'ties' caused unease in Paul's mind.

'Come on, Paul,' I urged, 'you need permission from Jerusalem for your mission to Rome. This visit could be useful.'

He rubbed his eyes, sighed, and carefully rolled up the scroll on his desk.

While Asphiel and I followed the two disciples through the busy streets of Antioch, my partner asked, 'What's Paul's problem?'

'I don't know. He seems to have something against *ties*.'

'Not that, Oriel,' Asphiel said. 'I meant his tiredness. It isn't usual for a human to find reading so tiring.'

At Barnabas' home we found four visitors waiting. As soon as we entered the room, a voice from the centre of Paul's spirit said, 'Uh-oh!'

Before I took over as guardian for Paul, I had little to do with that person of my Boss's being we call the Director. Now I have become quite familiar with his mysterious ways.

'What's up?' I asked.

'Trouble,' he said. 'Look.'

'I can't see anything,' I replied, studying the four Judeans carefully. 'I see four of your children, four Jews . . .'

'Stop there. Can't you see the tension in them, between those two identities?'

'No,' I replied, carefully.

'Oriel, for an Angel guardian, your understanding of humans is somewhat lacking. They are, indeed, my children. But there is one central family trait noticeably lacking.'

'Well,' I said, comparing these four terribly fragile and largely selfish humans to my all-creating, all-loving Boss, 'where do I start?'

I looked again and suddenly understood. 'Ah!' I said. 'Grace.'

'Well spotted,' the Director said. 'They have profound faith, abundant love, bright hope, comprehensive understanding – but they are seriously lacking when it comes to grace. That means trouble.'

This whole conversation was completed in a fraction of an Earth second. The visitors stood to greet Paul and began, 'Barnabas has been telling us all about your travels and there are some things we would like to clear up.'

The next day

The six men talked late into the night. This morning Paul took them to visit Titus, the non-Jewish leader of one of the city's many Christian groups. The Director and I looked on as traditional Jewish legalism clashed with the generous freedom that my Boss has brought to the lives of his Greek and Syrian children. Paul was irritated. He suggested that they all have supper at his favourite Greek restaurant. The visitors from Jerusalem flatly declined. Titus made his excuses and went home; the Judeans dined on stale bread and cold meat in Paul's room. It was during supper that Aaron, the spokesman for the four, suddenly announced, 'He must be circumcised.'

Paul choked on his salt beef sandwich. 'What!' he spluttered, trying to cough a fragment of cow carcass out of his windpipe. 'Titus? A grown man?'

'Yes.'

'Why?' Barnabas asked. 'What difference would it make? Aside from the pain.'

'It's the sign of our faith and has been for two thousand years,' Aaron stated.

'The Spirit of God is working in and through Titus,' Paul declared. 'Isn't that a clear enough sign of his faith?'

'Until he is circumcised, he will not be a Jew. Salvation, as our Lord himself said, comes from the Jews.'

A bees' nest is a place of ordered and productive beauty, one of the intricate glories of my Boss's creation. But when their nest is threatened, bees can be deadly. Aaron's misuse of Jesus' words set off every alarm in Paul's ordered and productive mind. A furious swarm of angry thoughts raced across his brain, sweeping away all trace of grace or patience. In seconds, a squadron of stinging replies was armed and waiting to be released by his tongue. I responded quickly, holding firmly onto the entrance of that livid hive to ensure not one angry bee emerged.

Barnabas was calmer. He stood, asking, 'With whose authority are you saying this?'

'We were sent here by James and Peter,' Aaron explained, 'to report on the life of the disciples here.' He paused for a moment, fully inflating his self-importance. 'Our judgement is that your Gentile *Christians*, as you call them, are tearing the family of Jesus away from the community of faith that our Lord himself belonged to – the Jewish nation.'

I doubled my grasp on Paul's mouth and asked Asphiel to keep Barnabas talking while I restrained Paul.

'We need to discuss this with the leaders of the different groups across the city,' Barnabas said. 'I will arrange a gathering tomorrow afternoon, when shops and businesses are closed.'

Paul was still buzzing with barbed and venomous replies.

'Get them out of here,' I implored Asphiel.

'I'm tired,' announced Barnabas through an enormous yawn. 'Let's go home. Good night, Paul.'

I called after Asphiel, 'Come and see me when they're all asleep.'

Next morning

It was not a good night. Asphiel brought with him the four Angel guardians of Aaron and his companions. Between the six of us we had the very argument our respective humans just failed to have yesterday.

The four visiting Angels were unswervingly committed to Jewish tradition. Perhaps this is partly my fault: I try to give Angels continuity in their assignments and these four have been serving Jewish families since the time of Moses.

'Don't think you can get your own way, Oriel, just because you are an Archangel,' Jeshaphael informed me at the height of our debate. 'Down here you are no more than one more Angel guardian – and a rather inexperienced one at that.'

Asphiel leapt to my aid, changing the subject. 'Are you seriously claiming,' he demanded, 'that our Boss put a tiny piece of extra skin on every human male just so he could command them to cut it off again?'

'Friends, please!' I interjected. 'When Angels fight one another, the only winners are the Opposition. Enough of this. Each one of us is overjoyed that our human is part of our Boss's new family. We must help our humans to live together as brothers. We must not allow ourselves to be dragged down into the muddy pools of human prejudice.'

'Amen!' The Director's voice resounded from within Paul's sleeping spirit but it appeared that I was the only Angel who heard him.

I continued, 'Tomorrow afternoon we Angels must work together for our Boss and not against one another for our humans. Do you understand?'

Silence. It appeared that an Archangel does maintain a certain authority down here on Earth, whatever Jeshaphael may think.

That evening

The human assembly this afternoon was just as ugly as the Angelic one last night. Everyone believed that they were right and therefore concluded the others must be wrong. The Angel guardians behaved excellently but were unable to help much. I sent a message to Raphael, asking him to join us immediately.

'What an unholy mess, my dear!' he exclaimed as he entered the room. He watched intently as the pendulum of discontent was hurled back and forth.

I needed the benefit of his wisdom. 'What can we do about all this?'

'Nothing,' he replied.

'What do you mean? *Nothing!*' I said.

'I mean *nothing*, old friend.' He drew my attention to the darkening storm of fear raging around the room. 'There is an abundance of opinion here,' he said, 'and a great, stinking pile of self-interest. But what is lacking is authority. Every human in this room is concerned for the future of our Boss's human family on Earth, but they are all limited by the horizons of their own experience. Not one of them has the authority to resolve this disagreement.'

'Should I go home and speak with our Boss?' I asked.

'No,' Raphael replied. 'You need to go to Jerusalem and resolve it with Peter.'

Now it was the hive of *my* mind that was shaken. 'Are you telling me,' I asked indignantly, 'that I have to consult a human about the affairs of Heaven?'

'Not at all, old friend,' Raphael replied, clearly amused by my reaction. '*Paul* does.'

I looked to the Director for some reassurance regarding Raphael's advice.

'Trust him,' he said.

Once I had settled my own swarm, I gathered the attention of all Angels in the room and explained that we would get nowhere until we had taken the issue to Jerusalem. We passed this message on to our charges and before long it was decided that Paul, Barnabas and Titus (a token Gentile) would accompany Aaron to Jerusalem and continue the 'discussions' there. They leave tomorrow.

The bank of River Orontes – lunchtime

Overnight, I gathered the Angels who would be travelling with me and, with the help of Raphael's calming influence, we agreed to do everything we could to encourage genuine friendship among our charges on the journey south.

As my fellow Archangel returned to Heaven, he said, 'What you need to do, Oriel, is get Aaron and that Titus together. Encourage them to become friends.'

'And how do you propose that I do that?'

'I haven't a clue,' Raphael replied. 'Humans are your speciality, not mine. Have fun.'

This morning, as soon as they were on their horses, I scanned the minds of both Titus and Aaron, looking for something – anything – they might have in common. It was not easy. Aaron is a teacher, Titus a businessman. Aaron has a large family, Titus has no family. And, most importantly, Aaron is a Jew, Titus is a Gentile. At last, with the help of both their Angel guardians, we found something they share – a common passion, or rather obsession . . . for cartwheels!

These two men between them know everything there is to know about cartwheels: different designs, different sizes, different uses . . . the list is bewilderingly long. It was Jeshaphael who spotted this first. He noticed both men gazing intently at the clumsy discs of wood and metal carrying all manner of cargoes around the streets of Antioch.

Once it dawned on us that they both shared this bizarre fascination, it was easy to draw each man's attention to the other's interest. They were off, like courting squirrels.

'I once saw a Phrygian Brace made out of cedar,' Titus proudly announced when their conversation was in full flow. 'It was being used on a hay cart, of all ridiculous things.'

'I've never seen a Phrygian Brace,' Aaron said jealously. 'I thought I saw one once on the road from Tyre to Sidon, but it turned out to be an Alexandrian Crossply that had been repaired by a Phrygian wheelwright.'

I was relieved to discover that their conversation was just as obscure to their other companions as it was to me.

A short while ago, the group stopped to eat lunch. They tied up their horses, took out their food and sat down. That's when things got complicated.

Aaron was in full flow, explaining how he had once seen 73 different types of cartwheel in one afternoon at the Jerusalem cloth market. Titus sat next to him. According to Israelite tradition, Jews must not eat with Gentiles. So Aaron, without pausing in his precise catalogue of all 73 wheels, stood up, moved several paces away from Titus and sat down again. Titus assumed Aaron was moving away from the disinterested non-wheelspotters, so he too stood up, followed Aaron and sat next to him for the second time. Once again Aaron moved, while extolling the praises of the apparently rare Carthaginian Plainside, and wedged himself in between Paul and Barnabas who both had to move to make room for him. In fact this meant Aaron sitting on a sharp stone, but he accepted the discomfort in order to avoid sitting next to his Gentile co-enthusiast. Titus finally understood what was happening, kept his distance and simply raised his voice so that everyone had the benefit of his reminiscences of all the Carthaginian Plainsides he has known.

Jerusalem

Arriving at the city earlier today, Aaron and his companions returned to their homes and Paul, Barnabas and Titus went to the *Lost Sheep Inn*, where Paul received a considerably warmer welcome than on his previous visit. In the evening there was a reception at the inn. Paul and Barnabas were invited to talk about their travels in Galatia. Paul had just got to his brush with Death outside the walls of Lystra, when Aaron arrived, accompanied by a delegation of traditionalist Jewish Christians. When Paul's narrative – his storytelling has improved enormously – reached the point when Alexander, the converted Lystran beggar, was appointed head of the Christian family in Derbe, Aaron could contain his indignation no longer.

'These Gentiles must be circumcised,' he declared. It was evident from the reaction of most people in the room that the matter of circumcision had not crossed their minds. They were delighted that so many former pagans were now joining the faith, but once the matter of circumcision had been raised, it had to be considered. The gathering was rapidly torn apart by differences of opinion and interpretation.

'Here we go again!' I observed to the Director.

Aaron spoke up over the growing volume of dissension. 'We are all followers of Jesus, the Messiah,' he said. 'Like Jesus himself, we must all live under the law of Moses. Jesus was a circumcised Jew, so his disciples must be. Whoever heard of a family where half the children were Jews and half were Gentiles?'

Had there been any grace in Aaron's argument, it might have shone some light onto the gloomy confusion of the evening, but there was none. I urged Paul to bring an end to Aaron's tirade.

Paul spoke to Peter. 'We should discuss this in private, not debate it in public.'

Peter stood on a table, rapidly gaining the attention of everyone in the room. (How that man has changed since his fishing days!) 'Brothers and sisters,' he announced. 'This is a matter for careful consideration. Our Lord has done more among us than we ever imagined possible. I am delighted that we have this problem to solve. Tomorrow, James and I will listen to Paul and Barnabas at length; we will also listen to the Spirit of our Lord. Until then, let's celebrate what God has done, not argue about it.'

He climbed down from the table and said privately to Paul, 'Bring Titus with you.' The former fisherman then slipped out through a kitchen door and into the street.

The next day

Paul, Barnabas and Titus crossed the city for their meeting with Peter. All three men were anxious. Barnabas was wondering if Aaron might not be right after all and Titus was frightened by the unexpected hostility being directed at him by the Jews. Paul was keenly aware that he needed this meeting to go well. I shared his anxiety. We still need Peter's blessing for Paul's mission to Rome.

Outside Peter's house I was surprised to find a high level Angelic security cordon, directed by Archangel Michael himself.

'This is all rather heavy-handed, isn't it?' I commented.

Michael glared at me as though I'd just declared the southern ocean to be a harmless puddle.

'Have you any idea what's going on here today?' he asked.

'Yes, a fair idea,' I replied. 'I've travelled at human speed all the way from Antioch for this meeting . . .'

'Oriel,' he interrupted, '*this meeting* as you call it, is a key moment in our Boss's whole plan and our elite troops and specialist advisors have been preparing for it down to the smallest detail.'

'Why?' I asked, bewildered to discover that this handful of humans should be attracting so much Heavenly interest.

'Where in all Heaven have you been, Oriel?' Michael was clearly exasperated.

'On Earth,' I replied. 'I've been to Cyprus and Galatia and back to Syria . . .'

'Well,' the leader of Heaven's army said testily, 'while you've been on holiday, I've been doing your work, planning the Council of Jerusalem.'

'The what?'

He was getting cross. 'I've cleared the entire city of Opposition spirits and established sentry points at regular intervals all across Jerusalem. I have arranged and re-arranged rotas because you weren't there to do it. I have chaired endless, tedious meetings of experts in Jewish interpretations of our Boss's guidelines for human living. And you glide up here at the climax of this vast operation saying, *This is all rather heavy handed.*'

Gabriel arrived. 'Oriel, lovely to see you! Have you brought the stars for Michael's little production?'

'I have Paul, Barnabas and Titus,' I said.

'Well, let the show begin.' He turned to the towering form of Heaven's greatest general. 'Come on, Michael, lighten up! Everything will be fine.' Michael grunted.

I entered the house, reflecting on the strange isolation of life as an Angel guardian. I had not realised how different the affairs of humanity look when seen from an earthly perspective.

Inside were some familiar humans: James – Jesus' brother, who had tried at one point to stop Jesus' work and take him back to their carpentry business in Nazareth; Simon – a reformed terrorist who had discovered the devastating power of forgiveness for disarming enemies; Matthew – one-time money launderer who was captivated by Jesus' simple honesty. Aaron was there too, again representing the city's traditionalist Jews. He looked at Titus with the icy hardness of one of humanity's most common fears, the fear of change.

Peter graciously invited Aaron to speak first. Fluent and articulate, he recited a breadth of Jewish scriptures to reinforce his case. His brain, which could so clearly remember the minute detail of countless cartwheels, was just as efficient at mastering every line from Jewish law that supported his opinion. Those present who were undecided began to lean towards his view. There was something of the young Paul in the power of Aaron's passion. Had Peter taken a vote at the end of his presentation, the call for all Gentile Christians to become Jews would have been quickly approved.

'This is grim,' I said to the Director.

'Be patient,' he replied.

Next, Peter spoke. He reminded his guests that it was the Director's initiative, and no one else's, to draw Gentiles into his family. 'He made no distinction between us and them,' he stressed. 'It is through the grace of our Lord Jesus that we are saved. It is just the same with those who are not Jews.'

The pendulum swung the other way. Aaron's argument was persuasive, but Peter exposed its lack of grace. He pressed home his advantage, inviting Barnabas to describe how my Boss's grace had been poured out among the Gentiles of Antioch and Galatia. Paul was restless. He was eager to dismantle Aaron's argument with the same meticulous care he applied to John Mark's book, but he didn't get the chance. When Barnabas finished his well-rehearsed stories, James stood up. He said nothing, but wanted to reserve the right to be next to speak. Everyone waited. Peter may be the leader of the Jerusalem Church, but James is the brains of the outfit. I watched him. That same careful consideration that has always been his was pulling together the broken pieces that make up his older brother's spiritual family. While he was silent, he was talking intently with his brother Jesus, and as their conversation became more intense, the Son's presence became brighter and brighter in the room. With the Son came Raphael.

James and Jesus were not in total agreement. Were they ever? James wanted to compromise. Jesus never compromised. That is why Jesus was executed by the Jerusalem Jews and James became their leader. The impasse was broken by Jesus.

'James,' he said, 'my Father has given you authority to help lead his family here in Jerusalem. You must decide.'

Jesus stepped back, leaving his brother with the full weight of responsibility. While James shouldered the burden of leadership, the room filled with Angels who had come to witness this important moment in the life of our Boss's family.

Suddenly, James shouted out to Jesus in his silent prayer, 'What if I get it wrong?'

Jesus did not reply but the Director spoke to him from the centre of his spirit, 'I oppose the proud but give grace to the humble.'

James heard. He made his decision. 'This is my judgement,' he announced. 'We should not make it difficult for the Gentiles who are turning to God.'

An Angel shouted out from behind me. 'Go for it, Jamie!' It was Maff.

The ice of Jewish tradition and prejudice was shattered. Life-giving Heavenly warmth flooded the room. Angels cheered, with relief as much as delight, and I struggled to take in the eternal significance of what I had understood as an informal meeting of a few Christian leaders. Among the humans there was only one more pleased than Titus; that was Paul. It was as if the sun had risen over his long intended journey to Rome, lighting his path. Aaron – poor Aaron – was stunned. He had built a house of sticks and fire had just been kindled under it. I asked Raphael to take him aside and help him grasp the ways of grace.

While James detailed a short list of basic moral pointers for Gentile Christians, the Son addressed the visiting Angels. 'This calls for a party,' he declared. 'Everyone is invited to my room as soon as we get home.'

He looked across to me. 'Oriel, will you join us?'

'I'd love to, but I need to stay with Paul. Lucifer is after him and I dare not leave him for a moment,' I said regretfully.

'You will be missed, my friend,' he replied, leading the large company of Angels heavenward.

'I'll fill in for you,' Maff offered excitedly as he passed me.

'You mean with Paul?' I asked, thrilling at the unexpected possibility that I might make it to the party after all.

'No,' he said. 'At the party.' He was gone.

Back in Antioch

With all the excitement, Paul never managed to get Peter to consider his Rome plan. At their last meeting, to collect the letter that Peter and James have written to all the believers in Antioch and Galatia, Peter said, 'We will talk about Rome some other time, Paul. I hope to come up to Antioch soon. We can talk then.'

Frankly, I was furious. The only thing holding us up at the present is the need for Peter's permission. Things were never this chaotic when Angels were overseeing our Boss's work on Earth. Paul, strangely, was less disappointed. He was very excited by the content of Peter and James' letter and is greatly looking forward to the day when he can introduce the big fisherman to Christianity Antioch-style.

Taking the letter, Paul and Barnabas returned to Antioch with two senior members of the Jerusalem Church. One was Judas – not the one who betrayed Jesus. (You see the confusion caused by the human abuse of names?) This Judas was another of Jesus' original twelve disciples. The other was Silas, a more recent addition to the family and the leader of one of Jerusalem's many groups of Christians.

Today, a week after our arrival in Antioch, Silas addressed a gathering of all the Antiochene Christians. He read out Peter and James' apology for Aaron's behaviour and affirmed all the work done by Paul and Barnabas. There was deep relief. In Paul's absence, there had been a great amount of talk about the matter of circumcision. Although many of the male Christians were reluctantly prepared to undergo the operation if required, plenty of others had declared they would abandon their new-found faith if such a drastic sacrifice was demanded. They walked to the meeting with tentative steps; they left with confident strides.

Some weeks later

Paul has taken Silas under his wing, personally training him in the subtleties of Greco-Roman culture, which has involved many visits to Paul's favourite restaurant, *The Potted Rabbit*. Silas is a keen student and Paul has turned out to be an excellent teacher.

Asphiel has asked me to add at this point that Paul is an excellent teacher for a certain kind of pupil and that he was not so effective when it came to John Mark.

Teaching has reawakened Paul's appetite for branching out into new territories – particularly in the Romeward direction – which, of course, takes us back to the Peter issue.

This evening Paul suggested that Silas and Judas should return to Jerusalem and tell Peter and James what they have seen. 'Do everything you can to get Peter to come and visit us,' Paul urged.

Months later

Peter is on his way! Hooray, hooray, hooray!

Paul has been increasingly depressed in recent weeks. At first he was happy to wait and to use the time to catch up on his studies. But there is definitely something wrong with his eyes. He finds reading and writing difficult. I raised the matter with the Director tonight while Paul was asleep. He attempted to explain it to me, but the intricate detail to do with the physical structure of the human eye was beyond my comprehension. I suggested he keep the technicalities to himself and asked if he could cure the problem.

The Director replied, 'Of course.'

Sensing a dislocation between his understanding and my own, I pushed my enquiry on Paul's behalf a little further. 'Will you please cure Paul's eyesight?' I asked.

'No.'

I was startled by his reply. 'Won't poor eyesight be a significant problem for Paul as he continues his work?'

'It certainly will,' the Director confirmed.

I was struggling to understand why he should be so negative about such a simple request.

He continued, 'Without his eyesight, Paul will have to rely on the help of other people, and that, in turn, will help him to depend on my grace rather than his own ability.'

This tactical use of human illness for the benefit of Heaven's work surprised me. 'Did you cause his eyesight to fail?' I asked tentatively.

'Most certainly not,' was the categorical reply. 'I thought you understood these things, Oriel. My strength is perfected in human weakness.'

'Do you mean that the more Paul relies on you, the stronger he will be?'

At that point Maff burst into Paul's room.

'I just dropped in to say that Peter is on his way to Antioch and should arrive in the next couple of days. But you're probably not meant to know that yet, so I'll be off. Bye.'

Two days on

Peter arrived today. He travelled ahead of the rest of his party because he was keen to meet with Paul in private and have an unofficial tour of the Antioch Church before the others arrive.

I needed to turn to the Director for a bit of interpretation. He explained that the Jew/Gentile issue is still a problem among Jerusalem Christians. Peter has brought some leading traditionalists to Antioch so they can see for themselves what a good thing Gentile Christianity is. He travelled ahead to forearm Paul about the delicacies of the visit.

What an asset it is to have my Boss on hand all the time like this!

I reminded Paul that he must talk to Peter about Rome. But Peter was distracted by his immediate concerns and said, 'We'll talk about that later, Paul. Can we go and see Titus?'

Peter spent the afternoon following Titus round the back streets of Antioch, informing the leaders of all the different Christian groups that there will be a city-wide gathering of disciples tomorrow – and informally inviting them to a slap-up meal at *The Potted Rabbit* this evening, when Paul will introduce them to 'a very special guest from Jerusalem'.

The party at *The Potted Rabbit* made up for the one I missed in Heaven after the Council of Jerusalem. Peter enjoyed the house speciality, reassured that Barnabas had taught the chef to kill his rabbits the Jewish way. There was even greater enjoyment, however, from the gathered Christian leaders, at meeting the man Jesus declared to be 'the rock', the leader of his Church. Peter thrilled them with stories of his life as Jesus' right hand man, and moved them to tears with an honest account of his own stupidity and failure on the day Jesus was executed.

While the audience listened in rapt silence, the Director whispered to me, 'Now here's a man who knows the value of grace.'

The next day

Today saw two arrivals. The first was a messenger from Timothy, the young leader of the Christian family at Lystra. Though the Angel who arrived with the messenger said nothing as he entered

Paul's house, he had, *You're not going to like this* written all over his face. He was right. An influential group of traditionalist Jewish Christians have been obstructing Timothy's leadership and visiting all the other churches that Paul and Barnabas founded in Galatia, insisting that Gentile Christians must be circumcised or there'll be no place for them in Heaven. Timothy is at the top of their list of those for the chop.

Paul was pacing up and down in his room, listening as the messenger read Timothy's letter for the seventh time. At the fore of Paul's mind was his life-changing encounter with the Son outside Damascus years earlier. He was quite certain he had done nothing – despite his devotion to Jewish tradition – to deserve the new start he was given. Most certainly he had been put right with God, but not by keeping the Law. His contemplations were disturbed when Barnabas came in to announce that the delegation from Jerusalem had arrived at Barnabas' home.

Paul was pleased to note that Silas was one of the Jerusalem visitors, but he cut short the polite introductions, presenting Peter with Timothy's letter. Everyone was shocked. Peter and Silas had brought their traditionalist brothers to Antioch to show them how well the decision of the Council of Jerusalem was working, but the letter revealed that the Council's decision was being ignored.

After a considerable amount of directionless discussion, Paul was in impetuous mood. 'Peter, you must come with me to Galatia and settle this matter finally. They'll take it from you.'

Everyone agreed that Peter's intervention was the way forward. Everyone except for Peter.

'I cannot and I will not,' he said firmly. 'Firstly, my wife and children are expecting me home by the end of the month. I cannot simply go galloping off round Turkey at a moment's notice.'

The married men and women present conceded that Peter was right to consider his family. Paul, Titus, Silas and the other single disciples considered it a weak excuse.

'But there's a more important reason for me not to go to Galatia,' Peter continued. 'James and I have agreed that Paul should be the Apostle for the Gentiles, just as I am for the Jews.' He looked across the crowded room to where Paul was standing. 'Brother Paul,' he said, 'this matter is your responsibility.'

This opened up further discussions which took most of the day. Paul and Peter spent some hours in private conversation, analysing the practical detail of his appointment as Apostle to the Gentiles. The legal training Paul received at university came into use as he sought clear demarcations between their separate areas of responsibility. Peter, who did all his studying with a fishing net in his hand, kept saying, 'You'll have to ask James that.'

When evening came, Barnabas announced, 'Sisters and brothers, how about some supper?'

Above the general murmur of agreeing voices and rumbling stomachs, Silas announced confidently, 'There's an excellent restaurant not far from here, *The Potted Rabbit*. Let's go there.' The Antiochenes enthusiastically supported the suggestion and the visitors from Jerusalem were happy to follow the lead of their Jewish hosts.

As they walked through the busy streets, Paul continued his conversation with Peter. 'As Apostle to the Gentiles, do I still need your approval to travel to Rome, or am I free to make that decision on my own?'

'Rome, I have to say,' Peter replied carefully, 'is a bit complicated.'

'Why?'

'I understand from Barnabas,' Peter explained, 'that our Lord has directed you to teach about Jesus there.'

'Yes?' Paul replied, questioningly, arming himself for the complication.

'I have a deep sense that the Lord has called *me* to lead the Church in Rome.'

Ahead, everyone had stopped outside *The Potted Rabbit,* waiting in uneasy silence for Peter and Paul to join them. As the two Apostles came within human hearing range, one of the Jerusalem Christians expressed the concern of his companions. 'Do they actually serve rabbit here?'

'Yes,' said Titus enthusiastically. 'It's delicious. Ask Peter – he had some last night.'

All heads turned to face the burly fisherman.

Peter blushed brilliantly, and whispered to Paul, 'We'll talk about Rome tomorrow.'

'Peter!' one of the Jewish visitors insisted, 'have you actually eaten rabbit meat in this Greek restaurant?'

Peter didn't reply, but whispered to Paul, 'Coming here wasn't a very clever idea.'

Barnabas, ever the peacemaker, stepped forward to rescue the situation. 'There's a pleasant little Jewish inn about a mile from here,' he suggested.

'They won't serve our Gentile brothers and sisters,' Silas quietly reminded him.

Titus joined in. 'Peter, you had a lovely meal here yesterday. There were Jewish brothers here as well as Romans, Greeks and Asyrians. You enjoyed it, didn't you?'

Once again everyone looked at Peter. So did I. He was eager to keep everyone happy but could not think of a way of doing it. He carved himself an escape route.

'Actually, I'm not really very hungry,' he lied. 'I'd be quite happy to buy some bread and cheese, and take it back to Barnabas' house.'

'You utter hypocrite!' Paul boomed, in full voice, in the hearing of everyone dining at the tables outside *The Potted Rabbit*. 'You are a Jew, but you come here to Antioch and for a day you live like a Gentile. Then, when James' friends arrive, you suddenly change your mind and pretend to be one of them.'

Paul's 'bees' were highly disturbed and, in the particular style of his unique mind, he armed them with theological stings. There in the street Paul harangued Peter – and everyone who cared to listen – about the true relationship of Jewish law to divine grace. Peter had no option but to listen.

'You know as well as I do,' Paul asserted, 'that no one can put themselves right with God simply by obeying laws. They have to trust Jesus and his death.' He ended by saying, 'If entry into heaven can be achieved by keeping the Jewish law, then Jesus' death was an utter waste of time!' He strode over to the restaurant doorway and announced, 'I shall be ordering pork chops. Who's joining me?'

I was the first to his side. 'You great idiot!' I told him. 'You still need Peter's approval for your mission to Rome. Did you have to humiliate him quite so comprehensively?'

The morning after

Silas and some of the Gentiles joined Paul for his seriously non-Kosher supper. The other Jews followed Barnabas to his home via the baker and the delicatessen.

This morning Peter came to see Paul early and explained that he was heading straight back to Jerusalem.

'There's no point staying,' he said. 'Anything we hoped to achieve here was destroyed last night.'

The two men looked at each other, both sad at the failure of the visit, both aware they had acted rashly, each waiting for the other to speak first.

'I'm sorry,' Peter said. 'I was wrong. Forgive me.'

They embraced and exchanged the separate stories of their different evenings. Neither had enjoyed their supper. When that conversation was exhausted, Peter asked Paul, 'What are you going to do about the Galatians?'

'I'm not sure,' he replied.

'You should write them a letter,' I suggested.

'I might write them a letter,' Paul continued, 'to explain everything clearly and thoroughly.'

Peter approved.

'And what about Rome?' Paul asked. 'What shall we do about Rome?'

Peter did not hurry to reply. Selfishness and graciousness were fighting one another for supremacy in his mind. He wanted to be the one to found a Church in Rome but he realised – with some help from the Director – that his motives were not entirely rooted in divine love.

'You're the Apostle to the Gentiles,' he eventually conceded to Paul, 'and they don't come more Gentile than in Rome.' Then he added reflectively, 'Maybe we'll meet there. I'll treat you to a rabbit stew.'

The two Apostles laughed, embraced again and parted.

Three days later

The Director and I have discussed the idea of Paul writing letters on several occasions. Even though he is now very experienced at public speaking, he still tends to panic and rarely does credit to the full depth of his understanding. When writing, however, his mind operates more clearly. Today, with the help of Silas – who did the actual writing – Paul composed a letter to the Galatians.

He didn't waste time on pleasantries but got straight down to business: *I am astonished that you are so quickly deserting the one who called you by the grace of Christ and are turning to a different message ... You foolish Galatians, who has bewitched you?*

While Silas struggled to keep up with the pace of Paul's dictation, the Director concentrated on holding his thoughts to the straight path of divine truth. Meanwhile, I urged him to lighten up his tightly-argued prose with a few good stories. Getting nowhere, I appealed to the Director for support.

'They won't be able to take it all in,' I explained. 'Poor Timothy is going to read this letter and they'll all fall asleep.'

'Is this Paul's letter to the Galatians, or Oriel's?' the Director asked me.

'Isn't it my job to help him?'

'To help, yes,' the Director said. 'Not to take over from him.'

I got the point. While Paul was busy comparing the significant difference between 'seed' (singular) and 'seeds' (plural) in my Boss's promise to Abraham, I scanned his mind in search of something to make his letter easier to understand. Gabriel would have been an ideal helper in this task but Silas was rapidly filling up the small parchment sheet, so I made do with the aid of Kalael, Silas' Angel guardian.

'Is he always this complicated?' Kalael asked.

'Yes. Why?' I asked innocently.

'I've never seen a human mind like it,' the Angel observed.

'I have not worked with many humans,' I confessed. 'I assumed Paul was fairly normal.'

Kalael laughed. Paul, meanwhile, was explaining that if the Gentile Christians allowed themselves to be circumcised, they would find themselves lumbered with the full weight of Jewish legalism for the rest of their lives.

'Lists!' Kalael declared suddenly. 'Paul often thinks in lists. He constructs lists of related things and compares them to other lists in his mind.'

'That's right,' I observed, looking with interest into my human's mental patterns. 'But how will that help illustrate all this business about circumcision and keeping ancient laws?'

'It won't exactly illustrate his point,' Kalael admitted, 'but it will give his listeners time to catch up with him and reflect a little on what he is saying.'

'Good!' I congratulated the Angel. 'Can you find a list that will fit into this letter?'

We both looked hard. Again Kalael was the first to find ripe fruit. 'How about that?' he asked excitedly. 'A catalogue of different effects caused by human selfishness, compared with this list of the benefits of listening to the Director – it's sort of related to legalism and freedom.'

'If it's the best we've got, we'll go for it,' I said. I drew Paul's attention to the two lists that he had often mulled over in his mind. He began to recite them to Silas and, for the first time in the whole day, Silas picked it up and began to chip in with his own ideas.

'Drunkenness?' he suggested when Paul paused for thought after *envy*.

'Yes, drunkenness,' Paul reflected. 'Why don't you add that in?'

'What about orgies?'

'Never been to one,' Paul replied. 'Anyway, aren't they already covered under *sexual immorality*?'

'They're very popular in Roman society, I believe,' Silas explained.

Paul was searching his mind for something suitable to end the list. 'Add them if you want,' he instructed Silas. He never did find what he was hunting for because while he was waiting for Silas to carefully write *orgies* he was distracted by the second list I was holding up to his attention – the list of spiritual characteristics. As Paul called out this collection and Silas scribed away, the Director joined our conversation.

'There's something missing from this lot,' he observed.

Silas got there before any of us. 'Have you forgotten gentleness?' he asked Paul.

'Gentleness,' Paul repeated thoughtfully. 'Yes, you're quite right. Put it in, between faithfulness and self-control.'

The lists added, Paul began to bring his letter to a conclusion with some general comments. He then nudged Silas off his stool and sat down at the writing desk himself. Straining his weak eyes he completed the letter. *See what large letters I use as I write to you with my own hand!* He wrote on, firing one last missile in the direction of those promoting circumcision among the Gentile Christians.

The letter was finished.

'Well done, team!' the Director exclaimed. 'That's everything I hoped it would be. Thank you Kalael, thank you Oriel. We must do this again sometime.'

Outside Tarsus – a year later

We are on the road again. On the road – not on the water, note – and heading west, towards Rome!

Paul waited in Antioch for news of how his letter had been received by the Galatians. None came. He became more and more anxious. He thinks of the Christians in Galatia as his own children and desperately wants to know whether they've resolved their differences. He is particularly concerned for young Timothy.

Also of concern, the friendship between Paul and Barnabas has become increasingly strained in the months since the drama of Peter's visit. Barnabas was angry with Paul for demolishing such a wonderful opportunity to build greater understanding between Jewish and Gentile Christians. Paul's respect for Barnabas was heavily dented by his collusion with Peter in snubbing the Gentile disciples. This crack developed into a clear rift when the two men started planning their return to Galatia.

'I'm assuming John Mark will come with us again,' Barnabas said innocently.

'Oh no, not Mark,' Paul replied. 'He had his chance and he abandoned us.'

'We both know why that was, don't we?' Barnabas responded pointedly, irritation rising.

I have seen it all before, among Angels as well as men. A major row was brewing and both men were bolting down the shutters of their minds against any help Asphiel or I could provide.

'Mark is a writer,' Paul stated. 'He is not an Apostle. He will slow us down.'

Barnabas rose to John Mark's defence. 'It has nothing to do with that,' he told Paul. 'You don't like him – you never have. You don't like the way he writes because he doesn't write the way you do, but that doesn't make his contribution any less important. Honestly, Paul!' Barnabas' irritation grew to exasperation with his long-time friend and colleague. 'If it were left to you, nobody would know a thing about the life and teaching of Jesus.'

Paul hit back. 'The trouble with you,' he told Barnabas, 'is that your concept of the Christian family is too organised and too comfortable. You're trying to make it just like the old synagogue service, with the one difference, that there is an extra reading from Mark's *Life of Jesus*. It is all too safe, all too easy, and all too Jewish.'

'So what do *you* think the Church should be like?' Barnabas asked aggressively.

'It's like . . . it's like . . . ' Paul could not reduce the intricate shapes and patterns in his mind to clumsy human words. 'It's not like . . . ' he tried to continue.

'What you mean is you don't know,' Barnabas judged harshly.

'Not at all.' Paul was indignant. 'The community of disciples is like . . . '

'What is it like?' I asked the Director in an attempt to help Paul.

'It's like a body,' he replied simply.

'It's like a human body,' I told Paul

'The Church,' Paul informed Barnabas, 'is like the earthly body of . . . Jesus. In fact it *is* Jesus' earthly body.' He grasped hold of the image. 'Every person, every disciple, is a different organ in that body. They each have a part to play; they each have their own purpose.'

Having latched onto this simple simile, Paul relaxed enough to tease his larger friend, saying, 'And they all work together with the same wonderful complexity as your impressive bulk, Barnabas.'

Barnabas smiled. Paul, a little awed by the shaft of bright insight he had just experienced, went on, 'I've no doubt that Mark has an important part to play in the life of the Church, but his part is not to travel to new towns, founding new communities of disciples.'

'I promised Mark my patronage,' Barnabas responded. He was also considerably calmer since the Director's intervention in their argument. 'If I go, he comes with me.'

Paul considered this ultimatum. He did not want the burden of the pile of scrolls that would accompany Mark. He anticipated repeated confrontations and more midnight escapes, and was keen to travel light. Neither did he want to carry with him the weight of Barnabas' traditionalist preferences.

The Director drew his gaze round the room towards the energetic young man who had just come into the room.

'Silas,' Paul said, 'will you come with me to Galatia?'

Silas had not expected the invitation. 'Yes,' he said, faint with surprise. 'I'd love to.'

'We leave in the morning,' Paul said. 'Meet me at the horse market at sunrise.' Paul looked across the room to his former travelling companion, Barnabas. For a moment he stared at the gentle giant, but said nothing. He picked up his coat and walked out.

Pisidian Antioch

Paul has fulfilled his objective of visiting the four cities where he and Barnabas founded new communities of disciples three years ago. In Lystra he discovered Timothy's leadership was still under a great deal of strain; some Jews distrust him because his father is Greek; some Gentiles distrust him because his mother is Jewish; and most of the rest distrust him because he is so young. Paul took Timothy for a long walk. As soon as they were out of earshot of the city gate, the young man let out a monsoon of tears. Paul, no stranger to strong emotions, half carried, half guided Timothy into a nearby orchard where he piloted his protégé through the deluge.

'I can't do it. I'm useless,' the distraught disciple sobbed. 'You should never have put me in charge.'

'I didn't choose you, Timothy,' Paul corrected him gently. 'God chose you. And he didn't choose you to be strong on your own account but to be strong in his grace.'

'But I've made a complete mess of it!' Timothy wailed.

'Think about athletes at the games,' Paul said. 'You watch them running their races and you cheer when one of them receives the winner's crown. What you do not see is the hours and hours of training, the daily agony of pushing their bodies to new limits. That brief public victory, Timothy, is built on months of lonely, painful, hard work. That's what you've been doing. This is what it means to be Jesus' disciple. If we struggle alongside him in this life, we will reign beside him in Heaven. If we die with him here, we will live with him there.'

It was a while before Timothy's storm had abated enough for him to respond. 'I can't take it any more,' he said. 'I've had enough.'

While Paul listened to Timothy, I was listening to his Angel guardian. It made grim listening.

'He's close to breaking point,' Terathiel informed me.

'Why don't you take Timothy with you?' I suggested to Paul.

He put the idea to Timothy. Immediately the rain of emotion stopped, the sun shone in his spirit and Paul's invitation stretched out before the young disciple's mind like a bright rainbow. The next morning Timothy packed a small travel bag, Paul purchased a third horse and they and Silas bid farewell to Timothy's mother, Eunice.

Timothy, with his strong organisational skills, has relieved Paul of numerous routine responsibilities, enabling Paul to spend more time in conversation with the Director, considering his future plans. It is these plans that are my current concern.

Paul has been enormously encouraged by the growth and commitment of the Christian communities in Galatia, despite continuing tensions over the Jew/Gentile issue. He has decided to travel to the north of Turkey and do the same thing all over again in the coastal region of Bithynia. In response to this, I have done my Archangel best to urge him to keep to bearing westward, towards Greece and, beyond Greece, to Rome.

It has all become rather complicated. Paul talks to the Director several times a day, unfolding his dream of new churches springing up all over Bithynia and Pontus. The Director talks to me because Paul, in his excitement, is not listening to him and the message from the Director is that we should continue towards Rome. I – in turn – talk to Paul, who rarely hears me clearly. He has managed to pick up a definite sense of opposition to his plan, but that has only made this stubborn man even deafer. So, with Paul not listening to the Director and not talking to me (he never does), we are going nowhere. The Moon has done nearly two full circuits of Earth since we arrived here in Pisidian Antioch and Paul is still waiting for the Director's advice to change.

He should know better.

The Mysian-Phrygian border

Guided by indecision, Paul, Silas and Timothy have been travelling in a north-westerly direction. It is an impromptu cartographical compromise by which he's managed to obey both impulses in his confused and stubborn mind. Tomorrow morning he has to make a decision; the compromise road has come to a junction. One way goes north, the other west.

Paul has become expert at arguing both sides of his dilemma. He feels drawn towards Rome (I should think so too after all the effort I have put into that campaign) but human logic tells him it makes more sense to go to Bithynia while he's in the area.

Tonight I decided I had to talk to my Boss, face to face. Though it is wonderful to have the Director always at hand in the spirits of his faithful children, sometimes one longs for a direct meeting. Reluctantly, I asked Maff to watch over Paul. Then I returned to Heaven.

I popped into my office to check that all was in order before proceeding along the corridor to my Boss's rooms. While I was glancing through the rotas that Michael had drawn up in my absence, the Son walked in.

'How can I help you, Oriel?'

'It's Paul,' I explained. 'He won't listen to the Director and he won't talk to me. He knows you want him to go to Rome and is determined to go to Pontus instead.'

'I know,' the Son replied calmly.

'Why on Earth won't he talk to me?' I asked, letting my frustration escape from its closet before the infinite grace of divine love. 'When you were on Earth, you used to talk to me,' I said to the Son. 'You used to ask for my help – but Paul never even acknowledges I'm there.'

'Of course he doesn't,' the Son said, to my surprise. 'Oriel, if I employed an Angel to look after my front office and handle all straightforward enquiries on my behalf, what would you choose?

Would you choose to talk directly to me, or to leave a message with my assistant?'

'I would speak to you, of course,' I replied.

'Exactly,' the Son said, smiling. 'So why are you surprised that Paul speaks directly to me rather than through you?'

There was some logic in this, but my latent pride was pricked. 'I am not some dumb secretary!' I exclaimed.

'Indeed you are not,' the Son reassured me, still smiling, 'but neither are you me.'

'What am I supposed to do?'

'Do what I asked you to do,' he said. 'Lead Paul to Rome so that he can tell the people there just how much I love them.'

'And how do you expect me to do that when he is determined to travel in the opposite direction?'

My Master's smile broadened, like the sun emerging from behind a cloud. 'Oriel,' he said, with more than a hint of amusement in his voice, 'as you are not *some dumb secretary* I expect you to work that out for yourself.'

Troas

The next morning, while Paul, Silas and Timothy ate breakfast, I set off early with Maff and Terathiel, leaving Kalael in charge of the travellers. We headed for the road junction which was causing Paul's indecision.

'What do you intend to do?' Maff asked.

'Block his way,' I said, bluntly.

'Are you really suggesting that we slow our spirits down to create a physical barrier across the northern road?' Maff sought confirmation.

'If necessary, yes,' I replied. 'Saul is taking the western road. I have our Boss's permission to put him on it.'

'I'm not sure I could do that,' Terathiel said uncertainly.

'Do what?' I asked.

'Slow my spirit like that,' Timothy's Angel guardian said. 'I've never done anything like that before.'

While I considered this potential setback to my plan, Lucifer arrived with three other Opposition spirits and took up position, blocking the western road.

'Now what are you going to do?' he asked me.

At that moment the three disciples came into view, riding towards the junction. I looked across at the Opposition line. With Kalael joining us, we would be evenly balanced in number. A fight could go either way. But Paul is far too valuable for me to take such a risk. I noticed a cart carrying a local family trundling down the northern road towards us. With the family of five came five more Angels; their leader joined me, offering his support.

'I haven't had a good fight with the enemy for aeons,' he said cheerily. I never feel cheery in the presence of Lucifer. I explained the situation, stressing my reluctance to engage in a straight battle.

Maff excused himself saying, 'You're not short of numbers, I'll go and see if I can sort something out.' This left the leader of the Opposition in a quandary: did he send a spirit after Maff and leave himself even more outnumbered, or risk leaving Maff to his own devices?

Just as Paul and his companions were reaching the junction, the family's chief guardian said, 'Here's an idea,' and flicked the wheel off from his family's cart. The ancient vehicle collapsed, spilling its human load all across the road. There were shouts and screams from both humans and Angels. Timothy and Silas jumped off their horses to help tend the bruised and bleeding children while Paul sat on his mount in the centre of the road.

Lucifer spoke. 'You don't train your guardians very well, Oriel. That one looks like he should be joining me.'

I tended to agree. It was certainly a careless way for an Angel to treat the humans entrusted to him. I said nothing. Lucifer and I both watched Paul.

Paul could sense Lucifer's presence. There was a darkness and a heaviness in his spirit as he looked towards the western road and a lightness when he turned north. He said to himself, 'We must go north.'

Lucifer laughed. 'I didn't realise your prize human was so stupid,' he shouted at me.

Paul isn't. He quickly sensed Lucifer's laughter and understood the cause of his misjudgement. 'My struggle is not just against human prejudice and disinterest,' he told himself, recalling the story of Daniel. 'It is also against the oppressive spiritual powers around me.' Then he added dismissively, 'Get out of my way, Satan.'

Lucifer's amusement faded rapidly as Paul rode straight past him. Paul stopped a few paces down the western road and announced to his companions, 'We're going to Troas.'

Now here we are in Troas, at the western end of Turkey on the Aegean coast. I have to confess that my enthusiasm for the westward trek has been dampened by the prospect of exchanging the horses for a boat. The question for both Paul and myself is: which boat?

I put my enquiry to the Director. His reply was clear. 'If you take the boat to Neapolis, Oriel, I'll go with you and work with you there. If you take the boat to Athens, we'll work together there. If you go to Corinth, we'll work together there.'

'So it doesn't make any difference?' I asked.

'It makes an enormous difference,' he said. 'They are very different places and Paul's work in each of them will be equally diverse.'

'Let me rephrase my question,' I said, realising the foolishness of my enquiry. 'Will you be equally happy, whichever destination I choose?'

'Possibly.'

I didn't like the *possibly*. It told me that I was oversimplifying the situation. Nonetheless, I couldn't resist asking the question in my mind.

'Which destination requires the shortest boat trip?' I asked.

'That is not the kind of criterion, Oriel, that makes me happy.'

I decided to call for the support of my fellow Archangels in searching for a way forward. As usual, we met at night while Paul was asleep.

'This is a stupid thing to do, Oriel,' grumbled Michael as he entered the cramped hotel room. 'Four Archangels meeting in the same time and place will be a gift to the Opposition.' He looked out of the window of the waterside hotel. 'And we're cornered with our backs to the sea.'

'Timothy chose the place, not me,' I said, defensively.

'You should have overruled him,' Michael said bluntly.

'You have no idea!' I struck back at the leader of Heaven's army. 'You have no idea how lonely it is here, hidden in a narrow ravine of Earth's time, unable to see or hear what is happening even twenty miles away, totally ignorant of what our Boss is doing in other parts of his creations.'

129

Raphael sensed my anger and stepped into the fray. 'I do believe it was Oriel who called this meeting. Therefore, Michael, my dear chap, don't you think you should listen before you criticise?'

Michael grunted. Gabriel arrived. 'This place is scary,' he exclaimed. 'Right on the very edge. What are you doing so close to the sea, Oriel? You might fall in.'

'I'm here,' I explained impatiently, 'because Paul and I have to cross that scary sea and I need your help to decide which way to go.'

'The shortest possible way,' Gabriel said quickly.

'I've already suggested that,' I told him, 'but our Boss would like a decision inspired by love, not fear.'

'Amen,' Raphael said, almost singing.

'Why don't you scoot round the coast and look for someone or somewhere who needs your Paul?' Gabriel suggested.

'An excellent idea,' I replied, still irritated, 'but, as Michael will appreciate, I cannot leave Paul undefended because the Opposition are taking a great interest in his progress.'

Raphael came to my rescue again, 'My dears, Oriel needs our help. I suggest we each take a different region, ask the Angels there whether they could use some help from Paul, and return with our findings.'

This was remarkably focussed for Raphael. Gabriel divided up the territories and they left. But only a very short period of Earth time later, Raphael came crashing back into the room dragging the disembodied spirit of a Macedonian man, followed by the man's highly agitated Angel guardian.

'This is Luke,' Raphael announced enthusiastically. 'A Greek doctor who has been reborn as one of our Boss's new children. I found him praying that Paul would go to Macedonia to help his little family of . . . whatever do you call them now?'

'Christians,' I said flatly, struggling to believe that Raphael would be so stupid as to remove a human spirit from its body and carry it to a different place. 'What have you done to him? You could kill a human doing that.'

'He'll be fine,' Raphael said vaguely. 'Gabriel has done this plenty of times.'

I stated the obvious. 'You are *not* Gabriel.'

'I am not,' the leader of Heaven's choir replied indignantly, quite missing my point, 'Gabriel is a useless singer. But what are we talking about Gabriel for? Luke has a message to deliver.'

Watched carefully by the doctor's Angel guardian, Raphael invited Luke's spirit to speak directly to the spirit of the sleeping Paul. While he was doing this, I said to Raphael, 'May I ask what you've done with Luke's body?'

'You needn't worry about that,' he said. 'Everything will be fine. Why don't I go and get it?' Before I could stop him, he was gone.

Gabriel arrived and I explained the situation. Gabriel offered to return Luke's spirit to Macedonia immediately, but I suggested we wait. Raphael soon returned, carrying Luke's limp body.

Gabriel was furious. 'You need special training for this kind of thing,' he reprimanded Raphael. 'Even fully trained Angels require specific permission from me before they attempt it.'

Raphael was too excited to be concerned. 'Well, *you* put him back together then,' he suggested, handing the dispirited body to Heaven's chief messenger.

Gabriel obliged and Luke was quickly reunited with his slowly expiring body. Paul, though asleep, sensed the presence of another human in his bedroom and woke. To see the very man he had just seen in his dream now standing by his bed was an unsettling experience. I ushered the excess Archangels out of the room and left these two humans to try and work out exactly what had happened to them. Thankfully, they concluded that it must have been the work of my Boss.

Neapolis

After two days at sea, my entire being still feels as though it's being tossed up and down, backwards and forwards by that vast fatal fluid, even though I am at the moment safely ashore. But there is good news which eclipses the unpleasantness of sea travel: this small Roman port, to which Luke has brought us, is the starting point of the main road to Rome, the Ignatian Way. It will take us by the shortest human route across this lump of land they call the Balkan Peninsula.

Luke is a travelling medic who was introduced to the Son by a wealthy patient called Theophilus. In his visits around Macedonia he has searched for fellow disciples, without success. Theophilus, who first heard the story of Jesus on a business trip to Pisidian

Antioch, also learned about Paul there. Luke and Theophilus were praying for more than two Earth years that Paul would visit their region with his message.

Learning all this, I said to the Director, 'So you've been planning this visit all along, have you?'

'Not planning it,' he replied, 'hoping for it.'

Paul, Luke, Silas and Timothy are staying in Neapolis tonight and will walk to the main town, Philippi, tomorrow.

Next morning

Archangel Michael visited me during the night.

'I have been carrying out a security scan of the area. There has been a noticeable increase in Opposition activity over the last two years.'

'Clusters of Opposition resources are quite common,' I said. 'Is there any reason for me to be particularly concerned?'

'Yes,' Michael said bluntly, irritated at me for belittling his discovery. 'The trouble began shortly after the rebirth of your Doctor Luke. It seems that Lucifer rates the man as a significant threat. There was a further scaling up of Opposition presence here when Paul set out on his second trip westward. Luke's guardian Lisael has done excellent work disrupting the Opposition expansion, but they have a greater objective than stifling Luke's growth. The majority of them have been put here to prevent Paul reaching Rome.'

This was disheartening news. 'What does this mean for Paul's plans?' I asked.

'I don't know at this stage,' Michael replied. 'I'll monitor the situation closely and keep you informed.' He thought for a while, then added, 'I will need you to keep a precise log of all Opposition activity you encounter.'

'I'm writing a diary of our travels anyway,' I told him.

'Let me see,' he demanded and I handed him this book.

He passed a swift Angelic eye across its content. 'Useless!' he announced. 'I need exact detail, not rambling stories.'

'I will do separate reports especially for you,' I told him, hurt.

As soon as it was light, Timothy roused his three companions and urged them downstairs for breakfast. Paul didn't eat; he chose to stand at the window and talk through his plans with the Director.

Philippi

Philippi is a strictly-organised Roman colony and does not have a synagogue; neither does it have the informal community of beggars that adorns most cities. While the four travellers sat in the pillared marketplace, wondering how to start their work in the city, I set Angelic eyes to good use. To an Angel's gaze, humans who love our Boss shine with a bright light that is absent in those who do not. Indeed, it is primarily the faith, hope and love in humans – especially their love – that we see. Human bodies are to an Angel's vision what a thin wisp of smoke is to human sight.

I sent Lisael, Terathiel and Kalael off to look for the brightest humans in the city while I watched and waited. Three Opposition spirits arrived in the marketplace with a European slave girl and her two Philippian owners. I studied them carefully. They were running a scam. People paid the slave girl's owners for her to predict their future. The Opposition spirits work their system like this: a customer asks the girl for some particular insight into their future, for example who they would marry; one spirit notes the personal details of the customer and passes them to the second spirit, the second spirit leaves that narrow stream of time humans call 'the present' and looks for the customer's life further down time's winding course. (This activity is forbidden to both Opposition spirits and Angel guardians.) The time-travelling spirit returns and passes on the findings to the third in the group, who speaks directly into the slave-girl's mind. The quality of information passed on to the customer is consistently distorted for two reasons: firstly because the second spirit's brief escape from time is necessarily limited; and secondly because the three spirits entertain themselves by deliberately twisting the truth they discover. This doesn't deter the people of Philippi at all. The girl has a reputation for accuracy and her masters have become significantly rich. I will have plenty to report to Michael tonight.

The Sabbath

My Angelic scouts did excellently, discovering a group of Philippian women with a deep love for our Boss. Inspired by some Jews they had met, they gather every Saturday on the bank of the River Gangites. This morning Paul joined them and they were very happy to listen to his message about a Jewish Messiah called Jesus. I spent the morning working on the brightest of these lovely ladies, a cloth merchant called Lydia. Familiar as I am with Paul's standard first sermon, I focused on preparing Lydia's mind and helping her follow the characteristic twists and leaps of Paul's argument.

The moment he finished, Lydia said, 'Paul, this is what I've been searching for, but could not find. This Jesus is my Messiah too! Will you please plunge me in the river just as you were plunged in that water trough in Damascus?'

Paul was somewhat startled by the speed of Lydia's response. While I tried to convince him that her enthusiasm was genuine, she was busy persuading her sisters, friends and staff that they too should get themselves dipped and become disciples of Jesus. Silas dipped seven of the women in the river there and then.

Everyone retired to Lydia's home for a sumptuous lunch and there the brand new Christian Church of Philippi had its first ever meeting. There was a very special guest of honour – the Son himself. His arrival ensured that there was even more partying among the Angels than among the humans.

When the party was over and all the guests departed, Lydia persuaded Paul to abandon the travellers' inn and stay with her. He was reluctant to lodge in a house populated entirely with women but Lydia is a forceful lady. Timothy and Silas returned to the inn to collect their bags, leaving the two older men talking together.

'What you need,' Luke informed Paul in his cultured Greek voice, 'is a book that tells the story of Jesus' life, which you can leave behind you as a primary resource for the new churches you found.'

I looked with interest to see how Paul would respond to this suggestion in light of his strong disapproval of Mark's writings. He has a respect for Luke's maturity and the quality of his education but he still harbours a distrust of stories, preferring the definable clarity of more traditional teaching. Paul thought for a long time, eventually replying, 'I'll consider it.'

Philippi Prison

This morning Lydia announced she was going down to the river to pray with some of her friends and invited Paul to join her. Luke, due to see a patient, took Timothy with him. Silas went with Paul and Lydia. The three stopped in the market to buy some fruit. The fruit stall happened to be immediately next to the booth used by the fortune-telling slave girl. The three Opposition spirits immediately recognised me and quickly worked out who Paul was. While they discussed our presence in the city, the slave girl picked up snatches of their conversation. Being accustomed to repeating what she heard the spirits say, she stepped out of her booth and shouted across the crowded market.

'These men are servants of the Most High God,' she declared, pointing straight at Paul and Silas. 'They will tell you the way to escape Death.'

To the dismay of her owners, the girl followed Paul as he made his way to the river. She continued to broadcast her announcement. 'These men will tell you about the Most High God,' she proclaimed.

Paul was unsure what to make of this strange turn of events. Silas was excited. 'This is great,' he exclaimed. 'I don't know how she knows, but you should take advantage of it.'

'I know exactly how she does it,' I interjected, 'and you don't want to have anything to do with her.'

Paul, already uneasy, picked up my advice and walked on. The girl and a fair-sized crowd followed. Michael arrived.

'Stop her, Oriel,' he ordered. 'Stop her immediately!'

'How do you suggest I do that' I asked, irritated at being ordered around by my colleague.

The girl continued to draw attention to Paul and Silas. The crowd were getting excited and their number was swelled by numerous Opposition spirits rushing onto the scene at the request of the girl's tormentors.

Over all the broad estuary of time I have rarely seen Michael panic, but there he was badly outnumbered. The Opposition would have no reservations about human casualties caused by a spiritual battle. Michael is not so reckless.

'Oriel, for Heaven's sake, do something,' he urged me.

I spoke to the Director. 'What do you suggest?'

'Have you forgotten,' he asked calmly, 'that as my child Paul has authority over the Opposition?'

I had. Prompted by me, Paul shouted, 'In the name of Jesus the Messiah, I command you to leave that girl alone.'

The game was up for the three spirits. They and their colleagues slipped disconsolately away. The people of Philippi returned to their business and the girl was dragged back to her booth. Paul, Lydia and Silas walked down to the river.

In contrast, on the east bank of the Gangites, Lydia's prayer gathering was peaceful. She argued the Son's cause quietly but at least as passionately as Paul. After a shared lunch of fresh fruit by the river, Paul was in the process of ritually dipping two more Philippian women, when the Son – who always attends these events – said to me, 'He had better hurry up or he won't get them both done.'

Before I could ask what he meant the two men who owned the fortune-telling slave girl arrived. Their dull spirits were simmering with anger as they stopped and stared at the unusual sight of two foreign men submerging two local women in the slow-moving water of the Gangites. As soon as Paul and Silas stepped onto the grass bank, they were grabbed and marched up the slope leading back to the busy marketplace. On the way, the owners irately explained that Paul had ruined their business. The girl had become totally useless, because she could no longer see into people's futures.

Paul and Silas were dragged directly to the public seats of the city's chief magistrates. 'These men are Jews,' one of the distraught entrepreneurs declared, as though that in itself deserved severe punishment.

'They are throwing Philippi into chaos,' the other continued, 'promoting strange foreign customs that are illegal in the civilised world.'

Other market traders joined the accusations. They had almost no idea what they were talking about, but that didn't matter. Paul was clearly a threat to the local economy and that, for them, was enough. The thoughts of the magistrates followed a similar path. One magistrate made a swift decision. He instructed the militia to take Paul and Silas, strip them naked, flog them severely and then hold them in the city's prison.

The orders were carried out and the head jailer was instructed to guard the two men with particular care. The disciples, sore and aching, were locked in the inner cell of the city prison, their legs secured in heavy wooden stocks.

Paul, strangely, viewed the entire episode with amused

detachment. He and Silas are currently singing their way through Paul's entire repertoire of re-worded Jewish songs. The other inmates in the small jail are listening, intrigued by the unusual behaviour of the new prisoners.

Back on the Ignatian Way

While Paul and Silas were busy singing and the jailer was checking that all his charges were securely contained for the night, we were paid a brief visit by Lucifer, the leader of the Opposition. He was satisfied to see that Paul had been so harshly detained and soon left. He did not care for Paul's choice of music.

At midnight Paul and Silas were still singing away, sometimes pausing to pray. Suddenly, without warning, the jail was stormed by an elite squadron of Angels. Each one emerged through a different wall or ceiling and their arrival was synchronised to perfection. No less than 23 highly-trained Angels appeared in Paul's cell at the same moment. Among them was their leader, Archangel Michael, who rose up menacingly through the cell floor. The walls and foundations of the building shook at the invasion. Before anyone else quite knew what was happening, every door was opened, every shackle and chain broken – but not a single prisoner moved. The physical restraints on the prisoners may have been destroyed but at that moment it was the most securely guarded jail in the Universe.

The head jailer was woken by the disturbance and ran in from his adjoining house. He took one look at the state of the building and assumed all the inmates had fled. Knowing the punishment for losing prisoners – condemnation to serve out the combined sentences of all who had escaped – he drew his short Roman sword and was about to kill himself when Paul called out from the darkness of his cell.

'Don't do it! We are all here.'

The man stopped, lowered his sword and roused his disorientated staff, ordering them to search the jail. One by one cells were checked. Paul was right. The chains and doors were re-secured, relieving the temporary Angelic guards. They reported to their commander in the inner cell where Paul and Silas were stretching their aching limbs.

By the time the jailer entered Paul's cell, it was stuffed to the roof with Angelic commandos. Something in the man's spirit responded to such company. He sank to his knees in front of Paul as though he, not Michael, was the commander of the troop.

'Get up, man,' Paul said, embarrassed at the jailer's actions.

The jailer escorted his two top security prisoners into the prison courtyard where, with the help of his wife and eldest daughter, he washed and dressed the wounds caused by the earlier flogging.

'Sir,' he asked, well aware that Paul had been imprisoned for his faith, 'what must I do to be saved?'

'You need to trust Jesus,' Paul informed him. 'You and all your family.'

While the two women carefully treated each wound and the jailer kept them supplied with boiled water and clean bandages, Paul talked to them about Jesus. He told them how Jesus too had been flogged by Roman soldiers, and how he had forgiven them before they crucified him, and how he had allowed himself to be killed to bring forgiveness and Heavenly life to everyone who follows him.

The treatment of their wounds took nearly two hours and Paul's lesson about Jesus matched it minute for minute. When the last cut was cleaned and covered the jailer brought his three young sons into the prison yard and asked Paul to initiate them all into this new faith straight away. Paul was not at all sure about dipping the children – neither he, nor Silas had done it before – but the boys' father insisted.

'We are a family,' he said. 'My children follow me, so if I follow Jesus then they will follow Jesus too.'

His daughter joined in. 'How can I be God's daughter and my brothers not be his sons?' she asked.

Paul didn't know what to say.

The mother spoke up. 'If this dipping is a sign of God's goodness, how can he not be good to my sons just because they are young? They need his forgiveness as much as I do.'

Paul was still silent. The mother spoke to her three sons in turn, starting with the eldest. 'Marcellus, if your father and I are followers of Paul's Jesus, will you follow him too?'

'Yes, mum.'

'Antonius, will you follow Jesus with us?'

'Yeah!'

She crouched down in front of her youngest, no more than three years old.

'Tavey,' she said gently, 'have you done naughty things?' The boy nodded his head coyly. 'Would you like Paul's God to wash away all the naughty things you have done?' He nodded again.

The mother turned and looked at Paul. Paul turned to Silas. 'What do you think?' he asked.

'You are the Apostle to the Gentiles,' Silas told him.

Paul stood up, grasped a full bucket of water painfully in his hand and said to the jailer, 'Do you promise to follow Jesus?'

'I do.'

'Are you sorry before God for all your selfishness?'

'I am.'

'I baptise you in the name of God the eternal Father,' Paul declared and threw water at the man from the bucket. 'And of Jesus, the Son of God.' A second slosh. 'And of the Spirit.' Paul emptied the bucket at the man's chest and head.

The gathered Angels let out a song of celebration and were joined by the richest of all voices, that of the Son. Paul uncomfortably handed the bucket to his jailer and asked him to do the wetting for the rest of the family.

When the prison yard was awash with water and Heavenly song and all six members of the family, including the youngest, had committed themselves to a life of discipleship, the mother led Paul and Silas into her house and served an impromptu midnight feast. The Son and Michael's commandos joined the party and we all sang some of Paul's songs. The celebrations continued until dawn when army officers arrived from the magistrates, ordering the jailer to release his two prisoners.

Paul was in no hurry to leave. 'These men had me publicly beaten without a trial,' he said, 'even though I am a Roman citizen.'

The words *Roman citizen* caused immediate embarrassment on behalf of both jailer and officers, since all Roman citizens are exempt from such humiliations. Paul continued. 'Yesterday they abused us. Today they try to sweep us quietly away.' Then he spoke directly to the officers. 'Tell your magistrates that I am waiting for them to escort me out of the city in person.'

The officers departed, leaving an uneasy quietness in the house.

'I'm very sorry,' the jailer said, knowing that Paul had not been treated with the dignity reserved for Roman citizens, even in prison. 'I didn't know you were a citizen.'

Paul reassured the man. 'They didn't tell you,' he observed, 'because they didn't bother to find out. They were much too concerned for their money.' He added reflectively, 'That's where all evil starts.'

The two chief magistrates arrived at the jail, apologised to Paul in generous terms, and escorted him to the market where they formally released him and Silas. With their next breath they asked the disciples to leave the city at their earliest opportunity. Paul and Silas walked to Lydia's house where they told their story, encouraged her to look after the jailer and his family, packed their bags, and left.

We are travelling on the Ignatian way – Rome-wards!

Thessalonica

Paul's suspicion that he would need to be ready for further secret escapes was quite right. He is currently hiding under a large pile of tent cloth, waiting for the darkness of night time to make his departure from Thessalonica.

He arrived here almost a complete orbit of Earth's moon ago. Being in need of more money for his travels he sought out the workshops of the city's tentmakers. With a little help from me and some excellent scouting by Kalael, Paul came across a tentmaker called Jason, an associate member of Thessalonica's only synagogue. Jason was delighted to learn some new techniques from a foreign colleague but he was even more interested to hear that the Messiah – long awaited by the Jewish faith he fostered – had finally arrived in the person of a fellow craftsman called Jesus.

Jason was a leading light of the synagogue's large group of Gentile adherents. In the days before the next Sabbath he introduced Paul to many friends, colleagues and relatives who had learned about my Boss from the city's Jews. These men and women were quickly drawn to Paul's message that their faith could be complete without having to undergo the physical trauma of circumcision. Come Saturday, Jason arranged for Paul to preach at the main synagogue service.

What a sight that synagogue was as Paul unfolded his claim that Jesus, my Boss's Son, was without doubt the promised Messiah! The building was constructed with three distinct sections: a small inner room reserved exclusively for Jewish men, which was half empty; an outer hallway in which the Jewish women were separated from their men by a wooden trellis, which was comfortably full; and a courtyard from which Gentile women and men followed the service through open windows. That courtyard was packed tight with shining humans desperate to hear more about the love of their Creator.

During the week that followed, those Greeks who called themselves God-fearers made regular visits to Jason's workshop. Mornings and evenings Paul worked hard, assembling tents for his host; Silas and Timothy assisting as unskilled labourers. In the afternoons Paul worked just as hard, talking about the Son, drawing people into my Boss's human family. There were a few Jews in his impromptu congregations but most were the God-fearers, and their pagan friends. Luke, meanwhile, had offered his services to a neighbourhood doctor.

On the second Sabbath I was not surprised to find some familiar faces in the inner room of the synagogue. The same group of Opposition spirits who caused so much trouble in Galatia had arrived in Macedonia. I knew what to expect. They stirred up the common jealousy that is found in all humans. Jewish men who, a week ago, had been pleased by the large number of associate members at their synagogue, began to see these enthusiastic Gentiles as a dangerous threat.

In the days that followed the Opposition spirits led these discomforted Jews to Jason's workshop and showed them how Paul was stirring up the God-fearers and pagans, telling them they did not need to be enslaved to Jewish law in order to be loved by the God of the Jews.

On Paul's third Sabbath in the city, the inner chamber of the synagogue was full. Jewish men had turned out in force to defend their faith and their tradition. The Opposition spirits were present, accompanied by their leader, Lucifer. The 'bearer of light' was darkening the spirits of the Jewish members. He quickly identified the most vulnerable point in the minds of these insecure men: money. He arranged for the news to spread that Paul had won some very wealthy Greek women to his cause. This was true. But to this information the 'father of lies' added a fear that Paul was using their money to build a rival synagogue which would not require its members to keep Jewish law. Untrue.

Unnoticed by the record congregation, Paul's sermon became a battle between Lucifer and me. Lucifer twisted everything Paul said as it entered the minds of the Jewish leaders so that it seemed to confirm the rumour that Paul was set to destroy the Jewish faith. I worked feverishly in Paul's mind, urging him to reassure the Jews he had no such plans.

'I am a Jew of Jews,' Paul told the confused men sitting around him in the synagogue's inner room. 'I was circumcised on the eighth day, according to the law of our people. I am a direct descendant of the tribe of Benjamin. In regard to Jewish law, I am a Pharisee. In terms of legalistic righteousness my life was fault-less. As for my enthusiasm for the Jewish way, I persecuted the Christian Church.'

These words, like all Paul's others, the Opposition spirits distorted. '*Was* faultless,' they emphasised, 'persecut*ed* the Church.' Then they added, 'Don't judge this man on who he was, see what he is *now*: he eats with Gentiles, he belittles circumcision, he is a danger to everything Jewish.'

The fruit of the tussle between Lucifer and myself was that a riot was avoided. The service ended peacefully, though there was no peace in the minds of those in the inner room.

Today, while Paul and Jason were making the final adjustments to a large Roman-style tent, Archangel Michael charged into the workshop shouting, 'Hide Paul, Oriel! Hide him quickly! The Jews are after him.'

I looked around the faint stone structure of Jason's house, wondering how I might conceal one of the brightest of my Boss's children.

Michael was insistent. 'Do something quickly, you fool.'

Terathiel, Timothy's guardian, gave me a clue, pointing to the dark canvas of the new tent. 'The humans can't see through this stuff at all.'

'Michael,' I instructed, 'we can hide Paul from the humans, but *you* will have to deal with the Opposition.'

As I spoke we heard the Jews push their way into the front room of Jason's shop. Michael rushed out to meet them. I snapped the main pole of the tent. The whole structure billowed to the floor, covering Paul, Silas and Timothy with several layers of thick canvas. When the irate Jews pushed open the workshop door, they could see only one person – Jason – standing alone in the middle of the room, holding a loose guy rope.

'Where's Paul?' the leader of the synagogue demanded.

Jason said nothing. Terathiel, Kalael and I were sitting hard on our respective humans, smothering all sound and movement. The Jews looked carefully around the room, saw no signs of life and decided that Jason would have to do. They grabbed him roughly and pushed him out into the street. When all was quiet I allowed Paul and his companions to emerge from the tent but would not let them out of the door. Michael, unaided, had all six Opposition spirits cornered in the shop.

Jason returned hours later, bruised and exhausted. He had been taken to the city magistrates and accused of harbouring dangerous political renegades, followers of a phoney king called Jesus. He was released on bail.

Paul offered Jason his share in the proceeds of the tent (which he had already repaired) to cover the bail. Then Jason arranged for Paul and his three companions to be smuggled out of the city as soon as it is dark.

Berea

As it was widely known that Paul was travelling along the Ignatian Way towards Rome, Jason's escape plan sent the four refugees south rather than west. After two days of swift walking, they came to the town of Berea. As usual, Paul made straight for the synagogue and introduced himself to the rabbi. The rabbi was fascinated by Paul's claim that Jesus is the Messiah and the two men have spent the last few days studying the Jewish scriptures together in minute detail.

Silas has been working as Paul's eyes, trying to compensate for their continuing deterioration. He spends every day reading and searching the synagogue scrolls for Paul, patiently carrying out his older companion's frustrated instructions. Timothy, meanwhile, has been teaching Luke to read and understand Hebrew script.

Tomorrow is a Sabbath and the rabbi has sent a message round the Jewish community informing his flock that there will be an extended service, owing to the visit of a rabbi from Jerusalem who specialises in Messianic prophecy. This, he assured Paul, is a favourite subject among the Berean Jews and will ensure a high turnout.

Five Sabbaths later

Never before has Paul been so well received in a synagogue. The Jewish community here is small and intellectual. They listened carefully and patiently as Paul spoke and Silas read. Many of the Jews turned, in faith, to the Son and decided to become his disciples. There was no great concern when a number of prominent Greek women and men showed interest, and Paul welcomed them into the family of Christians asking only the mild requirements of the Council of Jerusalem. The Berean Jews were simply pleased to share their spiritual wealth with their neighbours.

This morning, however, this loving harmony became suddenly discordant. News finally reached Thessalonica that Paul was now preaching in Berea. A delegation of Thessalonian Jews arrived in the town yesterday evening. At the synagogue this morning they openly and repeatedly disagreed with everything Paul said.

During a quiet section of the service, the Director said to both Paul and me, 'It's time to move on. You have laid a firm foundation here. Let others build on it.'

After the service, the Thessalonians went straight to the marketplace to stir up the same old accusations against Paul. Paul returned to his lodgings and prepared to leave. He has arranged for Timothy and Silas to remain in Berea, hoping that the Thessalonian Jews will not be interested in them. Luke is presently planning Paul's route. I have urged his guardian Lisael to ensure that the chosen itinerary will lead towards Rome.

Athens

Throughout the long journey south to Athens, Paul hardly spoke. Not to Luke; not to Jason's friends, who accompanied him all the way; not to the Director. And – no surprise – not to me. It was as if he had closed his mind. There was no joy in his spirit, only a uniform gloomy greyness. During the daytime he rode alone, usually ahead of his companions, seemingly hurrying them along and never looking back. At the evening meal he stared directly ahead, eating little. At night, when his travelling companions slept soundly, Paul cried, sobbing into his pillow.

When we arrived in the great and ancient city of Athens, Paul immediately sent Jason's friends back north to Berea, urging them to send Timothy and Silas to join him as soon as possible. Doctor Luke, well aware of Paul's condition, ordered him to rest.

'We need money for food and accommodation,' Paul complained. 'I must find work.'

'I will work,' Luke insisted. 'I can earn more in a morning than you can in a whole week. You, my friend, must rest.'

Paul conceded; he has a respect for Luke that he holds for few other people. Luke gave one more instruction. 'There's one thing I insist on. You must not stay in your room all day. You must get out. You're in the greatest city in the world – explore it!'

'I thought Rome was the greatest city in the world,' Paul observed dully.

'Rome was built with brute power and crude politics,' Luke replied cheerfully. 'Athens is a city of culture and philosophy. You could enjoy it here if you tried.'

The next morning, when Paul took his prescribed walk, he found a quiet corner in a cemetery, sat down and spoke to the Director for the first time since a quick 'thank you' on escaping Berea.

'I've had enough,' he said. 'I don't think I can carry on any longer.'

I was shocked. 'You can't stop now,' I told him. 'We're already two thirds of the way there.'

The Director reprimanded me. 'Oriel, please,' he said. 'Now is not the moment.'

Paul continued. 'Everywhere I go, they attack me. I have been whipped, I have been beaten, I have been in prison, I have been stoned almost to death. I can no longer read for myself, I can hardly write. And nobody likes me.'

He paused, systematically breaking a small twig into little pieces. I was not inclined to let him close his thoughts so negatively. 'You have to get to Rome,' I said. 'That's the task our Boss has given you.'

Perhaps he heard me, because he suddenly said, 'Rome! What is to be gained from going there? Luke claims that Athens is the centre for philosophy and religion. If he is right, then surely I am in the right place already.'

'If my Boss had meant you to stay in Athens, he would have said so,' I replied.

The Director brought my pep talk to an early conclusion.

'Oriel, will you please be quiet? You are here to support and encourage Paul, not to contradict and criticise him.'

I moved away, leaving the Director to reason with his depressed disciple. Feeling lonely and rejected, I asked Raphael to join me.

'I've told you before, my dear friend,' he said, 'you must love him. It seems to me that you are treating Paul like a project: deliver the man to Rome and then you can tick him off your list and do something else.'

'That's what my Boss asked me to do,' I claimed in defence.

'Not at all costs.' Raphael was thoughtful for a while, then said, 'The road of love is never straight; it twists and turns with every person it encounters. It is a road that . . . '

I perceived that Raphael's metaphor was likely to continue for several hours so I interrupted him.

'What do you suggest I *do* with Paul?'

'Be with him, my frustrated old thing,' Raphael replied. 'Be with him in Athens, be with him in his depression. Be with him wherever his mission takes him.'

'What about my orders to deliver him to Rome?'

'As I was about to say,' Raphael said, 'when you deliberately interrupted me, the road of love frequently turns right back on itself to meet another's need.'

Raphael left and I returned to Paul to find the Director talking to him about death. 'If you continue to live,' he was saying, 'then your work will bear more fruit. If you choose to die, then you will be welcomed into my home, eternally beyond the reach of all your enemies.'

'I don't know which to choose,' Paul replied. 'I would love to leave this life and be with you. That is better by far.'

'Rome, Paul!' I cried out. 'What about Rome?'

'But it is more necessary,' Paul continued, 'for the Church's sake, that I remain in this old body and continue the struggle.'

He dropped the broken twig, stood up and walked out of the cemetery.

Several weeks later

That was not the end of Paul's depression. Following his doctor's instructions he began to explore the city but, counter to Luke's opinion, Paul found Athens to be a distressing place. At almost every corner, certainly in every market square, there is a temple to some powerless deity or other. There are even several tumbledown sanctuaries whose deities have been long forgotten but where people still worship, 'just in case!'

As Paul pondered the empty soul of this energetically religious city, I guided his mind to the need of its inhabitants for news of the real deity for whom he is a chosen messenger.

Paul took to spending his days in the Agora, the main market-place in the centre of the city, just below the grand but vacuous temple to the so-called goddess Athene. I noted that the Opposition spirit who first set himself up as the prime object of this city's worship had long since abandoned his post. He left a note for any spirits who might be tempted to fill the vacancy. It read, *Human beings are tedious creatures. Their worship is bland and repetitive – little more than a habit they cannot be bothered to break.*

Paul found a small wine bar in the Agora, from which he watched the Athenians going about their daily business. One day he struck up a conversation with a man on his way to worship at the temple of Athene. Paul challenged the man about his religion, asking what he hoped to achieve from it. When the man finished a rambling and wholly unconvincing reply, Paul told him about my Boss – the one and only real God. He talked about the promise of a full and thriving life beyond Death which far exceeds the grim existence of departed spirits described in the mythology of Greek religion. The man was fascinated by Paul's conversation, but he eventually made his apologies, climbed up to the Parthenon building and worshipped the long absent 'goddess'.

On numerous other occasions Paul found himself in deep debate about the meaning of life and the value of religion. Religion is one of the primary industries of the local economy and everyone here has an opinion on the subject. This openness of the people allowed many opportunities for Paul to speak about the Son, but the majority of his listeners were so open-minded that one more doctrine, one more supernatural claim, was simply lost in the hubbub of spiritual chatter.

I shared this observation with the Angel guardian of one of Paul's many partners in conversation. 'It's so frustrating,' the Angel confessed. 'Sometimes I think our job would be far easier if the whole lot of them were avowed atheists! Then the truth would stand out in their barren landscape.'

The darkness in Paul's mind has lessened, but only to a limited extent. He has returned to his regular conversations with my Boss, but the memory of persistent opposition and the threat of continuing persecution still casts a long shadow in Paul's thoughts and feelings. He has not regained his appetite for visiting Rome.

This morning he found himself in complex debate with a group of highly educated philosophers who were fascinated by his claim that Jesus returned from Death. They insisted on taking Paul across the Agora to the Court of the Areopagus. This ancient Athenian institution passes judgement on matters of religion and morals and meets daily in the Royal Colonnade. Paul was invited to address a circle of learned Athenians.

'You are bringing some strange ideas to our ears,' he was told. 'We want to know what they mean.'

Paul was in no way prepared for this invitation. He still gets uncomfortably nervous when speaking even in the familiar setting of a synagogue. He would have spent many days preparing his speech for this famous audience, if he had known.

'Come on Oriel,' the Director said to me, 'we will have to carry this one.'

I brought to Paul's mind his memory of a ramshackle altar he had found in the city, dedicated to 'an unknown god'. He described it and then said, 'Now, what you worship as unknown I am going to explain to you.'

The Director projected into Paul's consciousness images of stars, planets and galaxies. 'The God who made the world and everything in it,' Paul continued, 'does not live in temples built by human hands.'

He was off. With dimly remembered quotes from Greek poets and a line of debate that was quite new to him, Paul spoke of divine judgement. The men of the Court of the Areopagus listened with polite interest. However, when Paul held before his audience the fact of Jesus' resurrection as proof for his beliefs, it was too much for their muddled minds to handle. The members of the court became restless. His time was up. He was invited to return another day and the Athenians turned their attention to different matters.

Two of the Areopagites, a woman called Damaris and a man called Dionysius, offered to buy Paul lunch. In all, nine Athenians gathered round a table with him, eagerly questioning about his Messiah. They talked all afternoon and when Luke arrived to meet Paul after his day's work, all nine committed themselves to become disciples of Jesus.

This evening, when Paul and Luke sank exhausted into chairs at their lodgings, Paul said, 'It's time to leave, Luke. Athens is not for me. Mine is a simple faith. I cannot manage all the philosophical gymnastics these people expect.'

Luke looked intently at his companion. There was a queue of questions and objections on his tongue but he kept his mouth firmly closed. He sat still and quietly planned how he would pass all his patients over to the care of other doctors. He had expected this at some point.

'Where do you intend to go?' Luke asked at last.

'Wherever the road leads.'

'It goes to Corinth.'

Corinth

The road took us south and west to this notorious city of fast money and even faster morals. Just as Athens had been duped into worshipping the so-called goddess of wisdom, the inhabitants of Corinth had been deluded by an Opposition spirit claiming to be Aphrodite, the goddess of love. This was strongly reflected in their lifestyle. Paul and Luke made their way to the central marketplace and stood there, surveying the detritus of a city obsessed with greed and lust. Luke went to find them some food, but Paul continued to look and listen, surrounded by noise yet immersed in lonely silence.

Corinth is built near the narrow neck of land that joins the Peloponnese peninsular to mainland Greece. The city boasts two separate ports: Lechaeon attracts traffic from Italy and Rome, and the eastern port of Cenchreae serves the Agean and beyond. I looked down the steep slope of the ancient city towards Lechaeon. From there, just one boat trip separates me from my goal.

Suddenly remembering Raphael's advice, I turned to Paul. He was looking in the opposite direction, to Cenchreae. He was surveying it with the same longing with which I had looked at Lechaeon. It took only a moment for me to understand the desire rising in his mind. He wants to go home.

I was tempted to harangue him about his duty to fulfil my

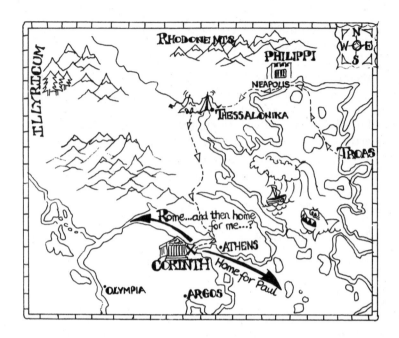

Boss's commission but I recognised that he and I have something in common. We are both lonely. In that moment I understood that my primary motivation for getting Paul to Rome is that I want our journey to be over. I want to be free to return to my own home, to the familiar routines of my usual work. I saw the same in Paul. He is tired of the constant stress of traditionalist Jewish opposition and the frustration of only ever sharing the basic principles of his faith. The very geography of Corinth presented us both with a choice. For me, that choice was either to satisfy my own needs or to serve Paul's.

Luke returned and roused us both from our homesick reverie. 'There is a thriving Jewish community here,' he announced. 'I found a smart new building with *Synagogue of the Hebrews* carved into its lintel in large Greek letters.'

This was bittersweet news to Paul. He was longing for the familiar pattern and structure of Jewish life, but most of his troubles in recent years have come from the provincial synagogues of the Roman Empire.

Lisael, Luke's guardian, spoke up. 'I checked out the synagogue leader, a man called Crispus,' he told me. 'He's one of the brightest rabbis I've come across. I think there might be some hope here.'

I passed the message on to Paul.

The two disciples ate their lunch in the synagogue grounds. They didn't meet any Jews but they had a long conversation with the synagogue's Greek next-door neighbour, Gaius, who is a regular worshipper there and an associate member. He told the travellers all he knew about the small community of Jews in the city. He also directed them to a Jewish family who regularly take in lodgers.

In the last few days, Luke sought work to pay their rent. Paul and I have wandered thoughtfully around the city. Paul has repeatedly stood on the Lechaeon-Cenchreae road, looking east then west, drawn towards Rome by his thoughts and towards Jerusalem by his feelings.

Today being a Sabbath, we went to the synagogue. Gaius introduced Paul to Crispus, the synagogue leader, and Crispus invited Paul to deliver the sermon. My attention, however, was focussed on a different matter. I scoured the congregation in search of suitable friends for Paul. It may be that my motives here were not entirely selfless; it had crossed my mind that if Paul found genuine Jewish friendship in Corinth it may lessen his yearning for home. Anyway, the fact remains that he is in great need of some genuine friends of his own age, race and religion.

So, while Paul was speaking to the assembled humans, I addressed their respective Angels. Angelic conversation can be highly efficient when necessary. It did not take me long to discover a middle-aged couple who arrived recently in Corinth from Rome and – to add triumph to victory – they are both tentmakers!

I am impatient for Paul to finish his sermon. I have every confidence that Aquila, Priscilla and Paul have the potential for becoming great friends.

Some weeks later

I was right. Aquila and Priscilla invited Paul to lunch after the service and he never left. He became a partner in their business and they soon became his partners in discipleship. Paul has been so much happier. It is a joy to see. He has continued to speak in the synagogue each week, at Crispus' invitation. His teaching is much gentler than before. There have been no argumentative proofs that Jesus is the Messiah and no mind-stretching talk about life beyond Death. Paul has focussed his mind on the person of Jesus and his violent execution – drawing heavily on his own recent experiences of rejection, arrest, trial, imprisonment and flogging. The Corinthians have listened in fascinated silence. Away from the public gaze of Sabbath worship, Paul has been praying intently for several members and associates of the synagogue community, almost all of whom have experienced rapid relief from their troubles as a result. It is this, as much as his teaching, which has led people to trust Paul's message.

However, the last two weeks have brought some less encouraging news. The same posse of Opposition spirits that hounded Paul out of Galatia and Macedonia have arrived in Corinth. Though severely chastened by Michael when cornered in Jason's tent shop, they are here nonetheless, quietly going about their destructive business.

At today's synagogue service their influence displayed itself in a muted protest at Crispus' decision to let Paul preach yet again. One of the older members of the Jewish community stood up and said, 'I have had enough of this jibbering idiot. He speaks so quietly I can hardly hear a word he says, and what I can hear is nothing but misery and suffering. We can read the book of Jeremiah for that.'

Paul, acutely sensitive to the prospect of being driven out of yet another city, stood up, shook the dust from his clothes in symbolic protest and replied, 'I have played my part. From now on I will go to the Gentiles instead.'

There was shocked silence. I quickly looked across to the Opposition spirits, expecting them to stir up another riot but all six of them were staring up through the ceiling of the building. I followed their gaze. Outside the synagogue, posted on its roof, was a small squadron of Michael's elite troops, some of whom I recognised from the jail in Philippi.

Paul walked towards the synagogue door. 'If any of you are interested, on future Sabbaths you will find me next door in Gaius' house.' He left.

Human eyes in the room all turned to Crispus, the synagogue leader. He too stood up, shook out his clothes as Paul had done, and said, 'You will find me at Gaius' house, too.'

I didn't see what happened after that because I left to follow

Paul. I've been told that a fair number of the members, and most of the associate members, followed Crispus. They didn't see Paul when they emerged into the light because I had quickly ushered him round the nearest corner. He needed to be alone.

Once out of human sight, Paul rushed to a secluded place and released a torrent of tears. This reaction was precipitated by the thick cloud of fear that has darkened his mind since we left Berea. I didn't know what to do with this looming storm of human emotion. I simply embraced Paul's spirit, protecting it from the downpour affecting the rest of his person. When the rain clouds had dropped their stock I escorted Paul home to Priscilla's house, in through a back door and directly to his bed.

The next morning

As soon as Paul was asleep, I gathered my Archangel colleagues to meet me in his room. I explained at length the delicate state of the man's mind and asked for ideas as to how I might help him. When I had finished, they looked at me without uttering a single encouraging word. I felt even more alone than I had done at the top of the Lechaeon Road on our first day in this city.

Eventually Michael spoke. 'What exactly is it that you want for Paul, Oriel?'

'I want him to know that he's safe,' I said calmly. Then the calm deserted me. 'For Heaven's sake! I don't see a lot, stuck here in one single time and place. I didn't know, for example, that Michael had assigned Paul a special protection squad. No one told me. I'm on my own down here, trying to do a job – a difficult job at that – while you lot are free to flit wherever and whenever you like. And as for Paul, for him it's even worse. He knows less of what's going on than I do.'

'Oriel! Oriel!' Raphael cried, trying to stem the flow of my passion. 'You are not on your own.'

'Well, not entirely,' I conceded reluctantly. 'There are all the regular Angel guardians, but they don't exactly feel comfortable with an Archangel . . . '

'Listen to me,' Raphael insisted. 'It's not them I mean. I mean us: Gabriel, Michael, me. We all check on you, every single fleeting Earth day, to make sure that everything is well. We have not abandoned you, Oriel. We are there for you, all the time.'

I was astounded. I looked into each face and saw three unique expressions of my Boss's love. I couldn't find words to share my gratitude.

'We have strayed from the subject,' Gabriel said gently. 'I suggest I speak to Paul and reassure him that he is in good hands. No offence, Oriel my friend, but I could probably get the message through more effectively than you.'

I nodded.

Gabriel continued. 'Michael's protectors will be with you all the way from now on. I'll go and clear the content of the message with our Boss and then come straight back.'

'No need,' I said, in a weak voice. 'The Director is right here in Paul's spirit, remember. You can ask him.'

Gabriel looked rather uncomfortable at the suggestion, reminding me that the regular conversations I have been enjoying with the Director are not within the normal experience of Angels.

'Let me,' I said.

The Director was strongly approving of Gabriel's plan. The final, agreed message was as follows, (in the Director's name):

Paul, do not be afraid. Keep on speaking, do not be silent. I am with you and no one is going to attack or harm you. I have many children in this city.

While Gabriel was speaking to Paul, Raphael said to me, 'Oriel, my dear friend, may I make another suggestion?'

'Of course.'

'I think you would value some support for yourself. Am I correct?'

I didn't need to respond; Raphael knew he was right.

'I suggest you ask your friend Maphrael to help you. That is, of course, if Michael has no objection.'

Michael said that he didn't.

'No human has ever had two Angel guardians,' I said. 'Is it allowed?

'That something has never happened before is never a good reason for not doing it,' Raphael responded.

'What about the security implications?' I asked Michael. 'Wouldn't it be a giveaway to Lucifer, saying, *Here's the one you're after?*'

'It would,' Michael agreed. 'But Lucifer is already onto Paul, so it won't make much difference.'

'Anyway,' Raphael added, 'this is for you, Oriel, not for Paul. I will send Maphrael down as soon as I get home.'

A year later

I had not intended to write again until we were leaving Corinth, but earlier today the Director's promise to Paul regarding his safety was severely tested.

Not long after my last entry, Timothy and Silas arrived from Macedonia with encouraging news of my Boss's new families there. They insisted on taking Paul's place in the tent shop, releasing him to spend all his time at Gaius' house, teaching the growing family of disciples in Corinth.

The success of this breakaway congregation became a persistent irritation to the remaining members of the synagogue and their new leader, Sosthenes. The Opposition spirits continued their blight – carefully and subtly – under the watchful eye of Michael's special forces. Their plan came to fruition today when Paul was summonsed to appear before Gallio, the leading Roman official for the province. Sosthenes brought an official complaint against Paul, accusing him of promoting illegal religious practices.

Five Roman soldiers broke into Gaius' house and forcibly escorted Paul to the impressive stone platform in the centre of the main marketplace, where the Proconsul's court is held.

Following Paul, I shouted up at Michael's marksmen, at their regular posts on the roof. 'Do something!'

'Nothing we can do, guv,' one replied.

'What do you mean, *nothing*?' I insisted.

'Our orders are to deal with the Opposition. We're not allowed to touch the humans.'

'Why, on Earth, not?'

'We'd mash 'em, sir,' he explained. 'In less than a human breath there would be nothing left of them but a mess on the road and we'd be up in front of the Gaffer for manslaughter.'

I didn't waste any more time on them. I sent Maff to fetch Michael and chased after Paul who was putting to the Director the very question I wanted to ask.

'You promised this wouldn't happen.'

As soon as the question passed Paul's mind, I knew what the answer would be. I mouthed it to myself in time with the Director's reply.

'Trust me, Paul.'

Sosthenes announced the charge against Paul. 'This man is

persuading the people to worship God in ways contrary to the Law.'

I looked at Paul; the old depression was oozing back up from the dark depths of his psyche. I looked at the Director, who was waiting calmly. I looked around, searching for some indication that a rescue was planned. Nothing. Finally I looked at Gallio, the proconsul.

Gallio was gazing intently at Paul, a serene smile on his weathered face. There was something familiar about his smile. It was a faint reflection of one I have often seen on my Boss's face.

'I will not judge this case,' he informed Sosthenes with gentle firmness. 'If you were complaining about some serious crime, I would listen to you. But this involves questions about your religion. You can settle the matter among yourselves.'

'Go Gallio!' a voice shouted from the gathering crowd. Maff was back.

Gallio apologised to Paul and told him he was free to return to his business. He then instructed the soldiers who had escorted Paul to the marketplace, to escort Sosthenes and his companions out of the court. The Opposition spirits were furious at their defeat and turned their anger against Sosthenes, causing the other Jews to assault him right there in front of the court steps. Gallio and his soldiers simply stood and watched, wilfully deaf to Sosthenes' cries for help.

Some months later – Paul's last day in Corinth

Paul became increasingly restless after the Gallio affair. He seems to have lost his appetite for his mission in Corinth. This is the longest Paul has stayed in one place through all his travels and the new church is strong in both faith and numbers. Luke has returned to Macedonia and Paul recently decided that he, too, will move on. He misses Luke's calm and mature friendship. The only thing that has kept him here since Luke's departure is his need to decide which of Corinth's two ports to leave from, west or east. Rome or home.

It was Aquila and Priscilla who ultimately persuaded Paul not to go to Rome. They had escaped from the capital of the Empire less than two years before, when the Emperor ejected all Jews from the city. They insisted it would not be safe to return while Claudius remains Emperor.

Paul sent Timothy and Silas up the northern road with a letter for the brothers and sisters in Thessalonica. He will be sailing from Cenchreae in two hours' time. He is going home.

But where is home? This he still has to decide. He ruled out Tarsus and booked a passage to Caesarea. At Caesarea he will have to resolve his dilemma, choosing whether to travel north to Antioch or south to Jerusalem.

Caesarea

Aquila and Priscilla travelled with Paul as far as Ephesus. While his ship was being unloaded and reloaded, Paul took the short walk to the local synagogue. Some of the Jews there had already heard about Jesus. They urged him to stay in Ephesus and tell them more about their fledgling faith, but Paul declined. He was tired of synagogues, even friendly ones. He did, however, promise that he would return to Ephesus if he could.

This has been Maff's first taste of sea travel. I must be getting accustomed to this precarious means of transport because I was only half as terrified as him. The one consolation of the voyage was that we were untroubled by the Opposition. They despise the sea just as much as we do.

On reaching the steady ground of Caesarea, Paul had to answer the question he had spent the entire journey avoiding: where is home? While he ate alone at a harbourside inn, I tried to help him.

'Where do you feel most comfortable?' I asked him. 'Among Jews and Jewish disciples, or among Gentiles and Gentile disciples?'

Paul searched his mind and his memories but found little that helped. I then directed his attention to the more powerful but less defined territory of his emotions and private fantasies.

One theme stood out repeatedly. 'I am a Jew,' Paul was articulating in his mind. 'I will always be a Jew. There are many great advantages in being a Jew.'

'Like what?' Maff asked rudely.

'The Jewish law is a treasure trove of wisdom and insight,' Paul replied, talking to himself rather than his two Angelic companions. Then his contemplation stumbled across a troubled pool of uncertainty. I held Paul's attention on this area of unease. He stared into its murky depths trying to discern its source. Eventually he said, 'But I don't feel safe among Jews.'

'I thought it was the Jews who don't feel safe with Paul,' Maff muttered.

Safe seemed to be the key word. If our mission to Rome is to have any chance of success, Paul's safety is high priority. Michael's security force, waiting for us at every port from Corinth to Caesarea, had been a constant reminder of this.

I didn't rush to make suggestions. I waited, watching Paul's thoughts, until his mind turned towards the Imperial City.

'Do you still intend to go there?' I asked.

He focussed on his mental image of the capital of the Roman Empire and reaffirmed it as the goal of all his travels.

'We need to keep you safe,' I said. Paul accepted my advice, repeating it across the numerous layers of his consciousness. I waited. I waited until he confidently asserted to the Director, in his prayers, 'I need to keep myself safe.' Then declared, 'Antioch is safer than Jerusalem.'

Antioch – some months later

We are going to Rome! We are taking the message of Jesus into the very hub of the Roman Empire, and from there his story can spread throughout the world. Paul has firmly resolved that his next trip will take him all the way.

Here in Antioch Paul has rested. Much more importantly, he has prayed. He has developed the practice of almost constant conversation with the Director. 'Conversation' is the key: talking *and listening*. In the past, Paul has kept to the Jewish tradition of observing set times for prayer during the day. In those times he used to recite ancient Jewish hymns to himself as well as singing some of his new Christian ones – all good stuff but he rarely paused to consider what my Boss might be trying to *say* to him. Through his months of depression he learned to be quiet and in that quiet he has come to recognise the Director's voice as it flows from his spirit into his mind. In the depths of his loneliness, Paul found that he has a friend, someone who loves him, who cares for him, who is always with him. Someone who is not afraid to tell him when he is being stupid. And that friend is living in his own spirit – the Director.

I have to admit that when Paul made this discovery, my first reaction was to feel rejected. After all, I was the only one who could get through to Paul during the years when he failed to hear the Director. I was his constant companion, counsellor and confidant. I wanted to be his friend. However, as Paul has drawn closer to my Boss in friendship, I have been gathered into their relationship and have begun to see Paul – at least a little – as my Boss sees him. Aside from that, it has been a great joy for me to see the fog clearing from Paul's mind and watch him basking in the heat of his Heavenly Father's love.

From this position of renewed strength Paul has resolved that the time has come to take on Rome, with or without Emperor Claudius. He is currently preparing for the journey and saying final farewells to the Christians of Antioch. (And, if I didn't already have enough to celebrate, he has resolved to travel overland as much as possible. Maff is even more relieved about this than I am.)

Ephesus

Paul retraced his steps through Turkey, briefly visiting Derbe, Lystra, Iconium and Pisidian Antioch. At each town and city he sought out his Christian sisters and brothers, encouraged them in their discipleship and collected money to support my Boss's family in Jerusalem, where there is still a severe shortage of rain, which has plunged the people into poverty and hunger.

Leaving Pisidian Antioch, Paul kept his promise to return to Ephesus. He took the great western road that led him directly to this elegant and wealthy port.

In Ephesus Paul met up with the small group of Jewish disciples he encountered earlier in the year. The meeting took place in the modest home of Priscilla and Aquila, Paul's tentmaking friends from Corinth. It was a strange meeting, rather like walking into a room full of beautiful lights where most were not lit. These men and women had all heard about Jesus; they had all concluded he is indeed my Boss's Son; they had all decided to follow his example and teaching. However, with the exception of Priscilla and Aquila, the dazzling light of the Director's presence – which shines from all his human children – was entirely absent. Even Paul noticed.

'What's happened to them?' I asked the Director.

'Not enough,' he replied.

As soon as introductions were complete, Paul asked these strangely dull disciples, 'Didn't the Holy Spirit come to you when you started to follow Jesus?'

'The what?' they replied.

Maff tried to help out. 'Look over here, you dimwits,' he exclaimed, trying to draw their attention to Paul's incandescent spirit. 'The Creator of your Universe! The one who sustains you through every beat of your flabby little hearts. Your God!'

Thankfully, they were even more senseless to Maff's presence than to the Director.

Paul proceeded more gently than Maphrael. 'Aquila told me you all had a ceremonial dipping,' he said. 'Didn't God's Spirit come to you at the same time?'

'We were dipped,' one of the Ephesians replied, 'by Apollos. He was dipped by John the Dipper back home in Judea. He heard about Jesus years later, in Alexandria. When he came here, he told us that Jesus was the Messiah and he dipped us all in the River Cayster just like John had dipped him in the Jordan.'

Paul considered the situation carefully.

'Someone is about to get horribly wet,' Maff observed.

'Where's Apollos now?' Paul asked.

'He moved on to Corinth,' Aquila told him. 'We sent him off with a letter of recommendation to Gaius and Crispus. He preached wonderfully in the synagogue here, and I thought he might be useful there.'

Paul was simultaneously excited and worried by the news: excited because he trusted Aquila's judgement; worried by his memories of Sosthenes and the other thugs who run the synagogue in Corinth. I was worried, too.

'Do I infer,' I asked the Director, 'that one of these unlit lamps is attempting to illuminate the grimy darkness of Corinth?'

'Oriel,' he replied, 'a human does not need to get wet in order for me to set up home in their life.'

'Are you fully on board with this Apollos?' I asked, seeking assurance.

'That, my friend, is not your responsibility.'

The Director spoke directly to Paul. 'Paul, my son, let's give these friends a good dipping.'

Aquila led them down to the River Cayster where he submerged each of his fellow disciples in the cold water on Jesus' behalf. Paul stayed safely on the bank. 'I see Paul has more sense than to risk the water himself,' Maff commented.

'Shh!' The Director called for our attention.

The soggy disciples stood in a row in front of Paul, their old spirits washed away. Paul stepped forward to place his hands on the first disciple's head. As he did, the Director stepped across the threshold of the woman's life and her body began to shine with my Boss's light like an unshuttered house on a winter evening.

'Stunning!' Maff exclaimed.

The newly enlightened woman spoke. She said the first words that came into her mind, words the Director had just put there. Each in turn – there were twelve in all – did the same.

A new church is born.

Some months later

As usual, Paul started his work in Ephesus at the synagogue. As usual, before long he was thrown out. As usual, he didn't let this deter him. He rented a daily session in a nearby lecture hall to which Jews and Greeks from all over the province have travelled to hear him teach.

Ejection from the synagogue being such a regular feature of Paul's life, I didn't think to record it at the time, but on this occasion there have been rather interesting consequences.

The people of Ephesus are dominated by their religion. Their temple is four times the size of its counterpart in Athens and the local 'deity' is very much in attendance. The locals believe that they are honouring the goddess Artemis – a many-breasted mother figure, supposedly the guardian of nature. The object of their worship is, in fact, a former Angel – now senior Opposition spirit – called Jagogue. Jagogue's claim to the guardianship of nature is founded on the fact that before he rebelled against my Boss he helped with the development of hoofed mammals. Now he leads a large team of Opposition spirits who have successfully duped the Ephesians into dedicating vast sums of money to Artemis. With their money has flowed the devotion of their hearts. Such devotion inevitably leads to slavery when the Opposition are involved.

Paul and the Director, between them, have banished a great number of these corrupt spirits, thus liberating the minds and spirits of many individual humans. This rapid improvement in spiritual health has brought with it a significant rise in physical well-being. All of this together has diverted many Ephesian minds away from Artemis and towards Paul's message about Jesus.

Paul's success in dealing with the Opposition spirits was noticed by the official exorcists in the Jewish synagogue, causing them to modify their own techniques. The Jewish exorcists, all sons of Rabbi Sceva, took to saying, 'In the name of Jesus, who Paul preaches . . . '

Maff drew this development to my attention and we consulted Michael about the practice. I left Maff in charge of Paul while Michael and I followed these Jews to watch them at work.

Michael surveyed the city in amazement. 'This has been a rout,' he exclaimed. 'It would have taken me months of ugly warfare to do the same. Has Paul really done all this on his own?'

'With the Director,' I said.

'I don't fully understand the Director's part in all this,' Michael admitted.

'And with a little assistance from these clowns,' I continued, returning Michael's attention to two of Sceva's sons, who had been called out to a local home.

It was a simple enough case. Jews are very strict about not buying meat from the Greek market because almost all the animal carcasses there come from the temple of Artemis where the poor beasts have been killed in sacrificial rituals. Such sacrificial meat is generally cheaper and this young Jewish couple had been routinely buying it, washing out the blood and selling it on to their fellow Jews as 'kosher'. Two Opposition spirits had pounced on the opportunity provided by their deeply secret guilt and given them a violent sickness which, unlike normal human sickness, had continued for many weeks.

The couple confessed their crime to Sceva's sons, who repri-manded them severely, fined them heavily, and then turned to the matter of dealing with the two Opposition spirits.

Starting with the wife, one of the exorcist brothers said, 'In the name of Jesus, who Paul preaches, I command you: leave this woman!'

'Will it work?' I asked Michael in a whisper.

'It shouldn't,' he replied.

The spirit, already disheartened by the battering his colleagues had received at the hands of Paul, surrendered immediately. He turned and wandered away, leaving the woman immediately freed from her sickness.

The other brother then took on the spirit afflicting the woman's husband – a much tougher creature. He recited the same formula: 'In the name of Jesus, who Paul preaches, I command you: leave this man!'

The spirit laughed. 'Jesus I know all too well, and I've heard more than enough about Paul. But who do you think you are?'

Driven by the Opposition spirit, the sick man lunged forwards and grabbed his visitor. He overpowered the exorcist, jumped on him and beat him thoroughly, tearing at his clothes. Michael laughed heartily at the scene but I could not find any source of amusement.

'I've seen enough,' I said, and left. I was followed shortly by Sceva's two sons who ran home naked and bleeding.

News of this spread across the city like wind over long grass. Bowed by fear, both Jews and Greeks took fresh notice of Paul and his message. The name of Jesus became greatly honoured and the lecture hall was full beyond capacity every afternoon.

Paul embraced the opportunity. He warned the pagan Ephesians of the dangers they faced whenever they engaged with spiritual forces other than those loyal to Jesus. He organised a large public bonfire in which the people burned hundreds of books and articles used in magical and mystical practices. Michael attended the event with a small army of Angels who dragged away the Opposition spirits trying desperately to stop their humans from destroying such valuable tools of darkness and Death.

A few weeks on

Four days ago, Apollos returned from Corinth with bad news. The disciples there have split into opposing factions, some associating themselves, with Paul, some claiming to be followers of Apollos and others – especially the Jewish Christians – aligning their discipleship with Peter. While Paul interrogated Apollos about the details of his visit, I spoke to the Director. He was greatly pained by this squabble within his human family.

'I love them all,' he told me, 'but each one believes that I love them more than I love the others.'

Paul was distressed too; he was also angry at what he considered to be the stupidity of the Corinthians. He was inclined to travel to Corinth immediately and sort them all out, but he recently sent Timothy to Macedonia to announce that he would go there next.

'Go round the other way,' Maff suggested. 'Start with Corinth, then travel north and east to Macedonia.'

'No,' Paul replied. 'I will need to stay at Corinth for several months.'

Without warning, Maff leapt into the air, turned a complete somersault and shouted, 'He talked to me! He talked to me! Oriel, Paul actually talked to me.'

'Settle down, for Heaven's sake,' I told him. 'We have a serious problem here.'

Paul, the Director and I focussed our minds together, considering the possibilities before us. In his anger, Paul had wanted to go to Corinth and sort them out, human face to human face. I attempted to cool his fury while the Director infused loving concern in him, replacing his injured pride.

'Write them a letter,' I suggested.

'I wouldn't know what to write,' Paul claimed, stubbornly.

'Tell them they're supposed to be following Jesus,' I told him. 'They're not your disciples, or Apollos'.'

'Help them understand how I work in and through their worship and their lives,' added the Director.

Paul began to listen.

Between us, we compiled a long list of matters to be addressed in a letter. Just when we thought we had finished, Maff said, 'And tell them that if they can't be bothered to love each other they might just as well take up playing the drums instead.'

I glared at Maff, but the Director calmly told Paul, 'You may wish to rephrase that a little.'

Macedonia

Yet again we have been forced to make a hurried exit. Two weeks before Paul was due to leave Ephesus, Archangel Michael informed me that Lucifer had paid a visit to Jagogue at the temple of Artemis. Michael admitted that he was unable to tell me the reason for the visit but he stressed that we had to assume that it was no coincidence Lucifer was in the city at the same time as Paul. In response to this, I gave Maff the task of keeping a constant watch on Jagogue.

Several days later, Paul, the Director and I were deep in conversation when Maff charged into the room with, 'It's happening!'

We were in the middle of considering the latest news from Corinth and it took me a while to understand what Maff was talking about.

'The silversmiths are out on strike,' he informed me. 'And just about the whole city has stopped work in sympathy.'

'So?' I asked, unimpressed.

'They've kidnapped Gaius and Aristarchus,' Maff explained, 'and are threatening to kill them both if Paul doesn't surrender himself before midday.'

This didn't make a great deal of sense and it was only later that I fully understood the whole story. A silversmith called Demetrius ran a business selling souvenir models of the 'goddess' Artemis to the city's many tourists. The increasing success of Paul's preaching had caused a significant downturn in the souvenir business which threatened the manufacturing jobs. That morning Demetrius had gathered all the smiths together and firmly laid the blame for their reduced income at the feet of Paul. The smiths were furious to learn this and marched to the market square chanting the city's anthem, 'Great is Artemis of the Ephesians'.

Almost everyone in the market, sensing the excitement – though not knowing what it was about – joined in the chant and followed the silversmiths through the streets to the theatre. On the way, they spotted two of Paul's friends – Gaius, who was visiting from Corinth, and Aristarchus who had brought news from Thessalonica. The mob grabbed the two men and dragged them to the massive amphitheatre where Jagogue and his much depleted team of Opposition spirits were waiting. At the sound of the city anthem being sung in the theatre, more Ephesians gathered.

This news reached Paul when Priscilla, who had been showing Gaius and Aristarchus around the city, ran into the house. He immediately resolved to go and hand himself over to the mob – but Priscilla and Aquila begged him not to.

'God will protect me,' Paul told them.

'What you mean is *Maff and Oriel will try to protect me*,' Maff corrected him. 'That's quite another thing.'

When did anyone manage to change Paul's mind once it was set? Maff and the two tentmakers tried their hardest, without the slightest success.

When Paul put on his cloak and was unbolting the door, Maff appealed to me. 'Oriel, for our Boss's sake, do something. Why don't you knock him on the head again?'

'Maphrael, if Paul has chosen to go to the theatre, I shall go with him,' I stated.

Maff appealed to the Director. 'This is madness. There are thousands of angry people in that theatre. Paul will be mashed.'

There was a knock at the door. Priscilla smuggled Paul into a different room while her husband cautiously opened the door. It was a messenger with a note for Paul from three provincial officials who regularly attended his lectures. Their message strongly advised him to keep out of sight. Remarkably, he conceded to their advice and turned his attention to praying for the safety of Gaius and Aristarchus – an encouraging turn of events.

I settled down to the relative safety of Paul's prayer but the Director said to me, 'Oriel, you will have to go and sort this out. Maff can stay and look after Paul.'

'What should I do?' I asked.

'Prevent Michael from doing anything rash,' he said. 'There are 22,543 three people in that theatre. It would not be a good place for Michael to pick a fight with Jagogue.'

'I can handle Michael,' I replied, 'but what about the however-many-thousand Ephesians?'

'Most of them have no idea why they are there,' he told me. 'Leave them to Gregory.'

I glanced at Maff and mouthed, 'Who's Gregory?'

He couldn't help.

At the theatre, Michael and his special Angel squadron were lined up on the top tier of the huge semicircle of stone seats. The curved benches of the theatre were covered with a thick mist of self-obsessed Ephesians. On the stage below, I could see the bright forms of Paul's two friends, closely guarded by Jagogue's spirits. I gave Michael our Boss's instructions and then asked if he knew who Gregory was. He did not.

Far below us, the Jews in the mob – who had been largely sympathetic to Paul since the sons of Sceva affair – pushed their synagogue secretary, Alexander, forward to defend him. The capacity crowd were pleased with this opportunity to find out what the impromptu assembly was all about. However, as soon as they realised Alexander was a Jew, they resorted to their anthem. The entire crowd rose to their feet and sang together. They sang, without pause, for two Earth hours and all that they sang, again and again, was, 'Great is Artemis of the Ephesians!'

After two hours their enthusiasm lost its edge, but a rumour spread through the many levels of the auditorium that someone was threatening to destroy the temple of Artemis, and they were determined not to leave until something happened.

'I can arrange that *something* myself,' Michael muttered.

'You will stay right here where I can see you,' I replied.

A thin, bald man scurried into the middle of the stage area. The chanting stopped. 'People of Ephesus,' he called out, in a high, reedy voice, 'doesn't all the world know that the city of Ephesus is the guardian of the temple of the great Artemis?'

This prompted the packed audience to strike up their anthem all over again, but after two complete renditions the thin man held up his arms for silence and his request was granted.

'Who is that?' Michael asked me.

I descended to the theatre floor to take a closer look. 'He's the city clerk,' I told Michael when I returned. 'His name is Gregory.'

'If Demetrius and his fellow craftsmen have a complaint against anybody,' Gregory continued, 'the courts are open. They can press charges.'

'He doesn't look like a Christian,' Michael observed while Gregory allowed the crowd to murmur their agreement.

'He isn't,' I said.

'So how does the Director know about him?'

I looked sharply at my Archangel colleague. 'That, Michael, is a very stupid question.'

'You're right,' he agreed, 'I'm sorry.'

Below us Gregory continued to reprimand his fellow citizens. 'We are in danger of being charged with rioting, and if that happens we would have no defence because this commotion is utterly pointless.'

Gregory dismissed the vast crowd and personally delivered Gaius and Aristarchus to Aquila's home along with an apology to Paul on behalf of the whole city.

Paul set sail the next day.

Corinth – three months later

Paul passed through Macedonia quickly, briefly visiting the churches there but eager to get to Corinth before winter. Aristarchus travelled with us as far as his home town, Thessalonica. Gaius, being Corinthian, travelled with Paul all the way to Achaia and invited him to stay at his home, next door to the synagogue. Michael and his security force also accompanied us. Michael is predictably grumpy about Paul staying quite so close to the headquarters of his human opponents.

After we arrived in Corinth, news came from Rome that Emperor Claudius had died and been replaced by Nero. It had been Claudius' prejudicial reign that prevented Paul from sailing to Rome last time he was here but, despite this encouraging news, his thoughts were divided. Ever since the synagogue leaders in Ephesus spoke up in his support, Paul has longed for one more chance to announce the Messiahship of Jesus in Jerusalem. At every stop on this journey he has collected money for the Christian community in that city. He is now inclined to deliver the gift himself.

Nonetheless, the news of Claudius' death makes the prospect of a mission in Rome more viable. Maff has repeatedly urged me to intervene and coerce Paul onto a Romebound boat. I have refused. Paul's desire to preach once more in Jerusalem is rooted and grounded in his love for the Jewish nation. His love for the Jews is rooted and grounded in his love for my Boss. I cannot resist such a motive. Instead, I helped Paul to write a long letter to the Christians in Rome. Most of his letters have been fired off at great speed. This one was quite different. He was writing to people he does not know and he composed his letter with great care.

'I want you to know,' he told my Boss's children in the empire's capital, 'that I planned many times to visit you but until now have been prevented. I wish to have a harvest among you, just as I have had among the other Gentiles. That is why I'm so eager to preach the good news to you who are in Rome.'

Throughout the letter Paul wrote about his Jewish faith and explained how it had been fulfilled, not replaced, by the coming of Jesus. As he pondered these themes, his desire to return to Jerusalem grew stronger. At the end of the letter he informed his Roman readers that they would be next on his itinerary, once he had delivered his collection to Judea. He then added a request that made me suddenly alert.

'I urge you, brothers and sisters,' he asked Tertius to write, 'pray that I may be rescued from the unbelievers in Judea.'

I had assumed he was going to Jerusalem in hope of a positive response from the Jews there. It would be crazy for him to risk such a visit otherwise.

'Have you told Paul something you've not told me?' I asked the Director.

Philippi

His letter to Rome completed and sent, Paul booked himself a berth on a boat bound for Syria. On the planned departure day I sent Maff ahead to check out the ship's crew for potential dangers – aside, of course, from the obvious dangers of sea travel. Maff had barely left Gaius' house when he returned. I could tell from his whole demeanour that something was seriously wrong.

'What do you want first,' he asked, 'the human problem or the spiritual one?'

'Are they different?'

'Not very,' he answered.

'Start with the spirits,' I suggested.

'Lucifer has put a line of Opposition spirits right across the mouth of the harbour.'

'On the water?'

'Yes.'

This was frightening news. I've seen Lucifer use that tactic before. He was planning to sink Paul's ship.

'What's the human problem?' I asked.

'The synagogue thugs have paid off the ship's captain, making him refuse passage to Paul.'

'Why?'

'To prevent him spreading his *poison* in their holy city.'

I arranged for this last part of the news to reach Paul quickly, and we ended up travelling overland instead, much to our relief and Paul's annoyance.

My Boss loves to bring consolation out of inconvenience. During this unscheduled detour, Paul more than doubled his collection for his hungry brothers and sisters in Judea and also acquired a large group of travelling companions to introduce to the family in Jerusalem. Among them are young Timothy and Aristarchus from Thessalonica, and – particularly pleasing to Paul – Luke.

Troas

Doctor Luke was so concerned when he heard of the plot against Paul in the harbour at Cenchraea that he insisted on chartering a private boat to carry the party safely round the Aegean coast. As this small craft has no sleeping accommodation, our plan is to hop from port to port and, thankfully, spend each night on solid land. Maff asked if he could be excused the boat travel altogether and follow us from the shore but, remembering the Opposition's plot at Cenchraea, I insisted he stay with me.

I am glad I did.

When the boat's skipper cut the corner between Macedonia and Turkey and we were at the furthest point from land, the Opposition descended on us. It was the same band of spirits that had cordoned off Cenchraea harbour. They stirred up a storm and rocked the small ship from side to side and end to end, trying to tip it over. While the skipper yelled instructions to his human crew, getting them to prepare the boat for a battering, I marshalled Maff and the ten Angel guardians, directing them to prise the Opposition spirits off the woodwork and throw them as far as possible across the sea.

It was a frantic struggle. In the middle of it all, Archangel Raphael appeared, keeping himself at a safe distance above the furious waves.

'Where in all Heaven is Michael?' I asked him angrily.

'Our Boss asked me to tell you that if you keep up what you're doing now,' he said in his calm way, 'you will be absolutely fine.'

'And if we don't keep it up?' Maff asked, at the same time spinning yet another Opposition spirit out over the violent water.

'You'll sink,' Raphael said.

That was incentive enough. When the last Opposition spirit had been repelled, I turned my attention to Paul. The Director had given him a similar message and he urged his companions to trust God and do whatever the skipper told them.

That evening the boat limped into Troas harbour, requiring a week of repairs before it can continue. Paul has been restless all week. His sights are firmly set on Jerusalem and he is impatient with every delay. Each day he visited the boatyard, urging the shipwrights to hurry.

Yesterday evening, being the first day of the week, he gathered the small community of disciples in Troas. Together they shared bread and wine to remember Jesus' gruesome death in Jerusalem 22 years earlier and, as happens every time my Boss's family join in this unique meal, the Son's life shone from the symbolic food and brightened the lives of his children who ate it. I have seen this happen hundreds of times in my travels with Paul and it still excites me.

While Paul himself was chewing his portion of the life-enhancing bread, the Director spoke to him, 'This is *your* last supper, Paul. You must prepare these disciples for your departure, just as I prepared mine.'

Paul followed Jesus' example and took the opportunity to teach his spiritual siblings. He talked and talked. One by one, the children present curled up in their parents' laps and went to sleep. Afternoon turned to evening, and still Paul taught on. Lamps were lit around the room. Paul continued to unfold the joys and demands of a disciple's life. By this time many adults were struggling to stay awake.

'It shows how he's improved,' Maff said to me, pointing out that one young man had fallen soundly asleep on the window ledge. 'A few years back he was putting them to sleep in a matter of minutes.'

'That's not exactly true,' I corrected my colleague. 'A few years back he managed to start a riot within a matter of minutes.'

Maff and I continued to chat while Paul continued to teach. Our attention was grappled back to events in the room when a great gasp went up from all the humans still awake.

'What's happened?' I asked Maff.

He laughed. 'Young Eutychus has just fallen out the window.'

It wasn't funny. We were in an upstairs room. I raced down to the ground to find the Son was already helping Eutychus' lively spirit emerge from his shattered body.

Maff joined me. 'Bored stiff!' he commented.

I glared at him and turned to my Master. 'Does Eutychus' story have to end so soon?' I asked.

'It doesn't end at all,' he corrected me. 'I have come to take him home.'

'But his parents,' I pleaded. 'They will be distraught – goodness knows who will be blamed – and for what? Can't you put him back together again?'

'That's up to Paul,' the Son replied.

'Get Paul,' I ordered Maff.

Paul hurried down the stairs to the street where Eutychus had fallen, along with the lad's family. Paul threw himself onto the crumpled corpse.

'In the name of Jesus,' he prayed deep in his spirit, 'come back.'

The Son was holding the hand of the dead boy's spirit. 'Do you want to go back?' he asked. 'Or would you rather come with me?'

The young man looked at the pain-engraved faces of his parents and sisters. 'I'll go back for now, please, Sir.'

While the Son helped Eutychus' spirit back into his body, the Director fused broken bones and torn nerves.

Paul sensed the life return and announced to those around him, 'Don't worry, he's fine.'

The assembly returned to their meeting room and Paul to his sermon. He talked until Earth's sun rose, its light smothering the feeble flames of the oil lamps. Eutychus stayed wide awake throughout.

Patara

Luke's ship sailed out of Troas that day – but Paul wasn't aboard. I persuaded him to walk across the narrow headland to Assos while the boat sailed round the coast. I did not want to risk a backlash from the Opposition spirits we had defeated the previous week. Much to Maff's annoyance, I insisted that he travel with the others in the boat, just in case there was another attempt to sink it.

While Paul walked alone, the Director used the opportunity to talk with him about his future. This was a deep and private conversation, most of which took place at the level of Paul's emotions – a language in which I am far from fluent. Paul spoke to the Director in low groans and profound longings. It was the Director who gave substance to these formless intercessions. I could only pick up the general theme – that trouble and opposition awaits Paul wherever he goes. At first it did not seem to me that this would be much different from our experience of recent years, but gradually I realised that the scale and significance of our struggle would be greatly intensified.

At Assos Paul rejoined his companions. They hopped from mainland to island to island to mainland, southwards down the coast of Turkey. Late yesterday evening, Paul persuaded the reluctant skipper to sail on in the darkness, straight past Ephesus, and moor up instead at the next harbour, Miletus. Paul – wisely – did not wish to risk the fury of the Ephesians. This morning he sent a message to the city asking Aquila, Priscilla and the other leaders of the Ephesian disciples to meet him at Miletus.

They sat on the harbourside. Paul's contribution to the discussion was passionate and urgent. 'I'm going to Jerusalem,' he informed them. 'I don't know what will happen to me there. All I know is this: prison and hardship wait for me in every city.'

These things have been true since his first visit to Pisidian Antioch ten years ago, but there is a notable difference in Paul's attitude. These traumas, to his mind, are now no longer obstacles he has to climb over in order to fulfil his call. He sees them as an integral part of his mission. He is resolved to follow in the very footsteps of his master Jesus. He has chosen to continue, in his own body, the gracious sufferings of the Son.

I gained uncomfortable insight into the detail of Paul's long conversation with the Director on the walk from Troas to Assos when he said to the Ephesian leaders, 'None of you will ever see me again.'

This caused the blood to drain from the faces of his listeners – if Angels had blood mine would have turned to ice. My itinerary was still destined for Rome, yet we were travelling in precisely the opposite direction. I had encouraged Paul to take this dangerous detour but I had no idea we were coming to the end of our road.

Paul's friends had heard enough; they begged him not to leave, literally holding on to him as he tried to make his way back to the boat. While Priscilla boldly clung to Paul's arm, forcing him to drag her along the quay, I spoke urgently to the Director.

'What have you been telling him,' I asked, anxiously.

'The truth.'

'I need to know this truth,' I said. 'How can I look after him if I can't see what's waiting round the corner of the next day? Should I slip out of time and look at what lies ahead for Paul?'

'You must not,' the Director said, sternly.

'How can I do my job if I don't?' I insisted.

'How can you do your job if you do?' he replied.

This tied my mind in a knot.

The Director addressed me, slightly less firmly. 'Oriel, you are responsible for all my Angel guardians, you know it is unwise and unsafe for them to look into the future of their charges, just as it is for the humans themselves. Humans are not able to handle such knowledge. Your task, my friend, is to travel with Paul, across time as much as across the sea. You may not put his future at risk by knowing it.'

Paul managed to prise Priscilla off his arm and clambered into the boat, leaving a group of distressed disciples on the harbourside.

'Can you answer me this one question?' I asked the Director, desperate for some guidance. 'Is it still my task to deliver Paul safely to Rome?'

'It is still your task,' he replied carefully, 'to deliver Paul to Rome.'

I noted that he had omitted one word.

We continued along the coast to Patara on the south west corner of Turkey. There the skipper put his precious cargo ashore and Luke and Timothy searched for a ship that was travelling east.

Caesarea

We boarded a large boat sailing directly to Tyre on the Phoenician coast. The weather was good and there was no sight of the Opposition. Throughout the trip Paul's mind was set resolutely on his plan to visit Jerusalem. As I watched and listened to his many hours conversation with the Director I gradually realised that though the Director is preparing him for further sufferings, the specific resolve to reach Jerusalem is Paul's. I discussed this with the Director one night when Paul was sleeping.

'Is it necessary for Paul to go to Jerusalem?' I asked.

'No.'

'Is it wise for Paul to go to Jerusalem?' I continued my enquiry.

'No.'

I understood that these blunt replies were intended to protect me from my own longing to know Paul's future. I also understood that I needed to limit my enquiry to matters to Paul's benefit rather than in my own interest.

I thought hard. Struggling with the limitations of my own mind, I realised what a wonderful gift Paul has, having my Boss – the Director – living in his spirit, inspiring and guiding him at every level of his being. Such intimacy with our Boss is not granted to Angels.

Eventually a question formed in the complex pathways of my mind. I tested it, shaped it and, when I was sure it was indeed the question I most needed a clear answer to, I asked it.

'If I tried to persuade Paul not to travel to Jerusalem, would I have your support?'

I would have loved to have been able to see my Boss's face, to read the subtle nuances of his expression, to sense the profound love that I always see in his eyes, but these things were not there for me to enjoy. I could only listen to his words rising unhindered from Paul's spirit. My Boss's voice, firmer and steadier than anything in all his creations, said:

'You may dissuade Paul, if you choose to.'

It was with a clear resolve that I landed, first at Tyre, then at Ptolemais and finally at Caesarea. I had briefed Maff as fully as possible about the task before us. We must keep Paul away from Jerusalem.

At Tyre, Paul spent a week with a family of disciples. Maff and I tried everything we could think of to persuade the disciples to persuade Paul that it was not safe for him to travel to Jerusalem.

'It was not safe for Jesus to go to the Garden of Gethsemene,' Paul reminded himself, 'but he still went.'

There were other disciples in the town. We tried them all. Paul would not be diverted from his path.

He spent only one night in Ptolemais. We had no joy there.

Here in Caesarea, Paul was greeted and welcomed by a disciple who had spent many weeks in the company of Jesus, during the Son's human lifetime. I realised that here was a man open to the Director's guidance. Even better, Philip has four daughters – all renowned for their ability to hear the Director's voice clearly, an ability Paul has almost completely lost at present. They heard me, loud and clear, but Paul could not hear them above the uncompromising voice of his own intentions. I also percieved in Paul a reticence about accepting the advice of four young women.

'We need a male prophet,' Maff informed me after Paul stamped out of the room. 'I'll go and get one.'

Some days later Maff returned, bringing a man called Agabus he had found in Jerusalem. Agabus came with the recommendation of the Christian leaders in the city. He is remarkably open to the Director's voice. He walked straight up to Paul as soon as he had dismounted from his horse. He grabbed Paul's belt, unfastened it, tied up his own hands and feet – all this without saying a single word – and finally announced to Paul, 'This is what the Spirit of God says to you, *This is how the Jews in Jerusalem will treat you. They will tie you hand and foot and hand you over to the authorities.*'

Maff and I stirred up all the Angels in the room, urging each to stir up their humans to plead with Paul not to go to Jerusalem.

'Why are you breaking my heart?' Paul asked the gathered disciples. 'I am not only ready to be bound, I am ready to die in Jerusalem.'

Maff couldn't contain himself. 'Oh no, you don't!' he boomed above the distress of everyone else present.

Luke attempted to settle the emotional turmoil. He called for everyone's attention and said, 'Let the Lord's will be done.'

At that, I could not contain myself. 'But it isn't *the Lord's will!*' I screamed.

I don't think any of them actually heard me, but all those in tune with their spirits felt my despair. There's nothing else I can do. As I have promised, so I will do. I will go to Jerusalem with Paul. Some of his companions are going too, though not all.

Luke, I am pleased to note, is coming with us. He, I think, is the only human who might have a chance of changing Paul's mind.

Jerusalem

Our journey to Jerusalem had the feel of a small army marching to certain defeat. On our final day Archangel Michael came out of the city to meet me. He was as grim-faced as I have ever seen him.

'The leader of the Opposition arrived here the day you reached Troas,' the chief of Heaven's security forces informed me. 'He brought with him the same band that's been dogging you from synagogue to synagogue since your first visit to Pisidian Antioch.'

I said nothing.

'Why don't you stop him?' Michael asked, crossly.

'I have tried,' I told him.

'You have tried to persuade him,' Michael corrected me. 'I said, *Why don't you stop him?*'

I looked at my colleague, amazed at his suggestion. 'What do you want me to do? Break his legs? Kill his horse? Whisk him away to some obscure island where boats have not been invented?'

'Any one of those would be preferable to marching straight into a large pan filled to the brim with simmering racial hatred.'

'Paul has chosen this road. Where he goes, I go.'

We continued to follow Paul in morose silence. 'What I need,' I said to Michael at length, 'is your help, not complaints.'

'Oriel, I do believe you're becoming as stubborn as this human,' he replied. 'I can protect you from direct attack by the Opposition. There are not many of them and I don't believe they are planning anything so simple. My main cause for concern is a group of extremist Jewish nationalists. Lucifer has lured them into advocating the total purity of the Jewish community. He has also helped them to identify Paul as the archetype of everything they fear and despise. They plan to kill him.'

'What are you doing about these people?' I asked.

'Nothing,' Michael replied. 'To use your own words: they have chosen their road. Angels fight Angels, humans fight humans. It's up to Paul. If you won't stop him, all you can do is help the fool.'

We arrived in Jerusalem late in the afternoon. Early the next morning Paul visited James and the other leaders of the church there. They shared stories about the massive growth of Jewish churches in Jerusalem and non-Jewish ones around the Roman Empire. Twice while the humans talked Michael visited me with up-to-date briefings about Paul's opponents. I urged James to inform Paul similarly, as fully as he was able.

James, we discovered, already has a plan to defuse the criticism of the nationalists.

'I suggest you undergo a full purification ritual,' he said to Paul. 'There are four other brothers here who have just arrived from Greece; they begin their purification tomorrow. I advise you to join them, and, as an extra declaration of your Jewishness, it would be helpful if you paid for them as well.'

Paul agreed. I was encouraged by this positive solution to our problem and congratulated Sharriel, James' studious Angel. Maff was less optimistic.

When I informed Michael on his next visit, he shrugged and mumbled, 'It's worth a try.'

The following morning when Paul and his fellow candidates for purification walked to the Temple to book in for the seven day ritual, Michael had their route lined with fully armed Angels. Everything went smoothly. Money was paid by Paul, forms were filled in and heads were shaved. The five men returned safely to their lodgings to fast and pray.

The days have passed easily for Paul. He is practised at surviving with little or no food, and is pleased to have opportunity to pray and consider the Jewish scriptures. His prayers now rarely surface into the inarticulate air of human language. They are an elegant duet between his spirit and the Director, played on the threefold instruments of love, faith and bright hope. At least twice a day Michael calls by to brief me about the activities of the Opposition and the fervent nationalists. Maff spends his time touring the city looking for what he calls *contingencies*.

The Roman Army barracks

Today, the sixth day of Paul's fast, he suddenly decided to go to the Temple for midday prayers. Paul has relaxed considerably during his enforced rest and seems to have forgotten the imminent dangers waiting for him in the city. I tried hard to dissuade him. Maff told him bluntly that he was being stupid. We called Michael.

'There are two options,' Michael said, after we had explained the situation. 'Either we commission a full scale security operation, in which case Lucifer will know immediately that Paul has broken cover; or the two of you go on your own and hope that the Opposition don't notice.'

'Does Lucifer still use the Temple as his headquarters?' I asked my colleague.

'No. He took a dislike to it once our Boss's new children started worshipping there.'

'You choose,' I told Michael.

'The two of you go. I will keep a close watch on Lucifer.'

Paul walked through the streets of Jerusalem alone – humanly speaking. I stayed above him to maintain a good vantage point and Maff travelled ahead, looking out for potential danger. We reached the Temple without incident. Paul basked in the familiar words of Temple worship he had not enjoyed for many years. As he relaxed, so did I. Perhaps if I had been more cautious, I would have spotted the danger three rows behind him. I will never know.

Two thirds of the way through the service, I was startled by a voice shouting above the rabbi, 'Fellow Israelites, help me!'

I turned to see Ben-Judah, the Iconian Jew who attempted to stone Paul to death outside Lystra.

'This is the man,' Ben-Judah informed the suddenly attentive congregation, 'who teaches people everywhere against our nation and our law.' There was a murmur of sympathy. 'He's a friend of Greeks,' the Iconian continued. 'He brought some of them into our holy city. He has probably even brought them into this Temple.'

That was enough. Ben-Judah lit the fuse which Lucifer and the nationalists had so carefully laid. Ben-Judah had barely finished speaking when Michael hurtled into the Temple. 'The flare has gone up,' he told me. 'Lucifer and his mob are on their way. Their human henchmen are with them.'

What had been a tranquil corner of the Temple's inner court was suddenly as busy as a wasps' nest. It didn't take the Opposition long to prick the insecurities of the Jewish people. I looked for an escape route for Paul, but there was none; Lucifer had every exit covered with nationalist Jews who rated Paul as Jerusalem's most wanted man.

Ben-Judah was the first to turn fear into physical violence. He lunged forward through the crowd and grabbed Paul by the shoulders, pulling him to the ground. Another man leapt into the fray and pulled Ben-Judah off his quarry. Considering this man as a potential ally, I quickly commissioned his Angel to help me.

'Try to get your human to smuggle my human out to safety,' I urged him.

'You're hopeful,' the Angel replied dismally.

The man in question stood up and took command of the situation. 'Men of Israel,' he called out, 'it's not right that we should kill this man here in the Temple.' The hubbub was momentarily subdued.

'You should have more faith in your human,' I told the sullen Angel beside me.

Then the man shouted, 'We should do it outside!'

There was a great roar of approval from the mob. They closed in on Paul and pushed, shoved and dragged him through the Temple gates, across the Court of the Gentiles, and out into the city. When they had manhandled him into the street, the gates of the Temple were symbolically crashed together to shut Paul out.

They took him no further. There on the street those closest to Paul started to punch and kick him, pushing him to the ground and stamping on him. I did my best to hold them back but with limited effect. I called for Maff to help me, but he had gone. I knew he would not have simply abandoned me, I only hoped that whatever contingency he was pursuing could be employed quickly. Paul was already bleeding heavily. He would be dead within minutes.

I was just about to reveal myself in dazzling Heavenly light to the murderous rabble, when Maff surged through the crowd, bringing in his wake a detachment of Roman soldiers. Paul's attackers quickly stopped when they heard the rattle of armour and swords approaching. They had no desire to get hurt. The Roman commander saw Paul groaning on the floor, covered in blood and dust, and ordered him to be arrested and securely chained. The commander then asked those standing nearest to Paul what he had done wrong. Everyone within hearing distance had an answer to this question and they all shouted at once. The commander realised he was getting nowhere and ordered Paul taken into custody for questioning. Off they marched. The crowd followed, growing as it went. Before the soldiers had reached their barracks, they resorted to carrying

Paul on their shoulders to prevent him from being crushed. All the while, the rabble were shouting, 'Kill him! kill him! kill him!'

At the top of the barracks steps, the Commander ordered his men to put Paul down. Paul found himself face to face with the Roman officer.

'May I speak to these people?' asked Paul, using the language of the Roman Empire.

'Who are you?' the official responded.

'I am a Jew from Tarsus,' Paul explained.

'I thought you were the Egyptian terrorist we chased across the desert last winter,' the soldier said.

'I'm not,' Paul assured him with a bloody smile. 'Please may I speak to my people?'

With the permission of his captor, Paul turned to face the agitated crowd and addressed them in the Jewish language. He raised his arms to gain their attention.

'Brothers,' he called out, 'listen to my defence.'

Remarkably, the people went quiet.

There was no time to prepare Paul for this speech; it was a contingency that neither Maff nor I had anticipated. Knowing how defensive the Jews get when Paul questions their beliefs, I said quickly, 'Tell them a story, Paul.'

He heard. 'What story?' he asked in a brief moment of prayer.

A different voice replied. It was the Director. 'Tell them *your own story*, Paul.'

He did, and the people listened. They listened as he reminded them how he had personally persecuted the disciples of Jesus. They listened as he told about his meeting with the Son in Damascus. They listened as he told them of his earlier trip to Jerusalem. But they stopped listening as soon as he mentioned his mission to non-Jewish people. The exclusively Jewish rabble immediately renewed their demand for Paul's death.

'Rid the earth of him!' they shouted. 'He's not fit to live!'

The Roman commander had heard all he cared to hear. He ordered his troops to take Paul inside. Once the armoured door to the barracks was firmly locked behind them, he instructed his centurion to give Paul a flogging and find out what he had done to upset so many people.

Paul's outer clothes were removed and he was secured to a stone pillar in the middle of the guard room. I have witnessed a full Roman flogging before; it is a gruesome spectacle. Maff joined me.

'Was this your idea?' I asked him angrily.

His reply was bright and confident. 'What do you think of it?'

'Maphrael,' I exclaimed, 'you have delivered Paul into the hands of a pagan army!'

'It's the safest place for him.'

'How do you work that out?'

The whip for Paul's flogging had been fetched.

'Think about it, Oriel,' Maff replied. 'Lucifer is after Paul, but Michael won't let him get anywhere near. That's why Lucifer has set the Jewish nationalists against Paul, but they won't get anywhere near him. The Romans will defend Paul with their lives when they discover he's a Roman citizen.'

'And how do they find that out?'

'Paul will tell them.'

Maff's plan was a bit complicated for my comfort.

'Have you instructed Paul to tell them he's a Roman citizen?' I asked.

'No need,' Maff replied. 'Watch.'

The flogging whip was passed to a mean-spirited specimen of the human species and a centurion gave orders for Paul's interrogation to begin.

Paul turned his head to face the man. 'Is it now legal to flog a Roman citizen before you try him and find him guilty?'

The centurion went rigid with shock. 'Are *you* a citizen?' he asked, incredulous that this battered, road-worn Jew could possess one of the highest honours of Rome's proud empire.

'I am,' Paul replied.

'Unchain him,' the centurion commanded urgently. 'I'll go and tell the guv'nor.'

'You see, Oriel?' Maff said, with a dangerously self-satisfied smile. 'Paul is quite safe.'

Next day

The Roman commander apologised to Paul numerous times and arranged for him to sleep in the guard room rather than a prison cell. This morning Lysias, the commander, ordered the Jewish council to convene a special meeting and formally present their case against Paul. Paul was taken to the council chamber under full ceremonial Roman escort, which did nothing to endorse his Jewish credentials among the nationalists.

I began to advise Paul how to manage the situation but he said, half to me and half to himself, 'I know how to handle this lot.'

After introductory formalities, Paul was invited to state his defence.

'My brothers,' he began confidently, with the characteristic sweeping movement of his arm. I perceived a trace of the arrogance that so dominated his personality when he was younger. 'I am a Pharisee and the son of a Pharisee.'

I turned to Maff. 'Why do I feel suddenly uncomfortable about this?'

'He's trying to divide the council,' Maff replied.

Paul paused to give the Pharisees in the Sanhedrin time to realign their prejudices in his favour. Then, 'Brothers,' he continued, 'I am on trial here because I believe there is another life beyond this life.'

The Pharisees all nodded with sympathetic agreement. The Sadducees in the council shook their heads in annoyance.

One of the leading Pharisees stood up. 'We find nothing wrong with this man,' he announced.

'Apart from being deluded,' a Sadducee muttered.

The Pharisee replied. 'Perhaps an Angel has spoken to him.'

'Perhaps you're deluded too,' the other responded.

In a moment, almost everyone was shouting. If Paul intended to divide the council, he certainly succeeded. His old talent for disrupting Jewish gatherings had returned in style. Never before has he caused so much chaos among so many people by saying so little.

Lysias had seen enough. He instructed his troops to rescue Paul from the floor of the council chamber and marched him swiftly back to the barracks.

In the relative safety of the guard room, Paul was rather pleased with himself. I was not. As far as I could understand the situation, we were stuck.

Earlier tonight, after the soldiers had retired to their beds leaving Paul alone in the guard room, I considered the possibilities of another dramatic jail break along the lines of the one carried out by Michael in Philippi. While I was busy calculating how many Angels it would take to shake a building of this size, the Son walked calmly into the Roman barracks.

'You don't want to do that, Oriel,' he said calmly.

'It worked last time.'

'You should remember, my friend,' he said gently, 'that I am not in the practice of doing the same thing twice.'

'I must admit,' I informed him, 'that I did not have much enthusiasm for the idea.'

'That is because I was not behind it.'

As I pondered his reply, an unexpected thought leapt to the fore of my mind. 'Have I been experiencing a human emotion?' I asked.

'You have been learning from Paul,' he told me.

'Can Angels learn from humans?' I enquired, rather surprised by the idea.

'I am human,' the Son announced. 'And now, if you will excuse me, I have a message for my brother, Paul.'

The Son walked across the guard room, looking more human, to my eyes, with every step he took. He stopped in front of Paul, who was sitting on his makeshift bed deep in conversation with the Director. He had not noticed Jesus' arrival. Jesus coughed gently and Paul opened his eyes, recognising his visitor immediately.

'You've done well, Paul,' the Son said. 'And I promise you that, just as you have spoken out for me here in Jerusalem, you will speak out for me in Rome.'

Paul savoured the experience of seeing his Heavenly Master. He didn't say a word. The Son smiled, repeated, 'You have done very well,' and left.

I followed, anxious to know how Paul might get to Rome. 'Do you know something I don't know?' I asked.

He just smiled.

Stupid question.

The Roman fort at Antipatris – the next night

Early this morning, Paul had another visitor – his nephew, Reuben. The young man had overheard a group of nationalists plotting at an inn, vowing to one another that they would neither eat nor drink until they had killed Paul. The lad told his uncle how he had followed the men through Jerusalem and slipped in among them when they stopped to gather more recruits for their mission. Reuben explained how he had gone with the men to the Temple. There they had asked the high priest to call Paul for a second council hearing so they could ambush and kill him on his way there.

Paul sent his nephew to Lysias with this information. While we waited, Michael charged into the guardroom.

'There's a plot to ambush Paul on his way to the council today,' he told us.

'We know,' Maff informed him.

I directed Michael's attention to the next room, where young Reuben was telling his story to the commander.

'What are you doing about it?' Michael asked urgently.

'Waiting,' I said calmly.

Michael was unimpressed.

I explained. 'Maff has subcontracted Paul's protection to the Roman army. We're waiting for them to respond to the news.'

Michael looked anxiously from Maff to me and back. He clearly hoped what I had just told him was not true, but Maff smiled and I nodded.

'What do you expect me to do?' he asked.

'What you are supposed to do,' I replied steadily. 'Keep Lucifer at bay while the Romans protect Paul from the Jews.'

Michael said nothing.

Lysias' response was swift and decisive. He wrote a letter to the Roman governor in Caesarea and sent Paul there with a squadron of 200 foot soldiers, 70 horsemen and a further 200 spearmen. Paul himself was supplied with two horses so that he could travel with a minimum of delay.

Maff was not able to resist a little gloat. 'That should keep him safe, Michael. Don't you think?'

We waited until it was dark and travelled through the night to this isolated mountain fortress. As soon as the soldiers have finished breakfast, the cavalry will continue to Caesarea with Paul, and the rest will return to Jerusalem. Thanks to Maff, we have escaped from the trap laid by the Jewish nationalists, but I have no idea how I am going to get Paul from a Roman jail in Caesarea to the city of Rome itself.

Caesarea

As Roman jails go – I'm no expert but have seen a few on these travels – Paul must be in one of the most luxurious. Governor Felix read Lysias' letter and ordered that Paul be kept under guard in his own palace, a very grand building with a panoramic view of the harbour.

Felix sent for Paul's Jewish accusers, who arrived promptly, accompanied by a Roman lawyer, Tertullus. Tertullus had prepared his case well. He boiled down the murderous venom of the Temple mob to one single accusation. 'We have found this man to be a troublemaker,' he told Felix on the priests' behalf. 'He has stirred up riots among Jews all over the world.' (That much I could not deny myself, were I called to give evidence against Paul.) The Jewish leaders were quick to agree.

Paul was invited to defend himself. He explained the reasons for his visit to Jerusalem, asserting he had done nothing to cause a disturbance in the Temple. He then turned to more important matters. He claimed that the main reason the Jews opposed him was because of his firm belief in a Heavenly life after human Death. Felix was familiar with the beliefs of Jesus' disciples and had no desire to be drawn into a religious squabble. He dismissed the Jewish leaders, telling them he would decide Paul's case when Commander Lysias next visited Caesarea.

Since then Paul has been kept under minimal guard in the palace. Philip and his daughters have visited daily, bringing food and news. Today's news was that Luke is travelling up from Jerusalem to join Paul. There is, however, no news as to when Lysias might visit the town.

Nazareth – two years on

Lysias has visited Caesarea several times, but Felix has never seriously considered reopening Paul's trial. The governor's wife Drusilla is a Jew and has become something of a fan of Paul. She often invites him to dine with her and her husband. Governor Felix has encouraged these meetings because he hopes Paul might offer a bribe for his freedom. Felix doesn't know Paul very well.

Paul is enjoying the most relaxed period of all my years with him. He knows he is safe from attack by Jewish extremists and is confident in the Son's promise that he will indeed reach Rome. He has written several letters to the numerous Christian families he founded. He spends much of his time in deep conversation with the Director, holding his many spiritual children up to his Heavenly Father's boundless love. One continuing frustration has been his eyesight, which is now very poor indeed.

Luke visits daily and reads to Paul from the Jewish scriptures. He has been a greatly faithful companion. He works during the day, sharing his income with Paul, and joins him each evening. Luke has lodged at the home of Philip, where he has feasted on his host's many stories about life with Jesus.

One evening Luke said to Paul, 'Do you remember me saying you need an orderly account of Jesus' life to leave behind in the new churches? I have decided to write it myself, using all the stories that Philip has told me.'

The memory of Paul assassinating John Mark's book flashed into my consciousness. I wondered how Paul would react to Luke's plan. I watched anxiously as the same memory floated into Paul's mind. He spoke quietly to the Director, saying, 'I'm sorry about the way I treated Mark. I overreacted.'

'What are you going to do about it?' the Director asked him.

'I'll write to him and ask him to visit me in Rome, when I get there,' he replied.

Paul then looked at Luke through his sick eyes and said, 'John Mark has been writing an account of Jesus' life. You might find it useful. I'll ask him to join us when we get to Rome.'

I entered the conversation. 'Perhaps I could take Luke on a tour of Galilee and Jerusalem,' I suggested. 'I could introduce him to some of the people who met Jesus.'

The Director approved of the idea and Paul followed suit. He was sad to lose his good friend and doctor but was comforted by the thought that it would deepen Luke's understanding of the Son's human life. I asked Maff to look after Paul for me.

So that's what has brought me to Nazareth – the Son's home for most of his earthly life. I took Luke to Jesus' old house and introduced him to Joanna, the next door neighbour, who was Mary's half sister and lifelong friend. With a little help from me and her own Angel, she has shared some of her former neighbour's most intimate secrets.

Tomorrow we head for Capernaum where I am keen to introduce the Greek doctor to Peter's aged and ailing mother-in-law.

Back in Caesarea

I had to cut Luke's tour short when Maff sent news that Felix had been replaced as governor by another Roman, Festus. When I arrived at the port town, the new governor had already left for a diplomatic visit to Jerusalem. Before leaving, he had promised Paul he would bring his long postponed case to a swift conclusion.

Two weeks later, Festus returned to his palatial home with a delegation of Jewish leaders. The very next day he convened a court and summoned Paul. This time the Jews did not have the benefit of an expert lawyer. They presented a selection of serious charges against Paul but could not prove any of them. Paul simply reasserted his innocence.

Festus quickly concluded that the trial was going nowhere, but he was keen to establish a good relationship with the Jewish authorities. 'Are you willing,' he asked Paul, 'to travel to Jerusalem and stand trial before me there?'

'Don't you dare!' I screamed into Paul's mind. 'Say *no* for Heaven's sake – and yours!' I had visited Jerusalem on my travels with Luke and knew all too well that it was no safer for Paul than it had been two years earlier. Paul asked Festus for a few minutes to consider the offer and quietly talked the matter through with the Director. I turned to Maff. His mind was in deep and distant thought. I didn't know what to do or what to say. I urged Paul to ask for more time but could see that Festus was in a hurry to clear up the mess left by his predecessor.

'Will you go to Jerusalem, Paul?' the governor pressed.

'Say *no*,' I advised uncompromisingly.

Maff butted in. 'Paul, appeal to the Emperor.'

'What?' I asked Maff.

Festus demanded an answer.

'Say nothing!' I commanded Paul. 'Maff,' I asked urgently, 'what do you mean by *appeal to the Emperor*?' But there was no time for his reply.

Paul looked into the new governor's eyes and said calmly, 'I appeal to Caesar.'

'What have you done now?' I demanded of Maff.

Paul slumped in his seat, weighed down by the gravity of what he had just said.

Festus conferred briefly with his advisers and then declared formally, 'You have appealed to Caesar. To Caesar you will go!'

The court was silent. The Jews were clearly disappointed. Festus was disinterested in Paul but pleased to have resolved his dilemma. Paul's mind, for the first time in many months, was focused once again on the prospect of death. Gradually, I began to understand what was happening.

I looked at Maff. 'Does this mean we're going to Rome?'

He smiled broadly. 'We are!'

Fair Havens, Crete

Festus made the arrangements very quickly. Paul was committed into the custody of a centurion called Julius, a member of the Emperor's private regiment. Julius had recently arrived in Caesarea with a number of Roman citizens, all bound for trial in the capital. Paul was allowed to take two companions to provide for him while he awaited his audience with Caesar. Luke was at the front of the queue and Aristarchus, who had travelled to Jerusalem with Paul from Thessalonica, happened to be visiting Luke and Philip, and volunteered.

Julius found a ship in the harbour bound for western Turkey and booked berths for his assortment of privileged prisoners. As soon as the ship was at sea, Paul took the opportunity to talk about the Son with his jailer, urging Julius to prepare for his own eternal future. At the end of the first day's sailing, as we were being blown into the port of Sidon, Aristarchus announced that he knew a family of Christians in the town. Julius had already learned to trust Paul and allowed him to stay the night with Aristarchus' friends.

The next morning the three men returned to their ship shortly after sunrise. Julius was arguing with the captain about which route to take. I listened intently, trying to work out the reason for their dispute, but the talk of wind speeds and sea states was quite bewildering. I asked Maff to seek clarification from the captain's Angel guardian.

From what we could understand, the problem was that the

wind was flowing in the wrong direction – which complicates things, apparently. Julius is in a hurry because he wants to be with his family in Rome for the midwinter festival. The captain, however, insisted on a longer route, round the north coast of Cyprus. That way, he claims, the opposing wind will be less strong. In return for this concession, Julius demanded that the ship sail day and night, not putting into port unless absolutely necessary. Maff and I both dimmed considerably when we managed to work this all out.

'Oriel, you're an Archangel, for Heaven's sake,' Maff blurted out, with more than a hint of panic in his voice. 'Surely you can fix the weather.'

'If I could, I would. I promise you.'

The journey was miserable. We zigged and zagged frantically, left and right, north and south, but our westerly progress was depressingly slow. While the wind tried to push our boat back towards Sidon, the sea itself tossed us up and down like beads on a drum skin. Drinks were repeatedly spilled, cups broken, clothing soaked and tempers shortened. The sense of privilege amongst Julius' prisoners was soon washed away. Angels and men alike simply endured the struggle, longing for it to be over. Every day the other prisoners begged Julius to let them escape into the nearest harbour and wait for more helpful conditions. He always refused. Paul though, well used to the complications of human life, volunteered to help the crew. He took his turn pulling on ropes and scrubbing decks – whatever his eyesight allowed. Maff and I sided with the other sick and solemn passengers, watching Paul as he threw himself into the routines of a sailor's life.

At last we reached the boat's destination, the port of Myra. Julius ignored the pleas and bribes of his seasick prisoners and found an Egyptian grain ship heading for Italy the next day. This boat was both larger and heavier, which meant that the vessel was more stable. Travel was less unpleasant, but our progress was even slower than before. Once again, Paul committed himself to the daily chores of the ship's company. I took the opportunity to speak with their respective Angels.

'How do you cope with life on the open sea?' I asked.

'By fixing your sights firmly on the spirit of your human,' one of them told me, 'and trying to think of nothing else.'

'The more you love them, the easier it is,' another added.

'But that doesn't stop the sea from being downright danger-ous,' Maff observed.

'What do you do if the ship itself falls apart?' I asked, facing my worst fear.

'You try to keep your human out of the water,' one said. 'Failing that, you try to keep them on the surface of the water.'

'Whatever happens,' another Angel volunteered, joining in our miserable conversation, 'never go into the water yourself.'

'What happens if you do?' Maff asked, the brightness of his spirit failing rapidly at the thought.

'You don't want to know,' the same Angel replied.

When the southern coast of Turkey ended, we looped south-wards and limped along the south coast of Crete. Our progress had been so slow that provisions intended to feed and water the humans all the way to Italy were becoming dangerously low. We were forced to stop at the small harbour of Fair Havens to restock the ship's stores. The prisoners, with the notable exception of Paul, were so eager to get ashore they almost managed it before Maff and myself. Archangel Michael was waiting for me on the jetty.

'I have bad news,' he said.

'It will have to wait,' I insisted.

Next day

Michael returned during the night.

'Has there been a change of plan?' I asked him when he arrived in the small room that Paul, Luke and Aristarchus were sharing.

'A what?' he asked.

'A change of plan,' I repeated.

'Oriel, you've been among humans too long. When did our Boss ever change his mind?'

'Right on both counts,' I admitted, pausing to consider how contagious human error can be. I looked up at Michael. 'What is your bad news, then?'

'Lucifer has greatly enlarged the band of Opposition spirits who tried to shipwreck you off Troas,' he informed me. 'They intend to destroy the ship and everyone on it long before it reaches Italy.'

'What should we do?' I asked.

191

'Don't go.'

'But we have to go,' I argued. 'The Boss has promised Paul that he will get to Rome.'

'I know that,' Michael said dismissively. 'What I mean is, don't go now and certainly don't go by boat.'

'We don't have a choice,' I insisted. 'Firstly, we're on an island. And secondly, Paul is a prisoner. He's not in a position to choose where he goes and when. Those decisions are made by Julius.'

'To whom, if I remember correctly,' Michael said with a pinch of sarcasm and a large dollop of irritation, 'you have deferred your care for Paul.'

'Julius is *humanly* responsible for ensuring that Paul is delivered safely to Rome,' I corrected him.

'Paul is not a parcel, Oriel,' Michael reprimanded me. 'He is one of our Boss's much loved children.'

'You and I are in danger of falling into Lucifer's trap,' I warned my colleague, conscious of the destructive turn our conversation was taking. We paused a moment and refocused our thoughts on our Boss and his love for his creatures. 'Lucifer is planning to drown Paul,' I said, returning to the issue. 'What can we do to stop him?'

'You escaped last time,' Michael reminded me, 'but the same method will not work again. Even with a total of 277 Angels, you will be dramatically outnumbered. There is only one option, Oriel, and that is to stay here on firm land.'

'Then we shall have to persuade Julius to stay,' I said.

As soon as Paul woke and spoke to the Director about his plans for the day ahead. I instructed him that he should persuade Julius to stay on Crete. He was due to meet with the ship's company on the quayside at sunrise. That was his opportunity.

The meeting was led by the ship's owner, an Egyptian entrepreneur whose sole concern was the safety of his boat. He cared little for the crew and nothing at all for its passengers. Paul spoke up.

'Fellow travellers,' he shouted, 'if we continue with this voyage, it will be disastrous.' As he spoke, I arranged his thoughts to match the priorities of the owner. 'I tell you, the ship will be lost, the cargo will be lost, and many of you will lose your lives.'

The ship's pilot spoke up. 'We can't stay at Fair Havens. It's not a suitable place to winter a ship of this size.'

The owner agreed.

Julius spoke. 'What's the nearest port that's suitable for the winter?'

'Phoenix,' the pilot replied.

'Then we'll winter in Phoenix,' the centurion declared. 'How soon can we get there?'

'We can leave as soon as the wind drops,' the pilot stated.

The owner added, 'Everyone must assemble here every morning in the first hour after sunrise. Whoever is not here on the day we leave will be left behind. No refunds.'

I reminded Paul that this compromise was no insurance against Lucifer's planned attack. He took Julius aside and tried to reason with him but Julius' mind was darkened by the realisation that he would not be with his family for the festival. He accused Paul of being unreasonable. In a final attempt to secure Paul's safety, I made one more suggestion.

'Why don't we travel to Phoenix overland and join the ship there in the spring?'

Julius was not interested in negotiation. 'Paul, I have paid for your berth on that ship,' he insisted, 'and, by Jupiter, you will use it.'

The island of Malta

Every morning Paul and his companions reported to the quay-side. Every morning Paul tried to change Julius' mind. Every morning he failed. Every night I informed Archangel Michael that we were still bound for the ocean.

'Lucifer knows,' he told me. 'This delay is helping him. He has mustered his forces close to the shore and every day you wait he uses to educate his spirits in the science of manipulating Earth's weather. We need an alternative plan.'

'You'll have to discuss that with our Boss,' I told him. 'My place is wherever Paul is.'

Finally, one morning the ship's owner announced that the wind had dropped. Everyone was bundled on board. As the huge vessel slowly swayed out onto the open sea, Michael called across to me, 'I will do what I can.'

For two hours we crept slowly along the southern coast of Crete. Every human on board was full of hope, with the single exception of Paul. I assembled all the Angels and briefed them about the situation. Maff gave a detailed account of our battle with the Opposition off the coast of Troas. I urged the Angels to get their charges praying, whether or not they were in the habit of doing so.

Just as I was finishing, the wind dropped completely, leaving a sickly calm. The ship drifted. Passengers looked hopefully over the sides of the vessel at the diminishing waves but the sailors glanced anxiously at one another, exchanging whispered messages.

'Where are the Opposition, then?' I asked Maff.

'I can't see them,' he replied. 'Do you want me to go up higher and look over the horizon?'

'No,' I told him. 'Stay with me.'

I wished Michael was with us. I have no appetite for battle and often wonder why my Boss doesn't simply dismantle Lucifer and his cronies, once and for ever.

The air began to move. It advanced from the north east, pushing us gently out to sea. Still no sign of the Opposition. The advancing wind quickly accelerated from a walk to a trot and before long it was charging us at a mighty gallop. The passengers fled inside but there was no refuge for the ship itself. Wave after wave crashed against our boat like a herd of frightened rhino. The ship fled before this assault. Sailors fought with ropes and sails to prepare for the storm. Maff and I clung tightly to one another. Paul refused to go inside. Once again he joined the crew, doing whatever he could to help. When there was no more to be done, he clambered round the creaking ship reassuring everyone that the God he served, who made the sea, had promised that he would make it to Rome.

For two terrible days nothing changed. The crew did everything in their power to secure the ship. They even threw some of its precious cargo overboard. Still there was no sight of Lucifer or his band of pirates, but the storm was so intense that my vision was little clearer than Paul's.

On the third day Michael appeared out of the gloom.

'Where are they?' I asked.

'Who?' he shouted. It was difficult for us to hear one another over the manic movements of the storm-tossed ship.

'The Opposition!' I bellowed back.

'Gone,' he yelled. 'As soon as the storm started up, they scarpered.'

'Isn't this their storm?' I asked.

'No.'

'Then who is doing all this?'

'The weather.'

'The weather!' I repeated. 'What can we do about it?'

Michael's answer was the very last thing I wanted to hear. He looked straight at me and shouted, 'Absolutely nothing.'

The light that beams from every creature who serves my Boss went suddenly dim in the centre of my being.

Michael spoke again, 'There's no point both of us risking our light,' he told me. 'I'm leaving. Maff should come with me. He's too valuable to lose in a meaningless storm.'

Of course, an Angel cannot be killed – we are immortal beings. But it is possible for our light to be so darkened that we become incapable of usefully serving our Boss. I have seen it happen. For the first time in all my travels with Paul, I realised that his was not the only life in danger.

Maff insisted on staying and during the days that followed his presence was one of only two lights in the darkness around me. We saw neither sun nor stars. The sailors had no idea where we were, nor which way we were being driven. The other significant light I could see was the brightness of Paul's total trust in my Boss's promise.

When Paul was not touring the boat urging his shipmates to pray, he was praying himself. On one of the incalculable days, while he was busy praying, Archangel Raphael suddenly arrived.

'Raphael!' I exclaimed. 'What are you doing here?'

'At Paul's suggestion,' he said, 'every single man and woman on this ship has been praying, even ones who have never uttered a prayer in all their brief lives. But there is one person on this boat whose faith is failing.'

'Who?'

'You,' Raphael declared. 'Our Boss has promised Paul he will get to Rome. He does not make such promises lightly. What's more, our Boss has gathered every single incoherent prayer that has risen from this precarious pile of wood. He has resolved to protect the life of every human here.'

I stared at my ageless friend and the warmth of his love pervaded the sodden depths of my dull spirit.

'You need to remember, my dear,' Raphael said seriously, 'you are never alone.'

When Raphael left, I gathered my remaining strength and slowed my life form down to the fragile level of human life. When I knew that Paul would be able to see me, I stood in front of him. He did not seem at all surprised. We embraced.

'Don't be afraid, Paul,' I said as the brightness of my Angelic form penetrated even his clouded eyes, 'You *will* go to Rome and you *will* stand trial before the Emperor.' I knew that he could feel me, hear me and see me; I could also feel him. I continued, 'God has graciously granted you the lives of every person on this ship.'

Exhausted, I returned to my usual form.

I completely lost track of the days. One night, the weather's assault having lost none of its violence, the sailors suddenly announced that we were close to land. They hauled their beleaguered bodies into action and took regular measurements of the sea's depth. We were getting closer. To prevent the ship from crashing against rocks, the crew lowered all the anchors and prayed feverishly for the light of dawn. I joined them, amplifying every scrap of faith and love for the Creator that these hardened men had. Then one sailor stopped praying, halted his neighbour and the interruption spread through the entire group. While human prayers are easy for Angels to hear, conspiracy is barely audible. I strained my attention to discover what the men were planning.

They were planning to escape. The sailors lowered the ship's lifeboat into the turbulent sea, on the pretence of dropping more anchors. I alerted Paul. Paul woke Julius. 'If these men leave the ship,' Paul told the centurion, 'we'll all die.'

Julius gave hurried orders to his soldiers, who ran onto the deck and slashed the lifeboat ropes with their swords. When the news spread of the crew's scuppered escape bid, an epidemic of fear swept through the ship's company. Rumour spread quickly that the ship would be smashed against rocks. Fights broke out between passengers and crew. Everyone was shouting and cursing.

The panic lasted at least an hour. Julius herded his troops and prisoners into one tight pack by the broken stub of the main mast. Above all the shouting and swearing I gradually became aware of my Boss's voice calling.

'Paul! Paul!' he was saying. The Director was calling Paul back to prayer. I nudged Paul's spirit several times until he too heard the voice in his spirit. 'These people are hungry,' the Director said. 'They need strength for what is to come. Get them to eat.'

Paul started to climb up what was left of the mast, which swung dangerously as the boat was pitched and rolled by tireless waves. Maff shouted to all the Angels who were struggling to either protect or restrain their humans.

'Shut them up!' he shouted.

It was crude but it worked. Everyone stopped what they were doing and stared at the grey haired man clinging to the broken mast.

'For fourteen days,' Paul yelled, 'you have lived in constant fear. None of you has eaten. Now you must eat. You need food to survive. My God has promised me that not one of you will be injured. But you *must* eat.'

In the colourless gloom preceding dawn, the captain and his crew opened up the ship's stores and invited everyone to eat as much as they wanted. Paul insisted that the first loaf of soggy bread be passed to him. He held it high above his head, broke it and thanked my Boss for his generous provision. It was as if he had kindled a bright light and hung it to that splintered mast. For a few precious minutes there was a party on the battered boat. People who had just been thumping one another now laughed together. When everyone had eaten, the Captain ordered them all to help him jettison what was left of the ship's bulky cargo. As they tossed sacks of waterlogged wheat into the waves, daylight slowly seeped across the dark sky.

The grey light revealed a rocky coast that not one of the boat's 276 souls recognised. The captain picked out a small sandy bay and instructed everyone to brace themselves against the ship while he attempted to run it aground on the beach. Anchors were cut loose, as was the rudder. A single sail was hoisted and the great vessel creaked its way towards the shore. No one spoke as the storm drove our ship towards its destruction and their own salvation.

'We're going to make it,' Maff whispered to me.

Suddenly the boat jammed into the sea bed. Everyone and everything in the boat was hurled forwards. The rear mast crashed down onto the deck and, but for the instant reactions of my Angels, many men and women would have been crushed.

The front of the boat was stuck firm and, for the first time since we embarked, was completely motionless. I said to Maff, 'This is the safest I have felt all journey.'

My optimism was short-lived. The constant creaking of the

ship's timbers suddenly changed its tone. What was a rhythmic groan became a horrendous ripping and tearing as the now rigid structure was massacred by a furious cavalry of unrestrained waves.

'Abandon ship!' the captain shouted and his crew echoed the cry. Sailors, slaves and paying passengers raced to the front of the boat and threw themselves into the angry water. Julius, however, still had his valuable cargo corralled against the main mast.

'We'll have to kill the prisoners,' one of his senior soldiers advised.

I was devastated. Even my Boss's promises give way to the wilful violence of selfish humanity. Maff grabbed Julius by the head and forced him to look at Paul. Julius' Angel guardian realised the urgency of the situation and brought to the fore of Julius' mind the considerable respect he had acquired for this balding Jew.

Paul said calmly, 'Not one will be lost.'

Julius was undecided. Part of him trusted Paul – though he could not understand why – but he also knew that if any prisoner should escape, he himself would be court-marshalled and exe-cuted. While the ship was being crushed to splinters beneath him, Julius searched his mind for a way to save Paul. Meanwhile, the back of the boat was rapidly disappearing.

'We have to kill them!' a soldier shouted, his voice laced with terror.

Julius still looked at Paul. Paul mouthed, 'Not one.'

Julius found the decision he had been seeking. 'Abandon ship!' he shouted. 'Swim for the beach.'

The soldiers were the first to plunge into the rabid water. Within seconds there was only one human left on the stricken vessel. Paul.

'Jump in! Swim for it!' Maff ordered.

Paul's mind screamed in reply, 'I can't swim!'

'If you don't jump, I'll push you,' Maff yelled.

Paul's mind was awash with despair. I looked down into the surf. It was dotted with little sparks of human life, each pulling their fragile forms through the water. I remembered how I had managed to teach Paul to ride a horse but there was no way I could teach him how to swim.

'Don't fuss over what you can't do,' I told him. 'Do what you can do. Jump!'

Paul filled his lungs with salty air and plunged into the liquid chaos below. I followed. Paul's ageing body fell quickly through the thin air and I expected that it would stop falling once it met the denser water. It did not. He continued to fall, sinking deep into the suffocating darkness of the sea. Still I followed. I quickly discovered the claustrophobic truth that the sailors' Angels had refused to explain. The salt water penetrated every part of my Angelic form. Where there was warmth, it brought coldness. Where there was light, it brought impenetrable darkness. Where there was hope, it brought blank despair. In the face of this creeping paralysis, three things kept me going and prompted me to force my ailing spirit even deeper into the cauldron of Death: first was a mental image of Paul standing in the centre of Rome, explaining the story of Jesus; second was a stubborn trust in my Boss's promises; third, and most important, was my utter determination to go with Paul wherever he went.

Although I could no longer see, I sensed Paul's suffocating body just below me. I forced myself downward, potentially nearer my own demise, and finally made contact with him. His limbs had gone limp and the tremor of life in him was close to the stillness of Death. My own light had become so faint that I could physically feel Paul's cold arms. With one last effort I dived below him and began to push upwards, carrying the near-lifeless form with me as I rose. I looked up and could see a bright light shining down onto the surface of the sea. I concluded it must be the Son, that he had come to welcome Paul's spirit into the long-anticipated life of Heaven. I pushed up towards that light until we finally broke through into the life-giving air.

I don't remember what happened after that. The light was not the Son, it was Maff. He tells me that he loaded Paul and me onto a large timber beam he had torn from the ship. He then guided us towards the shore, allowing the waves to carry us up onto the beach.

Doctor Luke saw to Paul's spluttering carcass while Maff, and a number of other anxious Angels looked after me. They carried me up the beach where I stayed, slumped like a stranded jellyfish, watching helplessly as Luke pumped sea water out of Paul's lungs.

The refugees from the sea were soon greeted by local islanders who built fires on the beach to warm their drenched visitors. Maff informed me that we were on a small island called Malta. Paul, true to form, was soon on his feet and, against his doctor's advice, helped the villagers gather wood for the fires.

What a remarkable man he is!

Julius assembled and counted his prisoners, ensuring that none had absconded. Once Paul had been accounted for, Julius allowed him to return to his task. I watched passively as he scurried to and fro, reassuring his fellow passengers and fuelling fires. Then, without warning, Paul suddenly let out a yelp and shook his arm frantically. He had just thrown a armful of brushwood onto the flames and a poisonous snake had jumped up from the wood, attaching itself by its fangs to Paul's hand. After the first shock, Paul calmly shook the viper into the fire. His shipmates and the Maltese villagers watched and waited, expecting him to swell up and die.

I groaned a despairing groan, deep in my drowned spirit. I tried to haul myself up, to go to Paul's aid, but I barely managed to move. In the cold darkness of my mind, I heard a distant voice. I cannot say whether there was, in actuality, a voice, or whether it was the sound of a memory. Whichever, it was the voice of my Boss. He was saying, 'Trust me, Oriel.'

I was no less a dumb spectator than all the humans on the beach. Luke rose and gently helped his friend to sit down. He knew, more than the others, that there was no cure for such a snake bite. There was no alternative but to watch, hope, and pray.

200

Islanders muttered to one another, 'This is a judgement from the gods. The man is probably a murderer.'

They watched Paul intently, waiting for justice to catch up with the villain. Nothing happened. Paul chatted calmly to Luke, sucked the wound clean and then returned to his task of providing drying warmth for his sea-soaked companions.

When the Maltese realised that Paul was not going to die, they revised their opinion of him. 'He must be a god!' they concluded. Clearly, they are a very confused people. Most certainly they need to hear what Paul has to tell them about Jesus.

Puteoli

We spent three months in Malta, passing the winter as guests of Publius, the Roman official who ruled the island. Paul quickly recovered from the traumas of the shipwreck and took every opportunity granted him to demonstrate my Boss's love. In the spring, when we set sail for Rome, the islanders generously provided clothes, food and money for Paul and his companions. We left behind many new-born children in my Boss's human family. Among them was Publius' father, healed by Paul at the Director's prompting.

My recovery was slower, despite the devoted attention of Archangel Raphael. I do not expect I will ever be completely restored to my former state.

We stopped only twice on our final voyage and the wind was behind us all the way. The ship – another Alexandrian grain carrier – was bound for the port of Puteoli. Julius assembled his prisoners on the harbourside and explained that now they're in Italy each of them must be chained to a soldier of the Imperial Guard. They will remain so, day and night, until they are called to appear before the Emperor. Julius then chained himself to Paul. He sent a messenger ahead to Rome to announce the arrival of the prisoners and to arrange suitable transport for them. Julius reminded his charges they would be responsible for arranging their own accommodation until such time as they were either condemned or acquitted. I sent Maff ahead to Rome to research some suitable lodgings for Paul and to ensure that the Christian disciples in the city were informed of his imminent arrival.

Meanwhile, in Puteoli, Luke sought out the Christian disciples and arranged lodging for himself, Aristarchus, Paul and, necessarily, Julius.

We expect to be here for at least a week. Paul has used the time to gather information about the Christian and Jewish communities in Rome. The rest of his time has been taken up by Julius, who hungrily interrogates Paul about his God and about his understanding of life and Death. The chain that connects these two men has not been removed at any point, or for any reason – a restriction Paul has accepted without complaint. When Paul has had opportunity to reflect on his situation – such moments are rare with a Roman centurion permanently attached to his wrist – he calmly considers it a privilege to follow the example of Jesus whose last significant journey, before he was executed, was as a prisoner of Rome.

Rome

At the end of a week, carriages arrived from Rome and we set off on the final leg of our journey, which took five days. There is no easier way to describe our arrival in this famous city than to tell the story twice, first as I experienced it and then as it appeared to Paul.

Archangel Michael stayed with us in Puteoli. Sometimes it seemed that Paul was manacled to two warriors: his body to a Roman soldier and his spirit to the commander of Heaven's army. Michael arrived with a huge battalion of warrior Angels and swept every trace of Opposition influence out of the maritime town. When we left Puteoli, our small convoy of luxury Roman carriages was accompanied by an extensive escort of Michael's finest troops. With scouts scouring the countryside for any hint of trouble, I had little doubt that Paul would reach his goal.

As we approached the outskirts of Rome, trundling steadily up the tree-lined Appian Way, I became aware of a distant hubbub further up the road. Though the source of the sound was too far off for me to identify, something about it caused my spirit to stir.

'What is it?' I asked Michael.

'I'll go and investigate,' he replied and left us.

I became frustrated by the slow progress of Earth time.

Whatever it was ahead on the road intrigued me and I was anxious to reach it. With Michael gone and Maff already in Rome, I consulted Paul, only to discover he could hear nothing. I prompted Paul to ask his companions what they could hear, thinking that his hearing was following the lead of his deteriorated eyesight. Luke, Aristarchus and Julius all listened intently but reported that they could only hear the twittering of birds and the rumble of carriage wheels. Their deafness to the sound was significant; it meant that the noise I could hear was spiritual, not human.

Earlier in my travels I would have left Paul and gone ahead to see what was happening but I had resolved not to leave Paul's side and would not have broken that vow for any enticement. Instead I sent Julius' angel ahead to investigate. He did not return.

The carriage seemed to be travelling slower and slower. I consulted Paul again. Within the familiar pathways of his mind my question was quickly answered. 'We're going uphill,' his thoughts informed me. 'That's why we're slowing.'

Whether or not the carts did in fact slow to a near crawl, I could not say, but it most certainly felt like it. I talked to Lisael, Luke's Angel guardian.

'My sense of time seems to have warped,' I observed.

'Humans get that,' he replied.

'But I'm not a human,' I reminded him.

'Of course,' he said calmly, 'but if you get deeply involved in the life of a particular human, you become a bit like them.'

I looked at Paul. There are aspects of his spirit that would be a credit to my own.

'Lisael,' I enquired, 'can you hear . . .?' I paused to listen again. 'Can you hear Angels singing?'

He changed the subject. 'Luke has come on a lot in the last two years, don't you think?' he asked me.

We were approaching the crest of the hill. There was now no doubt in my mind that I could hear Angelic music. I idly wondered if it was just one of the features of so great a city as Rome, but I knew that the sounds meant more than that. As we neared the hilltop, the noise became clearer. It was the sound of a party, a Heavenly party!

Suddenly there, laid out before us, was the city of Rome, glowing with the reflected golden light of the evening sun. However, between our hilltop and the city was a far more magnificent sight. The Appian Way was filled with Angels – thousands and thousands of singing, dancing, exuberant Angels. My tired spirit leapt like a gazelle. At the near shore of this beautiful ocean of Angeldom stood four very familiar figures: Raphael, Michael, Gabriel and Maff. They smiled at me with smiles that would illuminate a black hole. Then, at the moment that these four friends greeted me, the entire host of Angels turned in my direction. Every eye in that Angelic horde looked directly at me – at me, Oriel, the master of logistics, administration and all the other mundane ministries of Heaven! As one, the Heavenly host let out a great cheer. I struggled to understand that all of this could be for me.

Our carriage rolled on, gathering speed down the hill. My human companions were utterly oblivious to this vast welcome. As we progressed, the sea of Angels parted to let us through and every Angel shouted, 'Well done Oriel!'

I sat at the back of the carriage, marvelling to learn that all Heaven had taken such interest in my lonely odyssey. We rattled down towards the edge of the city, greeted by a hundred Angels for every turn of the wheels. At last the Angelic throng on the road thinned and I could see a stretch of clear track ahead. Here the Appian Way was lined by Raphael's choir, all the way to the first habitation of Rome itself. And there, standing in the middle of the road, towering over the exultant Angels, was my Boss.

My spirit burned inside me. 'What have I done,' I asked myself, 'that the Creator of all creations should greet me like this?'

When our carriage drew up to my Boss, he reached out a broad hand and lifted me out. He gathered me into a deep embrace and fixed his dazzling eyes on mine. Much of my depleted strength returned in that instant.

'Well done, my good and faithful servant,' my Boss said to me. The choir echoed his greeting in multiple harmonies.

'Is this really all for me?' I faltered.

'This is for love, Oriel,' he explained. 'There is no greater love than to sacrifice your life for a friend.'

Out of the corner of my eye, I saw Paul's carriage continuing on its way into the suburbs of Rome.

'I must go,' I said to my Boss. 'I must stay with Paul.'

'You have completed your task, Oriel,' he said. 'You may return home. Maff will look after Paul from now.'

'But I want to stay with Paul,' I explained. 'He's my friend. I have to prepare him for his trial.'

'That is for Maff to do,' my Boss insisted. 'You must come home with me.'

'Let me stay,' I begged, 'just for today at least, just to see him settled into his lodgings, just to make sure he's all right. I promise I won't interfere with Maff.'

My Boss looked deeply into me and smiled. 'We will go together,' he said.

And so it was, hand in Heavenly hand with my Boss, that I arrived at the centre of the Roman Empire.

For Paul, however, the experience was very different. He saw and heard nothing of the great gathering of Angels. He saw only the gnarled trees lining the ancient road. He heard nothing but the rattle and creak of his carriage.

Paul was greeted, though. Julius halted the carriages for supper at a place called *The Three Taverns*. By arrangement, four Christian disciples from Rome joined Paul, Luke, Aristarchus and Julius for the meal and travelled with them into the city. They took Paul to a small house near the city centre which Maff had found. I watched Paul as he unpacked the small bag of spare clothes given to him on Malta, and took in the sights, smells and sounds of his new home. Luke and Aristarchus were obliged to find separate lodgings – it is a condition of Paul's 'imprisonment' that he live alone. For this reason, Maff picked a house with only one bed. He had overlooked the fact that 'alone' for Paul, involves being chained, at all times, to a soldier of the Imperial Guard. Paul insisted that Julius should take the bed.

Paul and Julius were both weary from their journey. As soon as they had seen to the minimum of domestic arrangements, the two of them settled down for the night.

That is how I left my companion: exhausted from his travels, alone in a strange city but for a prison guard, asleep on a stone floor, his right arm held and lifted by a heavy iron chain. The chain will not be removed from Paul's wrist until the day he tells the story of Jesus in front of the Emperor of Rome.

An extract from ORIEL IN THE DESERT – to be published in Autumn 2004

The Sinai Desert – during the 19th dynasty of Egyptian Kings

I had assumed that it would be easy to find a human being in the middle of this desert.

My Boss had called Archangel Gabriel and me into his office and announced, 'The time has come to take Abraham's family away from their life of slavery in Egypt and deliver them to the territory I promised to Abraham, his son Isaac, and grandson Jacob.'

'Good,' Gabriel said cheerily. 'They've been praying for long enough.'

I looked anxiously at my colleague, whose department records every prayer any human ever offers. His comment seemed to betray a slight edge of criticism. My Boss also looked at Gabriel, his gaze as steady as eternity.

'Not one of those prayers has been wasted, Gabriel,' he said. 'They have been planted in my people's love and watered by their tears. Now the fruit is ripe.'

'What do you want us to do?' I asked, drawing my Creator's attention away from Gabriel.

'I've decided who will rescue Abraham's descendants from their slave masters,' my Boss explained. 'I would like you two to deliver a message for me.'

'Who have you chosen?' I enquired.

'A child of two Hebrew slaves, an Egyptian prince and a Midianite shepherd.'

I carefully recorded this information while Gabriel asked, 'Which one should we visit first?'

Our Boss smiled. 'You will find him in the Sinai mountains.'

This reply did not seem entirely helpful, but I have learned that my Boss always says what he means. While I tried to understand exactly what he was telling us, Gabriel went straight for another question.

'Who's in the Sinai mountains?' he asked.

'The man I have prepared.'

'You said there were three.'

I caught Gabriel's attention and frowned at him, urging him to think before he spoke. We both looked to our Boss.

'His name is Moses,' he informed us.

'So this is the Egyptian?' Gabriel asked uncertainly.

My Boss looked at me. 'Explain it to him, Oriel,' he said.

'If I have got this right, Gabriel,' I said carefully, 'Moses, the Egyptian prince, is the son of Hebrew parents and – if we are to look for him in Sinai – I assume that he is now working as a shepherd among the Midianites.' I looked across to my Boss. 'How did I do?'

'Very well, Oriel.'

Gabriel was slightly agitated. 'An excellent choice, Lord,' he declared, taking the initiative from me. 'Understands the Egyptians, identifies with the Israelites and familiar with the territory they will have to cross.' His praise had a hollow ring which betrayed its self-serving intention. 'What shall I tell him?'

Our Boss was unmoved. He accepted Gabriel's praise for its own meagre merits.

'Tell him I have seen the misery of my people in Egypt, that I have heard their cries for help. Reassure him that I am greatly troubled by their suffering and will rescue them. Tell him to speak to Pharaoh and lead the Israelites out of Egypt to the land of the Canaanites.'

'Sounds simple enough,' Gabriel said. 'Come on, Oriel, let's get on with it.'

Gabriel proceeded to the door where he waited for me. I stayed where I was, looking into the eternal eyes of my Creator. 'If it's so simple,' I was wondering, 'why did he ask both Gabriel and me?' Gabriel usually goes alone when delivering messages. My Boss's ageless face showed the same steady look he had maintained throughout our conversation. It was tinted with a gentle smile. He said nothing, and no Angel can read his thoughts, but I knew that he had invited me for a reason.

So what about Paul's message?

Twenty centuries after Paul journeyed the Middle East taking the Good News about Jesus to the non-Jews, the Christian faith has become a vibrant faith in many corners of the world. The beliefs for which he and thousands of believers down the years have been prepared to be persecuted, for which they have faced suffering, hardship and pain, are worth investigating.

CLOSER TO GOD FOR NEWCOMERS: MEET THE REAL JESUS by Belinda Pollard offers an encounter with Jesus through the Bible. It includes 40 brief excerpts taken from Luke's Gospel and the Book of Acts (the part of the Bible on which *Oriel's Travels* is based), with helpful insights. It describes Jesus' life and the effect he had on the people he met. It's straightforward, jargon free and you don't need to know anything about Christianity to read it.
ISBN 1 85999 459 8 £2.65

To order this and/or request a free catalogue of Bible resources from Scripture Union:
- phone SU's mail order line: 01908 856006
- email info@scriptureunion.org.uk
- fax 01908 856020
- log on to www.scriptureunion.org.uk
- write to SU Mail Order, PO Box 5148, Milton Keynes MLO, MK2 2YX

You might also like to **request free samplers** from our range of personal Bible reading guides:

CLOSER TO GOD – experiential, relational, radical and dynamic, this publication takes a creative and reflective approach to Bible reading with an emphasis on renewal.

DAILY BREAD – aims to help you enjoy, explore and apply the Bible. Practical comments relate the Bible to everyday life, combined with information and meditation panels to give deeper understanding.

ENCOUNTER WITH GOD – provides a thought-provoking, in-depth approach to Bible reading, relating Biblical truth to contemporary issues. The writers are experienced Bible teachers, often well known.

SU also produces Bible reading notes for children, teens and young adults. Do ask for details.

Scripture Union, 207–209 Queensway, Bletchley, MK2 2EB.